W9-AGB-109

THE MAN WITH THE FEB -- 2017
BALTIC STARE

Also by James Church

THE MAN WITH THE
BALTIC STARE

AN INSPECTOR O NOVEL

JAMES CHURCH

MINOTAUR BOOKS

A THOMAS DUNNE BOOK

NEW YORK

This is a work of fiction. All of the characters, organizations, and events portrayed in this novel are either products of the author's imagination or are used fictitiously.

A THOMAS DUNNE BOOK FOR MINOTAUR BOOKS.
An imprint of St. Martin's Publishing Group.

THE MAN WITH THE BALTIC STARE. Copyright © 2010 by James Church. All rights reserved. Printed in the United States of America. For information, address St. Martin's Press, 175 Fifth Avenue, New York, N.Y. 10010.

www.thomasdunnebooks.com
www.minotaurbooks.com

The Library of Congress has cataloged the hardcover edition as follows:

Church, James, 1947–
    The man with the Baltic stare / James Church.—1st ed.
        p. cm.
    "A Thomas Dunne book."
    ISBN 978-0-312-37292-7
    1. Korea (North)—Officials and employees—Fiction. 2.   P'yongyang (Korea)—Fiction. 3. Koreans—Fiction. 4. Political fiction. I. Title.
PS3603.H88M36 2010
813'.6—dc22

                                                                    2009047482

ISBN 978-0-312-56941-9 (trade paperback)

First Minotaur Books Paperback Edition: August 2011

P1

Acknowledgments

Thanks to Mike Chinoy, whose insistence and enthusiasm finally convinced me that Macau was a perfect setting for Inspector O. Thanks to Joji for providing a wonderful, quiet place to write and reflect. Thanks to John and Jackie for reasons too numerous to mention.

Apologies to hotel front desk clerks, who are badly treated as a group in these stories. In life, almost all of them are kind, eager to help, and well informed. Apologies, too, to my sister, for not acknowledging sooner that she has been a wonderful first editor always correcting my many missteps and awkward prose with graceful encouragement.

Some acknowledgments, as always, must remain unspoken. They are no less heartfelt for being wrapped in silence.

When I started the series, I knew there was much I did not understand about North Korea and its people; little did I realize how much. I thought there was always more for the heart to learn. Now I know there is not much time in which to do it.

PART I

Chapter One

When the engine died, the silence of the mountain climbed down from the tall trees. Nothing stirred, no buzz of insects, no breeze to break the afternoon heat rising from the valley below. The car, parked on the far edge of the clearing, tilted slightly to the east. From there the land fell away, gently at first and then more steeply, the thin cover of soil giving way to a few steps of smooth, bare rock before it vanished into seven hundred meters of untroubled air.

It wasn't a surprise, seeing the car. I hadn't expected them on any particular day, but it was always clear they would show up. Even if there had been some way to avoid them this time, some way to open a door to the past, I wouldn't have tried. Sooner or later everything was meant to lead to here. I could reconstruct all I'd ever said, redo all I'd ever done, but it would only lead back to this moment, looking out at that car. Maybe this was as good a time as any. It was autumn, and autumn marked the spiral down.

I watched from the window, waiting to see how the process would unfold. They would do it by the book, I felt sure, no surprises. That was how these things were done.

The telephone rang. I picked up the receiver.

"You see them?" It wasn't a voice I knew. "Don't go outside."

"Who is this?" We had never done this sort of thing, called before we went to pick someone up. It always led to fretting.

"Worry with that later. I repeat, don't go outside."

The phone clicked, dead.

When I went back to the window, there were two of them, leaning against the car, their jackets off in the stifling air. People forget that on a mountaintop in October, it can still be so hot. The one on the left, the driver, looked toward the trees when he saw me. The other one said something out of the corner of his mouth; then he stuck his chin out and stared straight ahead. After a while, he shook his head, and they went away. Odd, I thought to myself. Not the way we used to do it.

2

A week later, the phone rang again. The wind had been blowing hard all day, but now it stopped abruptly, so it seemed even more quiet than usual, the way an autumn afternoon can get when the year has nothing left to say. Late afternoon quiet, late afternoon light; you could blow your brains out at that time of day in October and nothing would happen. Everything died in autumn. The afternoon wouldn't notice.

"O here."

"They'll be at your place in a few minutes."

It was the same voice. This was annoying, this abrupt familiarity. "You have a wrong number again."

"Yeah, must be. I'm just dialing at random, making obscure comments to pass the time."

"Do we know each other? I don't recognize the voice. You called before, right? Maybe we should introduce ourselves, if this is going to get regular."

"That's fine. Listen, this time when they drive up, you go out to meet them."

"And if I don't feel like it?"

"There's no interest in your preferences, comrade. Put on a

coat and tie, and be outside when they pull up. The whole thing won't take very long. You'll be back in time to fix dinner and to sand wood far into the night."

I hung up. Even if the driver was suicidal, he couldn't get to Pyongyang and back in time for dinner. He probably couldn't even do it the same day. It didn't matter—I wasn't putting on a tie.

As I closed the door behind me and walked out to the car, I could see that this time there was no "they." The driver was by himself, sitting in the front seat, staring out the front windshield. It wasn't even the same driver who had been here the week before. From the side, he had the pointed face of a ferret. When he turned toward me, I could see he was very nervous around the eyes. His lips were jumpy as well. I thought about sitting in the back, but that would have looked strange—me in back as if a car and driver had been sent for my convenience. With a two-man team, there wouldn't have been a question about where I sat. That made sense; it's one reason why we always sent a team. We gave some thought to these things. It was never simply routine. Before we left, we'd sit in my office and go over what to say, how to handle questions, how to keep things from getting out of hand. It wasn't easy, bringing people in. They were upset. Some of them stared out the window, thinking about their lives, but quite a few babbled, pleaded, made offers if we would only pull over and let them go. We did what we could to calm them down. We never copied SSD's approach, though. SSD liked to make them show up voluntarily. They'd call and tell so-and-so to show up at thus-and-such address at ten in the morning. They thought it was a good way to break people's spirits, making them drag themselves in. Maybe that was more honest, in a way. Even if it was, that wasn't why SSD did it.

"I don't know anything, and I'll recognize less after all these years," I said as I opened the passenger side door. "I don't even want to try. Leave me alone. Tell them I went away and wasn't around when you got here."

The driver's hands shook. He gripped the steering wheel to make them stop. "Not possible. You can't stay out of what's happening. Anyway, it will only be this once. You have the memory, the bridge that goes across the—"

"Nope. No bridge, no key, no memory. Look at me."

He glanced quickly in my direction.

"I'm older than my grandfather was when he died. What do they want with me anymore?"

"Get in the car. Tell them yourself. I'm tired of arguing with people."

3

It took thirty minutes down the winding road to the floor of the valley, past the shack with the covered porch where the guards sat on their haunches and watched the flowers grow alongside the fields. When we got to the river, I told the driver to turn around and go back.

"Why?"

"Either we go back or I get out right here."

It took another half hour, past the guard shack again, up the winding road to my house. I went inside and took my time going through the box of wood chips. I already knew the choices were limited. Pine, oak, and chestnut—not an ideal mix under the circumstances. Something—some part of the ancient brain—warned me to keep looking. I rooted around for whatever could cope with complexity or anxiety, or both. Pine was too simpleminded; oak and chestnut were both stubborn in their own way. I remembered a piece of larch, a very calm tree, leaning against the back wall and was thinking of cutting off a couple of chips when a horn sounded, four impatient blasts. Back in the car, the driver was annoyed, eyes blinking furiously like a ferret that has been told it is not an ox.

"Late," he said. "We'll be late and they'll want to know why."

"Tell them it was my fault."

"That's what I plan to do. Don't say we went back to get your damned wood chips. They warned me about you and wood."

Down the winding road again, the turns taken close to the edge; past the guards, who were now alarmed and trying to bring their telephone to life; across the river, which was reduced to an autumn trickle over the rocks; another three hours on rutted dirt roads to the highway, and almost two more to Pyongyang. The sunlight was gone by the time we hit the outskirts.

"Why so many checkpoints?" I stared out at the line of cars on the side of the road. "We never needed this many before. Even those we had were seriously overmanned."

"They're not checkpoints. They're places people stop after they go out for a drive. They get food and gasoline."

"Go out for a drive? You kidding?"

"Relax, why don't you?"

Up to now, neither of us had said much. But silence can weigh on a situation. That's why we always tried to keep up some sort of conversation when we brought people in. Nothing too complicated, very normal conversation in a normal tone of voice. A couple of the cars had tape players in them so we could listen to music if we ran out of things to say. This was a new car, but I couldn't see a tape player.

"You sure nothing is going on?" We'd sped past another checkpoint–rest stop.

The driver didn't break his blank expression. From the right side, he looked even more like a ferret. I could tell he was ignoring me from the way he watched the road real intently, lips twitching every so often. I tried again. "You got enough gas?"

He kept his eyes glued to the road.

"You're new," I said. "I'd guess you're the most junior, because they assigned you to drive. That's how we used to do it most of the time. Good practice for the junior ones to drive. Gets you familiar with the roads in a way that doesn't happen when you're sitting next to the driver. Drivers pay attention. Passengers don't. You ever notice that?"

He was still breathing, so I knew he had heard me.

"But then again, you're by yourself, so you can't be completely green. There must not be much to do these days if they could spare you to come all the way up there for me. Funny, they didn't send you up the first time. It was two others. Maybe they were friends of yours? In the old days, we used to like to keep some continuity once an operation was underway. Even if the team had to be changed, we kept at least one of them involved; that way the subject felt the whole thing was connected—kind of a psychological leash, that sort of approach. Usually very effective; calmed the subject in a funny way. Do I look calm to you?"

His lips tightened.

"What happened to the other two?" We bounced over a railroad crossing. "Went on vacation and left you with the chores?"

We were well into the city by now. The driver made a sudden right into a narrow street and pulled over. "Shut up." He swallowed hard and stared at me.

"Sure," I said. "I'm only making small talk."

"Well, don't."

We drove slowly another thirty meters down the street before he honked the horn, just a tap. A light went on over a gate, the gate opened, and a tall man wearing a long black coat appeared. He motioned for the driver to get out. The two of them spoke briefly, keeping their voices low. The ferret disappeared inside the gate; the man in the coat got behind the wheel.

"Long time, Li," I said, and looked away. We'd worked together for a while, but then there had been trouble—hard to remember exactly what—and he was sent away to the east coast. It hadn't been an amicable parting, a few days of nasty looks and tough words before his orders showed up. He came back to Pyong-yang, assigned to the Minister's retinue, shortly before I left for good.

"Friendly, as always, Inspector. You bring a change of clothes?"

"Meaning what?"

"Meaning after a few weeks maybe you'll get tired of that shirt you're wearing and wonder about changing into something else. Another shirt, maybe even a tie, would help. It's a nice touch to change clothes occasionally when you're with other people and not pretending to be a monk on a mountaintop."

"Who said I was pretending to be a monk? The deal was I go away and they leave me alone. I kept the core of it real simple so there wouldn't be any problem with misinterpretation—no complications, no loopholes or contingency clauses. I go up on the mountain and stay out of everyone's way. They don't bother me; I don't bother them. It was supposed to ensure peace and quiet all around. You know that was the deal; you were there when we signed the papers. I've lived up to my end all these years." I brooded for a moment. "Why did you send a ferret to get me?"

Li made a slow left turn onto a wide street.

"I'm not hanging around here for a few weeks," I said. "No one gets to change that agreement. I went back and forth on the language for weeks. It's very precise." I looked at the line of street-lights down the avenue that led to the big square. They were all on, every one of them. "Visitors? Who are we trying to impress?"

"We have lights on most streets now, except where we need it dark. Things have changed a little."

"I'll bet."

He shrugged. "Have it your way."

"If I had it my way, I wouldn't be here right now."

"Yeah, I know. You'd be sawing a piece of wood. People still talk about you, O."

"Nice to be remembered, I guess. Nicer to be forgotten."

We drove across the square; just past the party's offices, we turned into a narrow street. The car slowed at a guard post long enough for the guard to read the plates and wave us through. More lights, a turn into a long driveway, then down a ramp into an underground garage, very dark.

The car stopped, but Li let it idle. "Let me give you a piece of advice. For a change, maybe you'll take me seriously."

"Turn off the motor, will you, before we suffocate."

"You don't know what you think you know." He turned the key and the engine quit with no complaints.

"That's it? I don't know what I don't know? That's helpful. I can put that in the bank. Maybe I'll carve it in wood and hang it over my door. I'll use beech if I can find any. Beech is the most inane wood on the planet."

"We're going inside for you to meet a few people. They out-rank me."

"You got rank? I'll throw a party."

"Save it for when this is over. Don't forget—these people breathe different air from us. One of them is especially important; you'll recognize whom I mean as soon as you step in the door. He doesn't put up with crap. Can you remember that, after living on the mountaintop?"

"It's only been four years."

"Five."

"Five. You make it sound like I've been away for centuries."

"Amazing." He shook his head. "You can't even guess what you don't know, and you're not smart enough to realize it. Nothing much ever changes with you, does it? Come on; we're late for this thing." He took out a flashlight and pointed it at a door. "That way."

Inside was a narrow hallway, another door, then an elevator with a silent girl who looked straight ahead at nothing, pushed the button with a white-gloved finger, and bowed as we stepped off into an anteroom with thick carpets and a high ceiling. A small man stood waiting, his hands behind his back. He nodded, took my coat, and ushered me into a room with tall, uncurtained windows along one wall and a long table in the center. There were floor lamps in two of the corners. They produced all the illumination the room had, other than what peeked in from the security lights along the perimeter fence about five hundred meters away. A big chandelier hung over the table, but this was its night off.

There were only four men in the room. Three sat in a row along the table, facing the door. The fourth stood in one of the dark corners, smoking. I didn't recognize any of them. The man sitting in the center, apparently in charge, indicated I should occupy the chair across from him. Then nothing happened. The smoker gave no indication he'd seen me come in. No one spoke. Finally, he put out the cigarette in an ashtray balanced on the windowsill. He took a seat at the end of the table, apart from the rest of us.

"Good," I said. "Everyone comfortable? I suggest we introduce ourselves. As you may know, I've been in the countryside for a few years and haven't kept up with personnel news."

The man across from me fingered the edges of a folder. He was military, he sat like a military man, but he was wearing a civilian suit and you could tell he didn't like it. "We know who you are," he said. "And we know who we are. That should be sufficient."

"Sufficient for you, maybe, not for me." Something else would have been smarter to say, but that's what came out. Living alone on a mountaintop, you lose a little social grace. "This meeting, it isn't what was agreed. I agreed to stay away; you agreed never to call me back."

"We know what was agreed, Inspector. What was agreed is right here." The man slid the folder across the table. "Go ahead; look at it. Make sure that's your signature and everything is in order, exactly what you signed. Nothing has been altered. This isn't a copy; it's the original, same bloodstains on page three." The man to his right nodded slightly. The man sitting to his left, his hands folded over each other as if they were a pair of gloves, stared at me. It was one of those mean, I-could-make-your-life-miserable stares that colonels practice in the mirror.

Stares don't bother me, but bloodstains? Blood I usually remember, especially if it's mine. I seemed to recall that I had bled but only metaphorically in the struggle over the agreement's final wording. They could have dictated the whole thing if they had wanted. That would have made it easier, but the battle was as important to them as the words. So we wrangled for a couple of weeks over details until I finally said, "Put down whatever the hell you want," and they took that as surrender enough, even though they knew I didn't mean it.

The signed document—the one in the folder on the table—allowed me to leave the Ministry of People's Security in 2011, a year before my official retirement, get out of Pyongyang, and withdraw from everything that was about to happen if I promised never to speak of what I'd seen or heard during my years of service—or, equally important to them, anything my grandfather had told me. My grandfather had fought with the anti-Japanese guerrillas. He knew the founding members of the new government; he knew what went on in headquarters during the war; he watched the postwar years unfold. They named him a Hero of the Revolution and buried him with high honors, but that didn't mean they hadn't always worried every time he opened his mouth.

I had thought they would pack me off to Yanggang, drop me as far away as they could, so the only ones who might listen to the old stories about people and events that were never supposed to be told would be a few pheasants and the ghosts of the tigers that had gone away long ago. But instead of Yanggang, someone picked an empty mountaintop near Changsong with a view of a little river valley. I don't think it occurred to them that, as far as I was concerned, the view was a plus.

An old truck carrying a load of scrap lumber took me up the road to the top of the mountain one foggy morning in April. The driver and I had to get out a few times to move big rocks that had tumbled down the hillside and blocked the way. Near the top of the mountain was a small clearing, surrounded by a few tall trees. In the center was a hut that wouldn't last another winter, so from the moment the truck drove away until the first morning of autumn—sharp with cold and crystal clear—I was mostly alone, building a one-room house using my grandfather's carpenter's tools. One afternoon in July, after three days of rain that made it impossible for me to work, a team of soldiers appeared. They had strung a phone line up the side of the mountain, and when I said I didn't want it they told me they couldn't care less. Two men in a Ministry car drove up with the phone three months later, just before the first snow. I told them I didn't need a phone, but they said it was implied in the agreement and it had to be hooked up. In any case, the army had already installed the line and it would be a waste of the people's resources if it stayed unconnected, they said.

After that, the phone rang a couple of times a year—it was usually an operator ostensibly running a line check and not interested in speaking more than a few words. I knew what this really was, a routine check to make sure I hadn't disappeared. As further insurance, in case I fooled with the phone or learned to throw my voice really well, they put the guard shack on the road at the foot of the mountain. It was a waste of everybody's time—the phone and the guards—but time was what they thought they had plenty of, and someone in the Ministry had decided they had nothing better to spend it on than me. When the road was open, food came once a month in the old truck. Twice a year, on the big holidays, a Ministry driver brought two bottles of liquor.

"Happy day, Inspector," he'd say, stretching his legs and looking in all four directions at the view.

"I'm not an inspector anymore."

"Yeah, well, I'm not a delivery boy, but I drove all the way up here to give you those bottles, so sometimes we have to be what we aren't, I guess."

4

"First of all." I pushed the folder to one side. "Let's get something straight. I'm not an inspector. I resigned, handed in all documentation, badges, identification, keys, and privileges attached thereto." I checked to see if the mean stare across the table was still running; it was. "Second, maybe you can read in a dark room like this, but I can't, not anymore. It's the eyes."

"Perhaps you'd rather be somewhere the lights are on twenty-four hours a day." The staring man spoke up. He was younger than the other two, seemed comfortable in a dark room at a long table. I changed my mind. Probably not military, but I couldn't figure out where he fit. He looked too intelligent to be SSD. When they stared, their jaws went slack. "It's very tiring, I hear, having lights all the time," he said. His voice had a lulling cadence. "Then again, with constant lighting, you could read whenever you wanted."

The man at the end of the table stirred. The others glanced at him quickly, but he only looked idly into space, as if they weren't there.

The military man in the center frowned to himself. If I had been interrogating him, I would have said he was trying not to show how angry he was. The frown was covering something, but he wouldn't let it out. Finally, he pointed at me. "Go through that folder tonight. Study it carefully again in the morning when you wake up. Read through it as many times as you want during the rest of the day, in the sunlight. We'll meet here again tomorrow, after dinner." This was an order; it made him feel better to be giving orders, you could tell.

"I can't, regrettably," I said.

The younger man leaned forward. "You have another appointment?" There was a sneer hanging on the edge of the voice. I revised my estimate—he was definitely SSD. Sneering was something they all picked up after a while, like diphtheria.

"No, I'm returning home. I don't, as it happens, have a change of clothes."

From the corner of my eye, I saw the man at the end of the table smile, almost in spite of himself. "Maybe later, Inspector," he said so quietly that the others had to strain to hear. "But for now, you're needed here."

I could sense the discomfort across the table as soon as he spoke. There was nothing overt, no clearing of throats or tightening of lips, but the temperature in the room went down suddenly, and they sat like ice figures. It didn't seem to bother the man on the end. He lit another cigarette and leaned back in his chair, very much at ease. All right, I thought to myself, time to leave. I whisked the folder off the desk and stood up.

"An honor," I said, and nodded. The nod was a good touch, I thought. It came almost automatically. Social grace was trickling back into my system. "I'll study this closely."

As I backed out of the room, the general in the center closed his eyes and slowly exhaled. The other two, sitting motionless beside him, didn't seem to be breathing at all.

5

The little man outside the room was holding my jacket. Li was waiting in the elevator. The girl with the white gloves looked at the carpet.

"As usual, you didn't take my advice, I can tell," Li said.

"As usual, it wasn't very good advice."

As we retraced our steps, I remembered it had been a long time since I'd eaten. "You hungry?"

"No, but I'll watch."

"Don't worry; I'll buy."

Li shook his head. "At these prices, you'll change your mind, believe me."

We drove back up the ramp out of the garage into the night. "So find a cheap restaurant. I probably owe you. Where am I staying, by the way?"

Li took a piece of paper from his pocket. "You're an honored guest, O. Anything you want. Wine, women, color TV."

We drove a few blocks and then turned parallel to the river.

"That bad, huh?"

"I told you."

"So you did. Who was that character at the end of the table?"

The car pulled up to a building that was spilling oceans of electricity into a neon sign. "Here's your hotel," Li said. He'd heard my question; he wasn't going to answer. "Pleasant dreams. You can call room service if you're hungry. Put it on the room tab."

"I walk in, they smile and hand me a key?"

"We don't use keys anymore. Electronic locks. The room is stocked with liquor. Drink it up. Watch TV as much as you want; lots of stations from lots of places. It may amuse you." He looked at me, funnylike.

"What?"

"You ever heard of Rip van Winkle?"

"Dutchman, by the sound of it."

"Went to sleep, woke up in a different world."

"Sounds like a good idea. I'll set the alarm for five years from now."

"Don't bother; it's already here."

6

The desk clerks were expecting me, three of them, very bright eyed. The lobby was bright. The colors of the chairs were bright. The whole thing gave me a headache.

"I'm told I have a room waiting," I said, and looked at the carpet, red with orange fish dancing across a shimmering sea.

"Welcome." Three clerks, three heads bobbing in unison.

The first of them put a piece of paper on the counter and waved a pen. "Check the information and then sign, if you please. You're staying with us for six nights?"

"Who said I'm staying here six nights?" I signed the form without glancing at it. "I'm leaving tomorrow."

The oldest of the trio nodded vigorously and gave me a little folder with a plastic card in it. "This is your room key. Room Twelve Nineteen, that's on the twelfth floor. Breakfast starts at six thirty on the second floor." He delicately indicated the second floor, his arm extended just so. "And the bar is downstairs, to the left." Also delicately indicated.

"Your luggage is arriving later?" The third of the trio was pretty, like a little bird. She might at any moment, I thought, break out in chirps and whistles.

"No luggage. I was told . . . never mind." Since when did I explain myself to hotel front desks?

The bird rang a small bell; a young man in a tight-fitting yellow uniform appeared next to me. He put out his hand, which I shook. "How do you do?" I said.

He looked at the trio and then at me. "Hand over the key card. I'll take you to your room."

"No need," I said. "I know my way around these places."

"Sure," the young man said. "All the same, it would be my pleasure."

I shuddered inwardly. Unctuousness and neon—a killer combination I had thought would never make it this far up the peninsula, not to Pyongyang. I looked around. The lobby had a few chairs in one corner and a potted plant in another. Along the front wall, near the revolving glass door, was a single chair. Slumped in it was a man wearing a cheap suit and a vacant expression. He had the look of someone doomed forever to stare into morning fog off an empty coast. His eyes took me in, but I wasn't sure what had registered. It was all getting to be unnerving—the streetlights, the lobby, this man staring into nothing. Maybe Li was right. Maybe I really didn't know as much as I thought I once did. Maybe I didn't know anything anymore.

Chapter Two

The young man in yellow came up in the elevator with me, opened the door to a room, turned on the lights, and stood next to the bed. "The TV is there," he said. "The bathroom is there."

It was a big room, but not so big I couldn't have figured out either of those on my own. "Sure." I looked around. "Classy place. Wouldn't want to confuse those two."

"You can get music in the bath if you like. There's a TV screen there, too, if you get lonely. Don't worry; it only goes one way."

I nodded.

"Also, the drapes open electronically. Don't try fooling with them by hand or you'll break something. I can find you something if you get real lonely, better than the TV." He rubbed the fingers on one hand together.

"Why don't you go back downstairs and be slimy with your friends?"

He didn't seem offended; at least, the grin he gave me looked real enough. "I could do that." He held out his hand.

"I already shook with you. Is this a new hotel custom, shaking hands on every floor?"

"A tip, you know—a gratuity, service charge, payment in advance for errands to be run, a friendly barrier against unfavorable winds and life's unexpected turns. See what I mean?"

I walked past him to the door, held it open, and jerked my head in the direction of the hallway. "I'll give you a tip," I said. "Don't play with matches."

2

I sat on the bed and studied the place. It was square, and no attempt had been made to hide that basic fact. "You are paying to sleep in a box," each of the walls said. One of them had a window in the center, which might have broken the monotony except that the window was square. If I'd had a suitcase, at this point I would have unpacked. There was a certain satisfaction, I recalled, in unpacking a suitcase in a hotel room. On overseas liaison trips for the Ministry, I stayed mostly in cheap rooms. To open the drawers and put something in, even only a pair of socks, gave an air of permanence, of personality, to a place.

The bureau was pine stained to look like something else. It had three drawers. I opened each of them. Usually there was a piece of paper, emergency instructions, something in them. These were empty, a mini-universe of infinite nothingness. I took the wood chips from my pocket and dumped them on the desk. This place needed something. There was nothing homey about it, not like the Koryo Hotel. Why hadn't they put me up there? Maybe they were installing the neon lights and laying new carpets. I hated to think what had been done to its lobby.

A soft knock on the door brought me back. "What?" I wasn't expecting visitors.

"Housekeeping."

"Go away."

"Turndown service."

I walked over to the entryway. "Turndown what?"

"Turndown service."

I opened the door to find a middle-aged woman in a maid's uniform. "I'm supposed to turn down your bed and leave a candy on your pillow," she said. "You want it or don't you?"

"No, I don't." I started to close the door, but then a question occurred to me. "Who owns this place?"

"What?"

"Who owns this hotel? It's foreign, isn't it? It doesn't feel right. The fellow in the tight pants even asked for a tip."

She gave me a big smile. "I'm sure I don't know what you mean, sir."

"Sir? Who taught you to say that? I suppose you curtsey now, too."

She bobbed her head. "Good evening and pleasant dreams."

The phone rang, so I closed the door and went over to the desk. The phone was white, new, with lots of buttons on it. I took a chance and punched one of them. "Yes?"

"Inspector, I hope I didn't wake you."

"Who is this?"

"You don't recognize my voice?"

"Should I?"

"This is Major Kim. We saw each other briefly this evening, though we weren't introduced. I thought we might have a drink, talk a little, trade stories. That sort of thing."

"That sort of thing."

"If you're hungry, we can get a bite to eat. I don't think the hotel restaurant is still open, and the room service menu is not exciting, but there are other places nearby you might enjoy."

"Noodles."

"What's that?"

"I said noodles. I like noodles."

"Well, then, noodles it is." A silence. "You there?"

"Sure." This was the man who made everyone nervous. I didn't need noodles all that badly. "I was thinking. It's getting late; maybe I should skip eating tonight."

"Don't do that, Inspector. You never know when you'll get another chance."

No wonder he makes people nervous, I thought. "OK, where?"

"I'm in the parking lot in front of the hotel right now. Come down in five minutes. You'll find me; don't worry."

"I'll be wearing what I had on before."

"I know."

3

The restaurant was in a building that hadn't been there the last time I was in Pyongyang. It was in my old patrol sector, and in those days I knew every crummy structure, every crack in every façade, every doorway out of plumb, and every crooked window. This place was modern, only three stories high but very sleek. The front door opened to a small vestibule where a young woman in a low-cut long red dress waited.

"Good evening, Major Kim," she said. "Your table is ready." She didn't look at me, not even a glance, before turning to lead us to a corner in the back, where there was a triangular table surrounded by a lot of plants. We sat, and the lady in red disappeared.

"You look to be in shock, Inspector. Anything I can do for you? Maybe we should start with a couple of drinks." The major pressed a button on the side of the table, and a man wearing an austere smile and a white coat appeared.

"Your usual, sir?" he asked.

"Yes, Michael, thank you. And one for our guest, as well."

The white coat vanished behind a fern.

"Michael?" I said. "Have we stopped the pretense of Korean names at last? Do I get to pick my own? Or have you already selected one for me? Let me guess. Paul? No, probably not. Matthew, perhaps? At least we're not going for Japanese names again. My grandfather hated his. He never told me what it was."

"Do you know who I am?" The major sat at arm's length from the table, making clear to anyone watching that we were not trading secrets. "Why don't we start there? The rest of the conversation will flow much more easily."

An easily flowing conversation was the last thing I wanted with this man. "The girl in the red dress. Unusual accent."

The major showed me his teeth. "Very good, Inspector. Most people don't hear the accent. They're too captivated by the neckline."

"The accent, I can't quite place it. It's been nearly trained out of her, but something is still there, a faint echo. Sort of fetching, in its own way."

"Anything else?"

"Smarmy group in the hotel; a few of them are still shy a coat or two of hospitality paint."

"Something wrong with the hotel? The room not up to your expectations?" He leaned forward to show me that he cared.

"The room is fine. Everything is fine. Our meeting earlier this evening in that dark cave was fine. You've made a hit with those three house dogs, by the way. Maybe you should throw them a bone every so often, though."

The austere smile materialized from around a potted palm, and drinks were placed in front of us.

"Thank you, Michael," the major said. "We'll order in a few minutes."

The white coat disappeared into the jungle.

"Do you always circle around a conversation like this?" The major lifted his glass. "A toast to you, Inspector. Welcome home."

"Major what? Major who? Major from where? Is there a new special group operating outside the normal channels?" I clinked glasses. "Normal channels. Normal. You know what's normal? Dawn, the sun coming up over the next mountain. That's perfectly normal. But this, I don't get the feeling this," I waved my glass in his direction, "is normal."

"Off we go, circling again."

"OK, no more circles. I'll lunge. Where are you from?" I took a swallow of my drink.

"Seoul."

I took another swallow. "Do they have menus here, or do we make it up? Incidentally," I pointed over his shoulder, "whoever installed the wire in that ficus behind you didn't know what he was doing. It dangles, like a water snake over a pond." The drink had skipped my stomach and gone to my brain. "I wouldn't use a wire if I were you. If you use something like that snake in the ficus, it has to be transcribed. Transcribers always fill in what they can't hear, and they always get it wrong. Hire a note taker. I'll bet that woman in the red dress is a terrific note taker."

Major Kim shook his head. "Don't worry. We don't guess. We don't have to. Our equipment is very, very, very good."

Interesting, I thought to myself, he was from the South, and his girlfriend with the soft accent and the neckline was, too. That wasn't so odd, was it? South Koreans had been coming up north for years. So there were two of them here, so what? My inner voice tried to keep a normal tone, nothing alarmist, but it wasn't very convincing. Li's words of warning to me hung like a wreath from the branches of the ficus: You don't know what you think you know.

"You're back in Pyongyang because we need your help, Inspector." Kim swirled the liquor in his glass. "There is a little problem, and we think you might be able to fix it."

4

Whenever I hear "we" in connection with the word "problem," especially "little problem," I start to worry. First my nerves go on alert; then I start to worry.

"Sorry," I said, "I'm not in the problem-fixing business anymore. I'm in no business. I follow no professional path. I'm unencumbered, untroubled, and uninterested. To tell you the truth—and you are partial to the truth; I sensed that right away—if the price of dinner is listening to your problem, I can drink a beer in my hotel room. I hope that doesn't seem rude." I started to push back my chair. "Anyway, I don't think I'm authorized to talk to you." I wasn't authorized to talk to anyone as far as I was concerned. That's why I had gone up on the mountain.

"Please, sit, Inspector. This wasn't my first choice for an assignment, believe me. I was due for Paris, but this came up, unexpectedly, you might say." His eyes wandered the room without much interest. "Destiny calls; personnel decisions trump everything. So I found myself here six months ago. That's a long time to be sitting in meetings with people who hate your guts, don't you think?"

"Only six months? Six months is nothing. If it's so bad, why don't they send you home? Declare you persona non grata."

The major laughed, but it wasn't particularly pleasant. It was more like the sound of a dead limb coming off a tree on a hillside nearby. For the first time, I noticed he had a classic Korean face, the sharp features that opened the gateway to a thousand different expressions. My grandfather had warned me that people with these faces were real Koreans—the purest of the pure, he called them—and that you couldn't trust them because you could never figure out what was going through their minds. "The women are the worst," he'd say. "A woman with that face will be a princess one minute and a bird of prey the next. I don't like Chinese, but a little Chinese blood mixed in isn't altogether bad. Your grandmother had Chinese blood. Remember that, boy," and I'd nod, wondering if any of the girls in the next village were pure-blooded and, if they were, would they ever take the road in front of our house so I could watch as they passed by.

Kim's voice battered into my consciousness. "Kick me out?

How could they? I countersign all of their orders, and much as I would be tempted, I couldn't chop off on that one." He laughed; another limb crashed to the ground.

"You countersign all of the orders?" I lifted my glass and tilted it toward the major to show him how empty it was.

"Another drink?"

"Tell Michael to bring the whole bottle."

He pushed the button and Michael materialized.

"Shall I bring the bottle, sir?"

"As always, you read my mind, Michael."

"Michael, the mind reader," I said as the white coat vanished. "He also runs your very good recording machines and picks locks, am I right?"

"No, Inspector, the lock man is the busboy. You had a question about my countersigning orders?"

I did but decided to skip it for the moment. That was a detail. I didn't need to know details right now. I needed to know the guts of what this was, this man, this restaurant, the woman with the soft accent, the hotel room stocked with liquor. "Actually, my question was more fundamental. Who are you? After that, I might have a second question."

"Which is?"

"Let's do them in order. Who are you?"

"Put it this way: I'm your best friend starting today. Whatever happens, you can rest assured that I'm going to help you. Things may come unglued, but you don't have to worry, because I am your insurance policy."

"Very comforting. Or it would be but for one thing. You still haven't told me who you are. I don't mean your name. I don't mean your title. I mean, who *are* you? A few gaps in my knowledge I have learned must be accepted. This one, though, I'm not prepared to live with. I could fall into this sort of gap and never be seen again."

"Let me give you some background, Inspector."

"No background. Let's avoid background. Let's try facts. Or don't you recognize those?"

He took out a pack of cigarettes and put them on the table. "We are dealing with a situation of considerable delicacy. Facts are not delicate. They can be upsetting, a burden actually. Anyway, as you know, facts are often in dispute. And there is no time left for disputes. May I smoke?"

"The tune sounds familiar."

"Excellent. In that case, you probably know the dance, as well. You did it long enough, all through your life in this country as a matter of fact. All that's required at this point is a change of partners." He searched his pockets and found a book of matches. I looked quickly at the cover. They were from a hotel I never heard of. The picture looked like a space robot, something Gallic. Maybe it was where he planned to stay in Paris. "Don't worry." He put the matches back in his pocket. "You can't betray what no longer exists."

I pushed the chair back the rest of the way and stood up. Any alcohol not already in my brain hurried up to see what the excitement was about. It was a gamble, but I thought I might make it to the door without running into one of the other tables. "I think I have lost my appetite. Pass my compliments to the girl in the red dress."

"Your hotel is to the left as you exit, Inspector." The major tilted his head slightly but remained seated. "It's a fine walk at night; the sidewalks are well lit. Enjoy the air."

Chapter Three

The bed was comfortable enough, though it had more pillows than anyone could use and the light switch for the lamp on the bedside table wasn't where it should have been. I thought of looking over the agreement before falling asleep, just to be sure no one had altered it, but decided that would be useless. Everything I'd seen so far that night made clear that it didn't matter what had been agreed to four, no, five years before. I wandered around the room and looked at the furniture. It was mostly compressed wood—agreeable enough on the outside but nothing really to it. That was getting to be the theme of the day: unreality. I froze. Something was missing—my wood chips. They weren't on the desk. The desk drawer had a room service menu, a piece of stationery, and a flight schedule. Odd, I thought, and opened the top drawer of the bureau. There were two new shirts in it, both of them my size. The wood chips had been put in a neat pile to one side.

"Well, what do you know about that?" I said, and lay down. The next thing I knew, the phone woke me.

"Good morning, Inspector. This is your wake-up call."

"Did I ask for one?"

"Someone must have. It's early. Take a shower and have some coffee, you'll feel fine."

"Tea. I don't want coffee. I want tea."

"Breakfast is on the second floor. They have plenty of tea. It doesn't start for two hours, though."

"You mean it's only four thirty?" I gave up looking for the light switch and went to take a shower. This was low-level harassment, and I knew there would be more where that came from. Nothing too rough, but enough to make clear who was in the lead and who was supposed to trot behind. Trot behind for what, I still didn't know. I'd left the restaurant before finding out what the "small problem" was. Just as I stepped under the water, the phone rang again. Nice, I thought. I got out and picked up the phone. "Go to hell."

"Good morning to you, too, Inspector."

"What do you want, Major?" I put a towel over the TV screen.

"Simply wondering if you slept well."

I slammed the phone down.

Twenty minutes later it rang again. "Is this a better time? I thought we could have breakfast together in my office."

"Do I have a choice?"

"The driver is waiting out front. See you soon."

2

The office was large and deceptively plain, the sort of plain that comes only with careful thought. Nothing was there by chance, everything had a purpose, and the purpose of the whole was to make it clear that this was a place in which central levers of power were located. Here, the room announced, was not merely the appearance, not simply the trappings, but power in pure form. Pure power didn't need elaborate decoration. A simple blade cuts clean. All right, I said to myself, we're making progress—we know the man has power beyond making people nervous.

Major Kim sat behind a wooden desk so highly polished that

I could see his reflection. It was a solid piece of furniture, quite heavy from the looks of it. The message was clear enough. The desk wasn't going anywhere, and the man behind it was here to stay. The color of the walls was muted, the lighting subdued. The only jarring note I could see was the chairs. They were all different— different colors, different styles. In front of the major's desk was a brown chair, high backed and without arms. It looked uncomfortable, and my guess was it was supposed to be. Slightly behind the brown chair and off to the side was one with a green velvet seat and a low wooden back. Oddly, it was turned away from the desk, facing a group of folding chairs that sat in a semicircle facing each other. Farthest back, next to the wall that held the room's only window, was a lonely stack of black plastic chairs.

The man who had picked me up at the hotel had the air of a duty driver—cheerful, talkative, saying nothing. It was at least an hour before dawn, the streets were deserted, but every streetlight was on. We drove past apartment houses that had not been there the last time I was in Pyongyang, turned into a tunnel I never knew existed, and came out in a compound at the base of a wooded hill. There was a long walkway to a three-story building that had a heavy tank parked on either side. The barrel of the tank on the left followed our progress to the entrance. The driver escorted me past Security, up to the third floor, and all the way to Kim's door. He knocked twice and then left me alone. More psychology. Did I want to wait until a voice told me to come in? Or did I want to push the door open on my own? I walked in. To hell with psychology.

Major Kim was pouring a cup of tea. "Ah, good morning to you, Inspector. I see you're wearing a new shirt. It fits, I hope." He looked at me carefully. "Yes, it does. The neck size is good? Sit, why don't you?" He pointed to the brown chair. If I could see his reflection in the desk, he could see mine. He didn't need to look up to know how I was reacting. "Here I have tea. We can enjoy some fish, a wonderful bowl of soup, and whatever else you might like." He pressed a button under the desk.

"Is Michael on duty?" I glanced around the room. "Or will we have one of the morning crew? Paul, perhaps?"

A door off to the side opened and a middle-aged man in a suit and tie walked in. He eyed me briefly before turning his attention to Major Kim. "It's not going to get any better if we continue to wait. You know that already, I assume."

Kim took the top off the teapot and looked inside. "We have a meeting at nine o'clock." He put the top back in place. "That's why we call it a nine o'clock meeting."

The man grimaced. "Your decision, of course." He started out the door and nearly knocked over an aide carrying a tray.

"Paul." I waved him in. "Good to see you. Put the things down and get out your notebook. Tomorrow, no four A.M. wake-up call, understood? Not four thirty, either. Let's say nothing earlier than five o'clock. Go ahead, write it down; the major doesn't object."

Major Kim sniffed one of the dishes and handed it to the aide. "I don't want this served ever again. Am I clear?" The aide nodded. "Good. And take note of the Inspector's instructions about the wake-up call. If that's what he wants, that's what he gets." The aide nodded again. "Dismissed," said the major.

"Well," said the major, after the aide had closed the door, "nothing here is easy. But then, there's no reason to expect it should be. That's part of the challenge. In case you're wondering, the man in the suit is one of mine. The aide is one of yours."

Mine. Yours. Marking territory, like a dog walking along the street. "A division of labor," I said. "Very smart. Would you like me to haul a few buckets of water?" I looked around the room. "At the very least, let me arrange your chairs for the nine o'clock staff meeting."

"Jumping to conclusions, aren't we, Inspector?"

"You tell me."

The major laid the dishes out on the desk. "Eat first, business later. I'm always hungry in the morning. You?"

"At my age, appetite is no longer central to existence. I don't give it much thought anymore."

"A weary thing to say, Inspector. You aren't going to be glum all day long, I hope. We have a lot to accomplish, and we might as well be cheerful about it. If I weren't careful, I could be depressed all the time, but what's the use of that?"

"A new day dawns. The world is fresh, and yet we confront the same question as we did last night: What is this about?"

"Have some soup."

"I don't want soup. I want to know what this is about, because if I don't find out damn soon, I'm leaving." I didn't think Kim would be fazed. He wasn't.

"Leaving. Again. I would have told you last night, but you left in a hurry. Don't press your luck, Inspector. I'd hoped to give you a lot of space to get used to things, but that's not going to be possible."

"I see."

"No, I doubt that you do." There was the tiniest flash of steel in his voice. "The fact is, from here on out, you are under my direct command. You take orders from me; you report to me; you jump when I tell you to jump."

Really? What led him to believe such a thing? I'd just spent five years on a mountaintop not following anyone's orders. I was going back in harness at the snap of his fingers? Not likely. "Yesterday, you were my insurance policy, my best pal. Now you are suggesting I am a draft animal. Something happen overnight?"

The major smiled obliquely; I checked off one of his thousand expressions. "I'm still your pal; don't misunderstand. But I'll crack your skull open and cook your brains for breakfast if you give me trouble. Is that clear?"

"Finally, we're getting somewhere. Let me put two and two together. You're from the South, as you told me last night. You seem to be under the impression that you are my superior. Street-lights are on everywhere. And the room maid addresses me as 'sir.' Shall I take a guess at what has happened? Or what might happen?"

"No. You won't be doing any guessing, Inspector. There's no margin here for that. I move according to stone-cold facts. And that's what you will do from now on, too." He shrugged. "Confused? I suggested to you last night that facts are inconvenient, but so is reality. Facts may be a problem, but reality is a killer. There's no way around reality, in my experience. Admittedly, you seem to have spent a lifetime avoiding it."

3

"Let me get this straight." I reached in my pocket for a piece of pine.

The major frowned. "What's that? One of those wood chips you carry around?"

"This?" I held it up for him to see. "It's pine, that's all, a very uncomplicated wood. It helps me think uncomplicated thoughts. Nothing threatening about it, don't worry. It won't explode or anything."

"Uncomplicated thoughts? By all means, Inspector, let's keep things simple. Maybe I should pass out some of that wood to my staff. Do you have more?"

I considered that. "No, I don't think it would do any good. What works for me might not work for them."

"And what work is that? More adducing of the evidence assembled so far? Is this a reflection of your training or your temperament, Inspector?"

"The three dogs at the long table last night knew who you are. Paul the pliant waiter has a reasonably good idea. Everyone around here knows, I take it. Everyone but me."

"Not everyone. Let's say everyone that matters."

"So, do I matter?" I got up and walked over to the window. The view told me nothing. It was an inner courtyard with two wooden benches, a few flowerpots with bright yellow mums, and a stone fountain made to look like a mountain waterfall, but it wasn't turned on. The sky above the courtyard was still dark, but there was soft lighting around the fountain to illuminate the scene. "Must be pleasant, hearing the sound of water. It soothes the nerves; do you think that's why they put it there? Very stressful, I imagine, working here. This office, for example, it must have been for someone with real power. Whose was it?" I looked at the windows across the way. The curtains were closed. It reminded me of the Operations Building across the courtyard from my old office. Our courtyard had no flowerpots and no fountain. We made do with three old gingko trees and a pile of bricks. "Before you moved in, who had this building?"

"You don't know?"

"Never been here. Never even been near here, I don't think. I never had much to do with buildings surrounded by tanks."

"Let's just say that whoever was in these offices has moved. They were happy to pack up when they were offered something better."

"You're not going to tell me."

"At the moment, you wouldn't be interested even if I did, because you wouldn't know what I was talking about."

"I might."

"No, Inspector, I'm quite serious. This building was for a group formed after you left. Or is 'retired' the term we're supposed to use?" I didn't rise to that crummy piece of bait. "The group was put together for a very specific purpose. That purpose has been overtaken by events. A lot has happened since you left."

"People keep telling me that."

"Perhaps you should pay attention."

I went back to the brown chair. There was no way to relax in it, no way to strike a pose of nonchalance in front of Kim. "I'm listening. I'm not going to interrupt. Sit and absorb—will that suffice?"

"We want you to take charge of a camp." The idea came out of nowhere. It might have been better phrased, probably more effective, if he'd led up to it. But maybe he figured that the direct approach would catch me off balance. It did.

Sitting down again had been a big mistake, I realized. I should have remained standing. That way I could have walked out the door as soon as I heard him—out the door, down the walkway, over the hills, anywhere but here. But now I was sitting, and getting out of the chair would take those few extra few drops of will that his words had bled out of me in the hurry. Kim didn't add anything. He watched the reflection on the desktop, waiting for my reaction.

"You mean you haven't disbanded the camps?" The question was so obvious it was beside the point.

"No, not yet." Kim looked up at me in a curious way. "It's way too soon for that, don't you agree?"

It must have been a stray note in his voice that rang the bell. That's what he wanted; he wanted me to say yes to something—anything. Get a "yes" into the conversation, a tiny crack in the door. One single spark of assent, that's all it took to light the fire. I'd nearly forgotten. I'd grown stale, up on a mountaintop forgetting everything I had ever learned, while he had been in this office, sharpening his technique every day. He was better than I thought, and that meant he was dangerous.

Kim appeared relaxed, but I could sense he was wondering if he'd moved a half step too fast. That's why he followed up when he should have stayed quiet, let the idea simmer. "The camps, as you can understand, are a very delicate problem. We did try to disband a couple, but things turned disruptive. There were too many people walking around with too many bad stories. We don't want an increase in negative feeling toward the current regime, do we?" He smiled to himself, a sarcastic smile, a smile that said he could afford to be ironic on this question because he was sitting behind the polished desk and I was not. "Negative feeling—that wouldn't be very helpful. Besides, we had experience running our own camps not so many years ago, you know. And we've also learned from what other people have done, as well, to get ourselves ready for this situation. Running prison camps isn't easy; neither is getting rid of them. So much complaining! No one approves of them. No one wants to touch them. But, everybody gets their feet wet sooner or later. It's unavoidable. The result is, there's a large body of experience to draw from."

"Which means?"

"Which means we're improving the conditions a little at a time, retraining your guards, instituting new rules. But the camps themselves stay, for a while anyway. We figure what they need is leadership." This time he gave himself an extra beat for pacing. "That's you. You have the credentials, grandson of a Hero of the Republic and all that."

"What about the Prison Bureau? Are you going to leave those psychopaths in place?"

"How comforting to know you never agreed with what was going on in those offices, Inspector! A little rearranging is in the works; I can tell you that much. A replacement here and there."

"This is the little problem you wanted me to fix?"

He said nothing. I looked at my bowl of soup. My grandfather had made soup every morning, relentlessly, without fail. Every 6:00 A.M., there it was, even in the heat of summer—soup. I pushed the bowl away. That's why I was here, nothing to do with prisons. They needed my grandfather; they needed his blessing from the grave. Good luck, I thought. They weren't going to get it, not through me.

"I can give you the names of plenty of people who would take the job," I said. "You need someone with the right temperament for that sort of thing. You don't want me."

"Aren't you going to ask which camp?"

"I'm not interested."

"Of course, just like you were uninterested for the past fifty years in what went on inside those fences?"

This sounded very much like a knife cutting through flesh. A little soon, I thought, for him to make the move to the negative. He should have waited another round; he still had a few problems with pacing. Maybe they didn't spend much time on that sort of thing in the South. "Apparently, this is the moment for me to chop wood for you," I said. "Or maybe it is the day to polish one of the tanks?"

Kim looked at my bowl. "You finished with the soup? I'll have the dishes cleared."

"Yes, let's bring in the trained monkey again." We were done with the feint about the camp job, and he'd let the subject of my grandfather drop. So why did they send the ferret to fetch me from the mountain? What was so important that they needed me here?

The dishes were whisked away, and the first rays of sunlight came through the window behind me, glinting off a group of framed maps on the opposite wall. Somehow, they missed Kim's eyes. Maybe he repelled sunlight, I thought. We sat in silence. Kim pushed a button and the shades on the window went down halfway. "I hope you don't mind," he said. "But I find the morning sun this time of year a little hard to take."

Simple, I thought. Have Michael and Paul move the fucking desk.

Kim opened a file and began to leaf through it. He stopped with the last page, which he held flat on the desktop so I could see that it was a list of names.

"Tell me, Inspector," he said finally. "Do I have your cooperation, or don't I?" He had his pencil poised over the paper.

"No." I stood up. That wasn't the real question, and I didn't plan to wait another hour or two for him to get to the main point. He had something he wanted me to do, and I had no intention of doing it. If he thought he had some power over me, let him try. "If there will be nothing else, I have to get to the hotel to pack my things."

He made a mark on the list, a small *x* next to a name. "Returning to the mountain, Zarathustra?" He crossed out one name near the top, then another. "I can have a car waiting for you. It can't be done today. How about tomorrow? About noon?"

4

Downstairs, I realized I didn't know how to get back to my hotel from here, because I didn't know where "here" was. The duty driver was nowhere around, and no one offered me a ride. When I stepped outside and started down the walkway, I felt a tank gun barrel following me. Small-caliber weapons aimed at my back might not register, but a tank barrel—always. At the end of the walkway, a jeep sat idling, with a man in an unfamiliar uniform and a red armband at the wheel. He indicated I should get in, drove at high speed through the tunnel, and pulled over as soon as we emerged.

"End of the line," he said.

"How far are we from my hotel?"

"Beats me," he said. "This is your city, not mine. And as far as I'm concerned you can have it." He put the jeep in gear and roared back through the tunnel.

I tried to orient myself, but there were no landmarks on the horizon to help. Off to the right, several new, tall buildings were going up. In front of me, an entire block had been leveled. A brief walk around convinced me that I was in the far western part of the city, some distance from the Taedong River and a long way from any subway stop that could get me back to the central district, close to my hotel.

When west, walk east. Maybe I'd run across a traffic cop whom I could ask for directions. They didn't know much, but they could usually figure out which direction the river was. As far as I could tell, no one was following me. It didn't really matter; in fact, it might be better if there was. If I got too lost, my tail might get tired and give me a ride back to the hotel.

I wasn't in a hurry, I didn't need to be anyplace particular, and the weather was good for a stroll. If I had to be in Pyongyang, a bright October morning was as good a time as any. The trees along the streets were turning color, and in an hour or so smoke from roasting chestnuts and sweet potatoes would be drifting from the kiosks. Already the air was painted with faraway hope. It was an autumn sky remembered from years past, always sparkling in anticipation—in anticipation of what I never understood. My grandfather said autumn was a party, that most trees acted foolishly drunk in the fall and then wept at their loss all winter long. He didn't like evergreens, but he said at least they were sober.

I walked about a kilometer, taking in the sunshine and becoming more and more uneasy. The problem was that no matter which way I turned, Li's warnings from the other night trailed beside me. No, I didn't know what I didn't know, but I was beginning to get a few ideas. Major Kim had extraordinary authority, he was from the South, and Pyongyang had the indefinable feel of a tiny planet beginning to wobble on its axis. There were more babies, more children being pushed in strollers, more couples walking together. The traffic ladies weren't where they ought to be. There were fewer of them, and they were doing their ballet in the smaller intersections. They looked the same as ever— same blue uniforms, same pouty lips—but none of them blew their whistles when I crossed in the middle of the street instead of taking the underpass. Even the cranes at the construction sites had changed, the old, stubby dinosaurs replaced by long, graceful booms. It wasn't only how things looked. It was how they felt, how they fit together. A city can change in five years, I thought, but not like this. It wasn't until I went up a long flight of stairs and crossed high over a train yard that the growing panic in my chest subsided. I stopped and looked down. Here, at least, the grime was familiar.

From the train yard, I knew, it wasn't far to the subway entrance. A tall man leaned against the railing, watching the traffic.

"Don't tell me," I said. "You're waiting for a bus."

Li kept his eyes on the traffic. "My car is on the next street. Let's go for a ride."

"Let's not. I'm getting out of here, compliments of Major Kim."

"I'll take a wild guess. He said he'd send a car for you tomorrow at your hotel."

"He did."

"And you believed him?"

"The man gave me soup for breakfast. How can I not believe him?"

"Never take soup from strangers, O—always sage advice. Let's not stand around. It makes me nervous."

I followed him to his car. "What makes you think Kim won't have someone right behind you?"

"He will. He already does." We pulled onto a busy street. "But he won't for long. These people are very sure of themselves, very sure we are idiots."

We turned left into a small alley, raced through the courtyard of an apartment complex, flew across a bridge, and ended up behind three small trucks in the parking lot of a blue-roofed market overflowing with people.

"Out, Inspector. You're going to do a little shopping. Don't look around; go right inside."

"Am I missing something? I thought you worked for Kim."

"See you later."

Inside, the market was a crush of bodies. For a moment, in the fruit section, I was stranded next to the bananas. Bananas! I gawked at them. Since when did normal people even in the capital have bananas to eat? Then a man pulled on my arm and I broke through the masses into a small office. The door shut behind me.

"You can wait here." The man let go of my arm. A middle-aged woman with a baseball cap sat at a desk working a calculator. She frowned at the numbers. "Too many fucking zeros," she muttered.

"Busy place," I said. It was a cinch I was trapped, that Major Kim would come through the door at any moment, with one of his tanks close behind.

"Major Kim, if that's what is worrying you, has meetings today." The woman didn't look up as she spoke. "He has a nine o'clock. Also, today is Thursday. He gets a haircut on Thursdays."

"What about his minions?"

The woman turned and appraised me carefully, from head to toe. "His minions aren't looking for trouble. They live a cushy life up here, and they don't want to spoil things. If they make us mad, we'll see that things get difficult for them. So they ease up when they sense we're serious. Self-preservation ranks high on their list of priorities."

"So, are we serious?"

The woman turned off the calculator and put it in a small cloth case before she stood up and looked directly into my eyes. "We are, Inspector. We are deadly serious. Are you?"

The man whispered in the woman's ear. She gave him a little nudge and locked the door after him. "A question, Inspector." She moved closer to me, so close that the brim of her cap touched my forehead. "There's a question pending. Do you want to answer it? Or shall I answer it for you?" She was round, very confident about who she was.

"You asked the question," I said. "Maybe you should answer it. Seems only fair."

"You don't act serious. You don't sound serious. I don't think you are. But I think you will become serious, Inspector, sooner than you imagine. And I'll tell you why—because there is no other way for you to survive."

"Business is good?" I didn't think I wanted to stay too long with this confident woman. I certainly didn't want to slip into an extended conversation with her about survival, definitely not about my survival. "Maybe you should put up extra lights. Everyplace else in the city has more than enough. That way you can see how much the ladies behind the counter are stealing."

"The real crooks are always somewhere else, Inspector. Do you know what is going on in your Ministry these days?"

"It isn't my Ministry. I'm retired."

"So you say. You gave me some advice. Now I'll give you some: Open your eyes; look around." She finally stepped back. "Someone will be in touch." She unlocked the door and indicated I should leave.

I figured Major Kim would be waiting outside, but there was only crowd of people around a table loaded with shoes. None of them looked my size, so I headed toward the exit. When I finally made it into the fresh air of the parking lot, an elbow jammed into my ribs.

"Got a match?" It was the bellboy from the hotel, grinning. "Didn't think you'd be here with the rest of us poor stiffs. Want to buy something? I can show you around."

"Thanks, but no thanks." I started to walk away, but he grabbed my shoulder. "Not so fast, Inspector. You want to stay right here for another minute or two." He nodded toward the street that lay beyond the parked cars. Major Kim was craning his neck, searching the area.

"Is there another exit?" I shook off the bellboy's hand and stepped back toward the market entrance.

"On the other side."

Three young women formed a screen around me, pushed through the crowd, and deposited me on the other side. The bellboy followed close behind. "There are a couple of taxis lined up near that apartment house across the street," he said, "but I'd stay out of cabs if I were you."

"You're not me."

He shrugged. "Yeah, I'm lucky that way."

Chapter Four

When I got to the street, Li's car came around the corner and stopped in front of me. "Don't argue," he said. "Get in."

We drove for a few minutes before Li said anything else. "I don't suppose you're interested in knowing about Major Kim." He rolled down his window. "You notice how stuffy it gets in a car this time of year?"

"No, I'm not interested in the major. I don't know, and I don't want to know. Clear enough?"

We turned into the hotel parking lot. A big blue car with two men in the front and all the windows open was waiting not far from the hotel entrance. One of the men jumped out and opened the rear door. A woman emerged from the restaurant attached to the hotel, walked straight to the car, and got in. The car pulled away in a hurry.

"I don't suppose you're interested in that, either." Li watched the car disappear.

"Should I be?"

"The lady didn't catch your eye? Very fashionable, don't you think? Quite a looker."

"Fashion was never my style. Expensive shoes, expensive coat, expensive scarf, that's what it looked like from here. Everything looks expensive on a body like that."

"So, who do you think wears expensive clothes these days?"

"Could be someone with money." I got out of the car.

"What's your hurry, Inspector? No way he's going to let you go home. Incidentally, I hope you locked the front door on your mountain retreat. They took the guard off the road this morning."

I got back in the car. "All right, you win. Who is Kim? I'm interested, after all. And you seem to know something you're dying to tell me."

"Wrong. I'm not dying for anyone, not anymore. That's done with."

"Who is Kim?"

"I'm not sure about everything, even though I'm in and out of his office. They don't want us to know too much. He appeared about six months ago. After that, there were a lot of meetings up top, cars racing around, aircraft coming in at odd hours, street closings for high-speed convoys. I got pulled off my normal assignment and put into his group, or at least the group that sits up whenever he calls. We do a lot of bowing and scraping."

"He's a major. Since when do we cringe at majors?"

"Funny, isn't it?"

"Yeah, funny. He acts like he owns the place. This morning I met him in an office I never knew existed. You must know what it was before he got there. It wasn't a Ministry building; we don't have that many chairs." I opened my window. "The air smells different in autumn, don't you think?"

"I hadn't noticed. I just breathe the stuff. And I intend to keep breathing." He gave me a sharp look.

"Noble goal," I said. The conversation was over. If he knew anything else, he was going to wait to tell me. Maybe it was actually everything he knew, though I had a feeling he had something he was saving. Everyone was saving something. The lady in the market, the bellboy, maybe even the ferret. "What about the lady?" I said.

"Which one?"

"The one with the nice shoes we were talking about."

"Forget you saw her; forget you saw her come out of that restaurant and get into that car."

"What car? I think you need to have your medication adjusted."

He laughed. "You think I'm edgy, you should see the people in the Minister's office." He laughed again, only this time it came out more like dead leaves in the wind. Dead tree limbs, dead leaves—laughs weren't what they used to be. We used to laugh a lot in the office. It helped sometimes.

"Give me a call," I said, though I don't think he heard me. His eyes were on the rearview mirror, watching a black car creep into the parking lot. As soon as I closed the door, he gunned the motor and was gone. The black car didn't follow, though I was pretty sure the driver said something to the person in the back before he got out and looked at me. He was missing most of his left ear.

Strange, I thought. Nice-looking woman like that. It seems a shame to pretend she was never there.

When I went back into the hotel, the man with the vacant look was leaning against one of the pillars. He had on a red-checked shirt, but it didn't make any difference. As he shifted his gaze to me, everything around him turned gray; foghorns sounded in the distance; seabirds lost their way and plunged into the ocean. I nodded at him, and it appeared that he blinked, like the lamp in a lighthouse that swings around every minute to keep ships off the rocks.

2

Things seemed jumpy, but not in the normal way. People had always looked over their shoulders, and no one thought twice about it. That's why your neck swivels, we used to say, to see who's following you. This was different.

"You've been away a long time," Li said when we met in a noodle place the next day.

"A long time," I said, "but not forever. I can still tell the difference between a routine twitch and something more serious."

"You're imagining things. Relax."

Only I wasn't imagining anything. Li was nervous; each time I'd met him over the past few days, he'd become more antsy. Kim was nervous, too. That was harder to spot. From the few times I'd seen him so far, he was good at cloaking himself in an unflappable air. People who were scared didn't look too closely at the cloak. But Kim didn't scare me, so I could afford to watch him carefully.

I'd been out of my hotel a couple of times to get my mental bearings. Normal people walking along the street weren't on edge; whatever the problem was, it hadn't come down to their level. People had a certain stride, a certain way of moving when they sensed a big storm coming. I'd patrolled my sector long enough to spot that move, that odd swing of the shoulders. I wasn't seeing anything like that, and it wasn't just the particular part of town around my hotel. All the barometers were holding steady at street level, that's how it seemed. The problem—whatever it was—had so far been kept over the horizon, as if one circle was wound tight and wasn't interested in letting anyone else know. That usually meant things were going to get a lot worse.

"If you think you're fooling me," I said, "forget it. You're about to jump out of your skin. When you saw that lady heading for the car yesterday afternoon, I thought you were going to have a stroke."

"She's a looker, that's all."

"Sure, and I'm the King of Siam. You have secrets? That's fine with me. I don't like secrets anymore. They ruin the digestion."

"I told you before. I'll tell you again, O. You don't know what you don't know."

"Yes—and I can't even guess. How about you tell me a little

bit of what I don't know. Maybe it would help me keep my balance."

Li stared at the table.

"You want another bowl?" I said.

He shook his head. "You said you owed me a meal. We'll let this one count." An alarm went off, and he looked at his watch.

"You in a hurry?"

"Unlike you, Inspector, I have no choice." He pressed a button on the watch and the alarm stopped. "It's Swiss." He held it up for me to see. "I don't use all the dials, but it doesn't matter. I like to look at it sometimes. It makes me think I'm someone else."

I decided to sit at the table and relax for a while after he left. The restaurant was on a corner not far from the subway. That meant a steady stream of people passed by. Watching people relaxed me. It also kept me alert. That was the only thing I missed all those years living on the mountain, watching people. I like trees, but they don't move much.

Years ago, in Pakistan, I had learned something special about observing people. Pakistan was not something I wanted to remember. I was young and had been on an operation there that went badly. After racing away through the crowds and the dust and the awful heat, I had rested in the shade of a walnut tree, sweating from exertion and sick with fear.

"You are not well," a quavering voice came from the other side of the tree. "That disturbs the harmony of this place."

"How about water?" I said. "Anything around here?"

"Sit in the shade a moment."

A minute later, a gnarled old man slid over beside me. He held out several leaves. "These will slake your thirst," he said. "They'll also calm you down."

I didn't bother to ask what the leaves were. My mood was such that if they killed me, so much the better. Just then, a woman walked by, the pale scarf over her head flowing behind.

"Did you see?" asked the gnarled man.

The shade had deepened; it had become a being separate from the tree, something different from a mere shadow. I could feel myself relaxing.

"There is a trail of existence that follows everyone, threads of life that people spin out and leave behind wherever they go," said the old man. "Threads cross all the time. Threads cross and cross again—time and place, if in no other way—even when the people appear unaware of each other. That girl who walked by, did you see the thread?"

"You have a few more of those leaves?"

"You've had enough. Listen to me." His voice became musical. "No one pays much attention to others around them unless the overlap happens again. Sometimes, people miss each other only by a few seconds, yet they are connected. Sometimes place is the reason for the overlap, but time is not. Sometimes the overlap is purposeful, other times happenstance. The threads are there, no matter. When they glow, they are one destiny." He put his hand on my forehead. "Cooler now?"

I sat at the restaurant table, looking out the window. The threads stretched in all directions, shimmering in the afternoon sun, as unthreatening and deeply peaceful as the longest sleep. Maybe the threads were reality and people were merely the vessels containing their existence. A woman walked by. Something made me pay attention. She was dressed plainly, no fancy coat, no fancy shoes, no fancy scarf. I watched the thread. It glowed slightly as it crossed the one Li had left behind.

Chapter Five

When the mountain rumbled, it was usually on Thursdays around noon. Living alone, you pick up patterns pretty quickly. At first I thought it might be a passing train. The tracks were a distance away, but when I hiked to the top of my mountain, a couple of hundred meters above my house, I could see the rail line that went all the way to the Amnok River. There were rarely trains on Thursday, but the rumbling went on anyway.

I wasn't supposed to see anyone without permission, but it didn't take long for the farmers in a nearby village to notice the smoke from my cooking fire and come up to find out what was going on. There were four of them. They watched from a distance until I waved them over.

"Welcome," I said.

They nodded.

"May I offer you something to drink? You must be thirsty after the climb."

They shuffled their feet and talked among themselves.

"Perhaps you could clear up something for me," I said. "The rumbling, the way the mountain shakes—do you know what it is?"

The tallest of the four looked at a group of big pine trees that stood in front of my house. "It's the blasting," he said slowly. "They are building dams, supposed to stop the flooding we get in the summer, and maybe give us some electricity to run the pumps. The army boys are doing it." He pointed vaguely to the north. "On a clear day, you might spot it from up here when trucks and whatnot aren't raising a lot of dust. Take good care of those trees." He leaned back in order to see all the way to the top. "If you don't, someone will chop them down, sure as I'm standing here."

The other three looked anxious to go.

"It was good of you to come," I said. "But you'll have to leave. This mountain is badly off-limits."

One of the four laughed. He was short, red-brown from the sun, a little better dressed than the others, and quicker in his gestures. "I'm the manager of the farm at the foot of this mountain, and that means—in case you didn't know—this mountain is technically my responsibility. I have to make sure no one is breaking regulations." He looked at me with an expression so serious that anyone would have believed he was a serious man. "I can't at this point say that you are; I can't say that you aren't."

The others began to walk back toward the road, as if they had heard the speech before. "Also, we all know that this mountain has been here a lot longer than any of us, longer than any dynasty, longer than any king."

I nodded. He nodded. And the four of them went away.

That first spring, before planting season, the manager returned by himself. "You made it through the winter," he said. His face was still red-brown from the sun.

"I did."

"The others thought you might not. I said you would."

"You were right. That's why you're in charge, I guess."

"You could be low on food about now."

"I'm doing fine."

"That old man in the truck won't be able to get up the road for a few more weeks. If it gets bad enough, come down to the farm. We have a little extra this year. I hear there will be more coming from over there." He nodded toward the south. "Next week, we're having our spring music show. You like music?"

"What's not to like?"

"It's an accordion group. Six of them, very spirited. We won the county competition last year."

"Is that so? They must be good."

Accordion music was a Russian plot, the old men in our village used to say after a few drinks. It was something the Russians left behind to drive us crazy when it dawned on them that we weren't going to be like Eastern Europeans and lick their boots. When I was in the army, headquarters sent down squads of accordionists. It lowered morale alarmingly, though no one would admit it. Even the Ministry had its own accordion troupe that performed overseas every other year. They told me they needed someone to stand on the stage with his hat pushed back and a big grin on his face while the troupe played. The sound of even a single accordion set my teeth on edge. I told them if I had to smile during that much noise I'd murder someone.

During my first year on the mountain, in the spring after the snow had melted and when the road was passable again for a fancy car, my brother drove up to see me. My brother was now very prominent in the party. His name was listed high in the ranks at important occasions; he sat solemnly on the podium among other old men, gave speeches on holidays to schoolchildren. Despite all this, he must have known he had failed; he was not and would never be part of the inner group. If he had done something wrong, I couldn't figure out what it was. He seemed the perfect halberd. For someone like my brother, it was worse than nettlesome to face this knowledge every day. It ate away at him and boiled up the anger that he had carried inside ever since we were young.

When his car stopped in the clearing next to the pine trees, he said something to his driver and they both laughed. Then my brother came into the house. I could see that he was shocked.

"This is where you live? Is this a joke?"

"It's pleasant," I said.

"I thought they had provided you a place to live. I know dogs with better shelters than this. It doesn't even deserve to be called a shack."

"It is not a shack. It's sturdy. I built it myself."

My brother ran his hands along the walls; he reached up and touched the ceiling, which was barely two meters from the ground. "You built this?" He pulled himself together. "This is a disgrace. Why didn't someone tell me things were so bad? Why didn't that fool of a doctor put it in one of his chatty reports? I can help get you out of here. It will mean moving a few files and changing a few orders." He pursed his lips. "This isn't the best time for that, but it can be done."

I said that things were fine as they were and I planned to stay.

"Really?" The shock in his voice gave way to sarcasm. "I forgot; you must be in ecstasy, just you and these trees."

"I have my reasons for being here."

"Don't be ridiculous. They were planning to send you to a camp. The only reason you're here is because I convinced them to put you on this hill instead. They assured me you'd have a house."

"Am I supposed to be grateful? I don't need your help. I never did. We agreed we were not brothers anymore, or have you forgotten?"

He wasn't listening. "The longer you stay, the more they will be convinced that you deserve what you got. Maybe they'll be right."

"The longer I stay, the more I realize I don't want to go back to that madness."

This stopped the conversation.

"Never wise with your words," my brother said finally. "Lucky for you, no one heard it but me."

"Are we done?" I went to the door. "Because if we are, I'm sure you have things to do, memos to write, all of those things that the Center has to have or the world will grind to a halt."

"As always," he said, "you are your own worst enemy. Have it your way; stay up here until you rot." He never came back.

2

After the first load of lumber was used up, I decided to test the limits and phone for more. It wasn't clear who was on the other end of the line.

"Seasoned lumber," I said. "Galvanized nails, otherwise they rust. And wood screws—try to get the ones with the flat heads. That way I can countersink them. Wait, I also need sandpaper. Two sheets of fine, one medium, and one coarse."

"That's it? Nothing else?" The voice on the other end sounded surprised. "Screws and sandpaper?"

"Can you get them?"

"Sure I can get them. I'm a magician. I wave my magic wand and everyone gets everything they want. Last week, a man called from another place—I can't say where—and asked for fresh fruit. He said his gums were bleeding. I'm still looking for fruit. Screws will be no problem."

About two months later, the old man in the old truck was back with a shipment of boards, a box of nails mixed with screws of various sizes and types, and three or four torn sheets of sandpaper.

"The guards at the bottom of the hill emptied the box and looked at every damn screw. Normally, they wave me through without a second glance. There must be something going on."

"As long as it stays at the bottom of the hill," I said, "I could give a fine fuck."

"Yeah," said the old man, "that's what I thought."

One of the few things I had brought with me, besides my grandfather's tools and a few pieces of furniture he'd made, was a radio. Reception was poor, but I could hear something over the static the few nights a week I got electricity. At first there was only electricity a few hours a day and some days not at all, but by the third year the outages were only on Thursdays and usually only in the afternoons. At one point, I wondered if rumbling on Thursdays had anything to do with the power outages. Maybe every time they set off a charge, they blew over a power line by mistake. When I was in the army, things like that happened more than ever made it into the reports.

A doctor visited twice a year. He said they told him it was owed me because of my family's loyal service, but I had a suspicion my brother had sent him up to spy on me. If he was a spy, he was melancholy and soft-spoken. The second year, he brought books that he thought I should read. He brought Tolstoy and Chekhov in Russian, which I read slowly and with some difficulty. The third year, he carried in his pocket a small book that must have been read a hundred times.

"What is this?" I asked as he handed it to me.

"Kafka," he said. "Make sure it's a clear, sunny day and sit outside when you read it. Don't try to read it at night, and whatever you do, don't read it when the wind is blowing."

"Why not?"

"If I know you, you'll want to devour it in huge chunks. Don't. Sip it as if it were boiling-hot soup. If you're not careful, you can hurt yourself with Kafka. It can make you very cynical." He smiled.

3

The house had not been so difficult to build. It was a simple structure, basically a box with two windows in the front and one in the back, a front door, and a flat roof. The ceiling was low, but I didn't have many tall visitors. A few times every winter, I had to go up on the roof and shovel off the snow, so eventually I built a simple ladder permanently up the side. Rough carpentry was less a problem than perfecting the skills it took to make wooden toys. I didn't have all the right tools, but I had a lot of time. I made cars and trolleys and sometimes boats. I could make a trolley a week; a boat took longer. Sometimes, what started out as a trolley turned into a boat, usually an ocean liner. For some reason, it never happened the other way around. A trolley is relatively easy—a few dowels to make the windows, an open platform on either end, two long rectangles for the ceiling and the floor, and a couple of round pieces as the headlamps. Cars were more difficult. At first, the cars looked like the ones we used in the Ministry to pick up subjects for questioning, but I didn't want to think about that, so I started making them with only two doors, room for two people in the front seat looking out at the scenery. If the doctor noticed the change in models, he didn't say anything. He usually took four or five—whatever I had ready—when he left.

Living on the mountain, I trained myself to stand in one place and do nothing but watch the light move and the layers of the scene in front of me unfold. It was against all of my instincts, contrary to years of experience in the Ministry, to close down those nerve endings that had been put on permanent alert. I forced myself to become oblivious to distractions; I battled down the nervous habits of the hunted, the learned behavior of always shifting one's gaze, ears twitching at every sound, ceaselessly trying to escape danger, to twist away from the doom that moved from front to back, right to left, at every moment.

It took me almost a year, after I was finally settled, to purge myself of the urge to be completely aware of my surroundings each second. In the quiet, it was easier to do, to let the world pass without the overpowering need to recognize the shadow of the hawk, the soft beat of the owl's wings, the talons that were just above your neck. It was only when I learned to be so still and hear things without listening that I caught the pattern within the rumble of explosions—three in a row, several seconds apart.

The explanation from the farmer about the dam building had stopped making sense one crystal clear morning when I went to the top of the mountain and saw—across the valley that lay behind me—a heavy truck coming out of a building built directly against a hill. Big construction vehicles don't come out of buildings next to mountains unless the buildings are covering tunnel adits.

The old truck driver gave me a blank look when I asked him about the explosions. "I never hear them," he said. "I don't know about what I don't hear. Maybe neither should you."

When the doctor came up in September, I asked if he had an idea what the explosions could be.

"Blasting," he said. "Dams, mines, tunnels—could be anything. This is a funny part of the country. I'm surprised they let you stay here."

"Yes, very gracious of them. Anything special going on?"

"Always something going on. I've heard people say that Thursdays are a good day to stay off the roads around this mountain. But you don't know it for sure, and neither do I."

In addition to the books, the doctor also brought a few pieces of wood on his visits—mostly scrap and almost always pine. I didn't have the heart to tell him that used pine is almost never fit to be something else, and even then not without so much coaxing that it is rarely worth the effort. My grandfather wouldn't take scrap pine, and that was at a time when it was almost the only thing he could find. He had nothing against scrap wood as a rule, but he said he would rather do without than argue with a pine board that thought it already knew what it was meant to be. Some people in our village fashioned new furniture out of old boards. The old man considered this a form of prostitution. I told this to the doctor, who laughed and shook his head.

The last time the doctor showed up, he stood at attention and opened the back door of his car with considerable fanfare. He pulled out a long board.

"I don't know what it is," he said, "but I think it's a virgin."

It was hard to do much in winter. My fingers were too cold to hold the tools, and I didn't want to run out of wood while the road was impassable, which it usually was from late December until March. Summers were often too wet, and even when it wasn't raining, the wood swelled in the humidity and the joints in my fingers ached. Autumn was the best time to work. I started at noon and worked through the day until the sunlight began to fade.

Most mornings in autumn I went for walks along the ridge of the mountain. There was no one to stop me from going into the valley on the far side, but I went only once and decided I would not go again. The trees were bent in odd shapes, which made the wind moan like a man dying of a grievous wound.

Chapter Six

No one called at noon to say a car was waiting. No one called at one o'clock. Or two. At two thirty, there was a knock at the door.

"Room service."

Only it wasn't. It was Major Kim, and he didn't look happy.

"We've got a problem, O." He walked past me as soon as I opened the door. "I'm supposed to be in Paris. I *should* have been in Paris, but no, no, I ended up here. Here!" He closed the curtains by hand.

"You just broke something," I said. "Light bother your eyes?"

"I'll tell you what bothers my eyes. Looking at the mess you call a city, that's what bothers my eyes. Looking at that statue every morning on the hill, that bothers my eyes."

"So, don't look. Or take it down."

He sat on the bed. "Not yet," he said. "A problem, O, we have a big problem."

"How come every time we meet, you say we have a problem? Last time it was little. This time it's big. Doesn't matter to me— whatever it is, it's yours. I don't have any problems."

"Where are you, O?"

"In Room . . ." I went out and looked at the number on the door. "In Room Twelve Nineteen." I stood in the hallway and looked from one end of the corridor to the other. No one was hanging around. I came back in the room. "Makes you wonder. Does this hotel have guests, or did you build it specifically for me?"

The major took a piece of paper from his jacket. "Close the door," he said, "and read this." He handed me the paper.

I glanced at it and shrugged. "This is a State Security Department operational order."

"I know what it is. I want to know what it means."

"Do I look like I work for SSD?"

"Don't screw with me, O."

"In case you haven't noticed, Major, I don't owe you anything. I still don't know who you are. At this point, I only have a vague idea of what is going on. And for as long as I can remember, I have made it a practice never to inquire too deeply into SSD orders. They have their own codes, and they don't spread around the decoding instructions. SSD does not get high marks for sharing. One of those three dogs at the table the other night seemed to be from SSD. He'll roll over if you order him to, won't he?"

"Not him. You, you're going to tell me, and you're going to do it in the next thirty seconds."

"Or?"

"Don't push me, O. I don't have any patience right now. Why is SSD using code?"

"That's what they do. They do it all the time. It's in their nature. They think in code. They sleep in code. They probably make love in code. Don't let it worry you."

"What does it say?"

"If I knew what it said, it wouldn't be much of a code, would it?"

"What. Does. It. Say."

I looked at the paper. The grouping of numbers on the top indicated it was an alert order of some sort; of what sort I didn't know. The two letters at the end of the number group indicated it was an immediate-precedence message. I'd learned this much about SSD orders, because it was what I needed to keep my head above water when I was in the Ministry. Kim didn't have to know. "I take it you and SSD don't work together real close."

Kim looked down for a few seconds. When he looked up again, he wasn't even the same person. He had reached for an unpleasant expression, and he'd found one that beat anything I'd ever seen. "Do you know how a tree dies, Inspector?"

"I guess you're about to tell me." I'd seen a lot of dead trees, but there was no sense ruining his game.

"They die one branch at a time. Does that sound good to you? I'm not talking about a tree that has been chopped down, of course. I mean one that rots slowly, bark peeling, dying in the sun, dying in the rain. You've seen them, I'm sure. Very painful to observe."

"You should learn to avert your eyes."

"Aha! Something you know quite a bit about, I take it. Ignore your surroundings and they will not harm you. Ignore pain, it goes away. Maybe it doesn't even exist. Shall we test your theory?"

Kim was a compact man. Little effort had been put into creating his body. His shoulders sloped, and when he sat, his feet turned out at alarming angles. All of the craft and art of creation had been poured into making his face—and the frame that surrounded it. His ears were perfectly aligned, as were his eyebrows. His hair was perfectly clipped to resemble an expensive shaving brush. The setting was good, but the face was the jewel. There was no nuance it couldn't convey. There was no season, no phase of the moon, no combination of cloud and sun that it couldn't best; there was no joke it couldn't tell, no lullaby it couldn't hum, no verdict it couldn't hand down.

The face had put unpleasant away for the moment and was smiling again. Maybe it remembered something amusing, or something pleasing. I didn't like either choice, given the drift of our conversation.

"Don't misunderstand, Inspector. I'm here to do a job. You're only here because I received orders. Left to me, I wouldn't have summoned you from the mountain. You are an unknown quantity, and I don't like dealing with anything unknown in the midst of a fast-moving situation."

This came as a relief of sorts. At least I knew Kim hadn't handpicked me. My name had been put in front of him, by whom I didn't know. "I'm delighted to have your full confidence and backing."

"You could help me, but you remain skeptical about my commitment. Very well, I'm suggesting an experiment, if that will convince you how serious I am."

"That's surprising," I said.

"Really? In what way?"

"I thought you'd looked carefully at my file. I thought you'd studied me."

"Go on."

"You should know that I don't like experiments."

"Pain, Inspector." The stale smile lingered on his face. I definitely did not like that smile. I wanted it to go away. "Would you rather inflict pain or suffer it?" Kim let the question float on the currents of the moment. His pacing had improved. "Think it over this afternoon," he said. "We'll have drinks before dinner, and you can give me an answer; then we'll see where we go from there."

"Where we go from there? I thought I was going home. That's what you said yesterday."

"Simply a question of time." The face appeared thoughtful, but not the sort of thoughts that led to a comfortable walk in the park. "That's what this is all about, isn't it? Time?"

Actually, I thought as the door shut behind him, it's not about time. It's about running out of time. It's about being nervous because SSD is up to something and the people in the market are up to something and a gorgeous woman and one of your officers are up to something and you, Major Kim, don't know what it is.

I turned on the television. The announcer was listing the days on which people with respiratory problems should take extra care. I'd have to remember to tell Li.

2

The bar was in a building at the end of a small, deserted street. The side door opened to a narrow room, barely space for five or six tables. When it was full, it probably felt crowded, but there was no one else there at the moment. Kim indicated we should sit at the bar, where, on each end, there was a globe containing a fat white candle. In each globe, the flame stood straight up, barely a flicker, for a long time, then began a frantic dance, responding to a puff of air that swirled in the glass but nowhere else. Otherwise, the place was pitch-dark.

"Pain, Inspector. The question left hanging from this afternoon concerned pain."

"Is that the essence of your world?" I don't like it so dark when I'm talking to someone I don't know and have reason to think doesn't have my best interests at heart.

"I'm not sure you are concentrating. Are you? What are you looking around for?"

"A light switch."

"This isn't a game. I have a lot to accomplish, and only so much time to get it all done. An hour ago, I learned that the time is even shorter than I'd thought. You can imagine that I'm getting impatient, and when I get impatient I feel the urge to peel off some of the veneer of civilization."

In other words, he was under a lot of pressure and wasn't getting much help in solving his problem. "So the problem isn't really pain, after all. We're back to the question of time, that and these mysterious tasks of yours. Go ahead and get them done, why don't you? By all means, do what you have to do. Work eighteen hours a day. Skip dinners with your girlfriend in the red dress. Just leave me out of it. Whoever put my name in front of you must have pulled the wrong file. It happens."

The major signaled the bartender. "Two large drinks."

The bartender nodded and went somewhere into the darkness.

"Large." It seemed to me that he could at least have asked what I wanted to drink. "That is now an acceptable order, I take it. No need to worry with content, only size. Sign of the times?"

Kim patted my knee. "Get real, Inspector. We're about to have a conversation, a true exchange of ideas. No more fencing, no more banter. We're going to talk of pain and suffering on a large scale. Let me say at the outset, I honestly believe it would be good to avoid that if possible. If not, if it proves impossible, well, it won't be the first time."

When the drinks arrived, we moved to a table, deeper into the gloom. Other people's eyes adjust to the dark; mine don't. There was a young inspector in our office years ago with eyes like a cat. The darker it was, the better he could see. He would sit in the dark reading files all night long. If we were on surveillance, he could spot a suspect moving in the blackest night. It made the rest of us look bad. No one was sorry to see him assigned to another office.

"Obviously," I said, "neither the pain nor the suffering is to be yours."

A woman appeared, a shadow emerging from the emptiness of space, and handed the major a piece of paper. He moved back to the bar where there was at least a little light to read by, wrote something quickly across the top, and held it up for the woman to take away. She didn't move until he looked at her and nodded.

"I have enough suffering of my own, Inspector. You might not think so." He stared in the direction of the vanished woman. "Pain and suffering," he laughed. The room echoed with the sounds of a five-hundred-year-old gingko tree losing a limb in a storm. "Sign of the times."

"Overall, though, we aren't focused on your suffering."

"No, we aren't. Disappointed?"

"Then it must be mine."

The major sat down again and raised his glass. "Not yours exactly. Not in so many words. Let's put it in broader terms. Let's be grand in our vision, lofty in our ideals. Nation, race, family, individual—when one is in pain, all suffer, isn't that the theory?"

"Theories are junk." I picked up my glass. "To better times."

The major shrugged, but in the dark I couldn't be sure of the face. "To whatever comes next."

We drank in silence and sat awhile in contemplation. With barely enough light to see your own glass in a bar, there isn't much else to do. I was not inclined to say anything more. The man was baiting me. He was trying to ratchet up my interest. I took another sip of the large drink. It was gin, but I drank it anyway. The flame in the far globe flared enough so at last I could see the major's face. He was staring at me, not in a friendly way, but at least it wasn't a mean, practiced stare. I made a note to myself to start a file on stares. Laughter wasn't of much use. All it did was point to more pain. A typology of stares might be more instructive. Something to do with the eyes, I guessed. Maybe we were seeing the impact of all the light flooding the city, light that, for some reason, couldn't find its way into this bar.

"Things will change," Kim said at last.

"They do, sometimes."

"From what I've seen, that hasn't been the case here in the North for quite a while."

"Let's leave that discussion for another time. Purely for the sake of argument, we'll posit that things will change. And next you're going to tell me, that means for the better."

"You're doubtful?"

"Oh, not at all."

"Then what?"

"Loss, my dear major. Loss."

The light from the globe was giving out, but I could see that his face was appropriately puzzled.

"Now, truly, I am disappointed," I said. "In another minute you will tell me that we have nothing to lose but our chains. Yet freed we will become what?"

He waved a hand in front of his face. "And you, you're about to rattle on about the joys of the collective. Spare me, please, Inspector."

"Freed we will be what?" I asked again. This was something I'd thought about on the mountaintop, watching shadows climb out of the little valley and then fall back. "Smarter? Richer? And, in the end, why do you care what is best for us? Is it your business? Do you really care at all?"

At this the major shook his head. "Apparently, not only is it my business; it is my unhappy fate. To make you happy, all right, I'll admit it. No, I don't care what happens to you, because of everything you and your friends have done—or allowed to be done—to this place for the past fifty years. You can all hang as far as I am concerned. I'd spring the trapdoor myself, but I have no choice in the matter. I am here to deliver you into freedom, and that is exactly what I am going to do."

"I know you were bound for Paris. A pity you didn't go."

3

"The game is over, Inspector. It comes down to that. All of the planning and plotting and maneuvering—all done. For some reason, your side has decided the best offense is to give up." We were back in the major's office. The night before in the bar, after I had finished my large drink, a man had appeared with a message in a locked black dispatch case. The major had read the message and left in a clatter. "We'll continue this tomorrow morning, Inspector, in my office," he said before disappearing.

The driver was waiting in front of my hotel at 5:00 A.M. We were back to the ferret. He told me to get in the rear seat. "We aren't pals," he said. "I'm a driver; you're the passenger. Keep it that way, OK?"

When I walked into Kim's office, breakfast was already on his desk. He handed me a bowl of soup. It was pumpkin, but I put it to one side.

"I don't believe you," I said. I'd mulled it over through the night and decided this would be my opening line. It wasn't strictly true. I did believe him. What he'd said about surrender at the top was the only explanation possible. All that I lacked was evidence. Not counting Kim himself seated behind the big desk, the neon sign on my hotel, and the low-cut red dress, where was the evidence of such surrender, exactly? The woman with the baseball cap in the market was actually evidence to the contrary. She didn't sound like someone who was giving up. Besides, from everything I'd seen, there was a lot that hadn't changed. Buses continued not to run on time, in some cases not to run at all. People walked across the bridges as they always had. A few new buildings stood here and there, and yes, there were all of those extra streetlights, but did that really suggest anything as sweeping as Kim was laying out—wholesale surrender?

"Fortunately for all of us," Kim picked up his bowl to drain it, "the state of your belief is unimportant."

This, I could be sure, was untrue. I was of no utility to Kim and his people unless I bought into what he was telling me. He needed me for some reason; that much was clear. That, I knew in my bones, was my leverage. It was not the heavyweight crowbar I would have liked, but it was something. It was more than something; it was all I had.

Kim looked at my bowl. "Are you sure you won't have any? It's pumpkin, and it's pretty good. The cook is one of yours. I'm glad to see your people haven't forgotten how to cook."

"I'm always pleased when you're glad, Major. Nothing for me, though."

"Well, as I think I mentioned before, it wasn't my idea to bring you into this. I didn't even want you in the city. I said you'd be trouble, and it turns out I was right."

This did not seem to be adding to my leverage.

"But you're here, and things are moving. You can be useful, as long as you don't get in the way."

"I've heard the same thing said about doorstops."

"We have decided that talking of 'surrender' is a bad idea. The problem is not simply in use of the term but in the concept as well. Bad idea, bad concept, bad approach—that's why you won't hear me talking about it. Surrenders lead to vacuums; things become unstuck; people wander aimlessly and go bump. Some of them get crazy ideas about history and destiny. It makes for a lot of noise."

"And blood."

"Yes, that, too. Messy, ugly, painful."

"Costly."

He was silent, but I could see I had hit upon the word that swirled up from his cable traffic every morning. Cost. Expense. He needed calm and quiet, he needed to avoid bloodshed, because chaos ran up the budget.

"There we are," I said. "You do need me. For some reason you need me to save your skin."

"Never overestimate your place in the universe, any universe. Yes, your skills," he looked as if the word caused him some pain, "might prove useful. And whether you believe it or not, for a change you will actually be doing something good, in the long run."

"An interesting place to live—the long run. What do you suppose they're serving for lunch, in the long run?"

"You mean to tell me that you don't care about the future?"

"In case you've forgotten, Major, at one time you and I were the future. Now, here we sit."

"Yes, here we sit. And there's a way yet to go."

"Not for me."

"Ah, I keep forgetting. You're no longer part of the human race. You are some sort of new mountain-dwelling species. I saw something to that effect in your file."

"I don't think you've seen my file, not the whole file."

"You'd be surprised, Inspector, what I've seen. You'll be pleased to know that your file and all its annexes have been pulled from the inactive archive and put back into active status."

"In other words, I'm to be paid."

"In other words, you take orders."

"From whom?"

This earned a broad smile, a number one on the chart. "Lucky you."

4

"For one thing," the smile fell from the face as if held on with old cello tape, "it's time to stop playing the angles, stop acting like a rat in the shadows."

"Rabbit."

"Another thing, stop contradicting me. I said 'rat.' I meant 'rat.'"

"So, I should be more like . . . what?"

"When you're sitting here, you're working for me. Don't try to figure out how to get around me, or play me off against someone else. There *is* no one else. For all intents and purposes, I am it. I am the party center." He paused and glared. I could tell he was gauging my reaction. I only glared back, so he went on. "You don't have to check with anyone else; you don't have to worry about orders being countermanded, or signals being switched, or my waking up one day with a new agenda."

"You say jump, I jump. Fairly simple."

"You jump, and you don't come down . . ."

". . . until you finish your soup. You still expect me to believe you've read my file? I'm not by nature a jumper. Everyone says so. There are whole chapters in my file filled with complaints about how I failed to jump."

"No, but you will. You will. And you know why?"

"I can't guess."

"Because I could snap your backbone right here, Inspector. I could throw your guts out the window and let them hang there until . . ." He had to think about it, just for a second, but that was all it took. It told me he wasn't as tough as he wanted to be. I didn't need to get around him. When the time came, I could walk right over him, but only when the time came. If it came. Meanwhile, there wasn't much I could do.

He fixed me with a baleful stare, his entire being concentrated in his eyes, sending probing rays into my skull. "I know what you're doing. You're calculating, Inspector. Don't." He stood up, switching off the ray machine. "Follow me. There's something you need to see."

We went into a hallway lined with old photographs: a woman walking down a dirt road, the village in the distance behind her, the sky overhead heavy with summer's heat; two men sitting in the shade on a wooden bench in front of a house; a line of trees at midday; a bridge in the late afternoon with a woman and a young boy standing together, looking over the edge. I stopped at each photo. It was impossible not to fall deep into each one. They were from the 1930s, judging from the clothes the people wore and the way the trees leaned against the sky. When I looked up, Major Kim was watching me.

"They're very good, don't you think?" He put his hand on my shoulder. "I brought them with me. Another age."

"The light is pure, almost liquid. It breaks your heart."

Kim turned and led the way down the hall. He took out a key and opened a door to a small room. Inside was an old wooden armchair, a small table with a file on it, and, next to that, a green teapot. The colors were jarring after the black and the white of the world in the photographs. Against the far wall sat a young man with alert eyes. He didn't stand up when we walked in. The major didn't seem to notice.

"This is the file room. That is the file. Here you will read the file all the way through. No notes. Commit it to memory; make riddles or songs of the key points to help you remember if you like. Whatever you want, as long as it stays here." He tapped his forehead.

I looked at the man who hadn't stood up. He was pretending not to care, but he was studying me closely. His eyes moved bit by bit across my face. "Sometimes," I said, "my lips move." I nodded toward the man. "Should I read with my mouth open?"

"This is not someone you need worry about." The major looked at his watch. "The file on the table is dense. It may take you a while to get through it. I don't want you to become lonely."

"You mean, you don't want me alone. Already we are without trust?"

The man in the chair suddenly relaxed. "You got that right, pal," he said.

"Inspector O is a colleague." Major Kim's voice was flat. "Remember that, Captain. He gets every courtesy—and 'pal' is not his name or his title."

The captain gave me a mock salute. "I am at your disposal." He turned to the major. "Better?"

"It may take you the rest of the day to absorb the file." Major Kim moved to the door. I had thought he would hand the captain his head. It was odd to see him retreat. "We'll talk later," he said, frowning again. The door shut. It clicked, locked.

5

The file took all afternoon to finish. I had hoped it would be possible to skim most of it, but the major was right. The information was dense. Many names. Many connections. I didn't bother to try to memorize anything. Whatever stuck, stuck. The captain didn't say a word the whole time. He looked at his watch now and then but did nothing else that suggested impatience.

"All done," I said finally, and stood up to stretch. The room was cold, windowless, no pictures or mirrors on the walls. No decoration of any kind. It was a room. It had a door that locked from the outside. Either it was soundproof or the rest of the world had gone away. This was an interesting thought: The captain and I were the last people on earth, in a cold room with no windows.

"No one could hear your screams," he said.

"They couldn't hear yours, either."

"Well then, let's not scream, shall we?"

"Like I said," I closed the file, "I'm done. You want me to sign anything?"

"Sign? Sign what? No one gets to see that file. Ever. You didn't see it. I didn't see it."

"The major didn't see it."

"Especially the major."

"If no one has seen it, it must not exist."

"You might be right."

Chapter Seven

Two days later, the captain and I stood about a meter apart, not far from the border with China. After I finished reading the file, Major Kim had made clear that he wanted me to drive to the border to see exactly where the problem was centered. The file mainly focused on Chinese plans to move into the North to stop a collapse. There were wild rumors that Chinese were already flooding into the country, though no one could ever seem to spot them.

"I don't know what's sparking these stories or who is helping to spread them, but they have to be stopped," Kim said. His people in the South were alarmed, and they were making his life a nightmare. He was doing his best to keep them calm, he told me. For the time being, that was possible by playing down the more alarmist of the reports, but it wouldn't work forever. He needed someone to go up there and look around. He didn't trust his own people on such a mission, because he didn't know which ones were really loyal to him and which were reporting to his many detractors in Seoul. He wasn't overjoyed to have to use me, he said, but I'd been highly recommended and he didn't have time to search for alternatives. "Your pedigree is considered impeccable, you were never in a responsible position, and you've been thrown out of Pyongyang. All that looks good on a bio sheet. Remember, one thing you don't want to do is double-cross me," he said. "But I think you already know that."

The captain came along because Kim didn't trust me, and I was there because Kim didn't trust the captain. It was simple. The captain said he wasn't supposed to let me drive, but would I mind because he had a bad headache from drinking too much the night before. So I drove, and he tried to sleep. We went through the mountains near Hyangsan, where the maples looked like a forest fire burning on the hillsides. I went off the main road to avoid a couple of ugly towns, then sped through Hu-ichon to Kopun, where my grandfather and I sometimes went shortly after the war for wood from a special stand of oaks.

Past Kopun, the valleys had a few farms with goats on the hills and fruit trees along the road but nowhere really to stop, so I drove until I found a pavilion on a mountain thick with pine trees, overlooking a river. Not far from the pavilion was a glade of Erman's birch, beautiful trees, almost twenty meters tall and at peace in the afternoon sun. I sat underneath them and closed my eyes until a couple of old women showed up, pushing bicycles loaded with apples.

"What are you going to do with those, Grandma?" The captain seemed better; he was picking his teeth with a silver toothpick.

"What do you think I'm going to do with them?" The first woman put her bike against a tree. "What does anyone do with fruit? Where are you from, anyway?"

"Never mind him," I said. "How about giving us a couple of those apples. It will lighten your load."

"I don't want the load lightened. As soon as we get to the top of this hill, I'll need the extra weight to keep me from going too fast down the other side, won't I? Unless you want to buy more than two. I'm not against sharing, you understand, but a person's got to make a living. And that's not easy these days."

"More complaints," the captain said. "Nothing but complaints from you people." There it was again. Even the captain was afflicted with Kim's compulsion to mark the territory, to draw a thick line between the "you" and the "us."

"Do you want the apples or don't you?" The old lady shifted the load on the seat of the bike. "I haven't got all day. The Chinese only buy in the afternoon, and I'm already late for the market."

The captain sat up. "What Chinese?"

"What Chinese? They're strutting all over the place."

"You've seen them?" The captain had a notepad out and was searching for a pen.

The old lady shook her head. "If you don't want the apples, why don't you just say so?" As she pushed the bike onto the road, she turned to her companion, sitting on her heels a few meters away, watching closely. "I was right," she said. "Wasn't I right? As soon as we spotted them I said they were a couple of deadbeats from Pyongyang."

"Time to go." The captain took one last look around. "How long until we get there? I don't want to be roaming around at dusk. It's hard to see Chinese in that light. Step on it, will you?"

It took another five hours, going up mountains, down mountains, around mountains. The captain dozed; each time he woke with a start. "Where are we? Did we cross into China?"

"What makes you think that?"

"More trees, and then more trees. Where did they come from? I thought you didn't have any left."

"Got to get up early to fool your people," I said. "I called ahead and told the farms to mobilize everyone to plant these big trees in a hurry. But you spotted it right away."

"Let me offer a suggestion," said the captain. "It would save a lot of time if you people would build a few bridges over these valleys. A nice, straight highway would probably cut an hour, maybe two, off the drive. You might build some tunnels, too, while you're at it. We could send some of our engineers up to show you how to do it."

"Captain, tunnels are one thing we know how to build."

"Then why don't they do something about these roads?"

"Nothing wrong with these roads," I said. "They're scenic. Why don't you look at the scenery?"

He looked and I drove as fast as I dared as we descended from the mountains down to Chosan, toward the shores of a lake formed by a dam on the Amnok River. We arrived before dusk, but not a lot before. I suggested we wait until morning to look around, but the captain seemed in a hurry.

"Let's go out there now, get it over with," he said. "There's plenty of light left, and I don't want to hang around."

2

"This is nothing like the descriptions in those reports in the file. I wonder if they were talking about another location."

"If I were you," the captain had a pair of small binoculars to his eyes and was scanning the horizon, "I wouldn't mention that file anymore. Forget you saw it."

"What file?"

"That's more like it."

"Still, it's peaceful. I don't know what it is about the country-side in the fall, but it has a lulling effect on everything. If there was anything to worry about earlier in the year, you've forgotten what it was by October. You know, this area was separatist a long time ago. It pulled away from one of the old kingdoms and wouldn't come back. Maybe that's why we're up here, to see if that sort of thing has stayed in the gene pool. Stubbornness is a dominant gene, I think. You only need one."

The captain put the binoculars in his pocket. "Stop musing, Inspector. It's going to get one of us killed."

"Not likely," I said. I turned my attention to a line of lindens that defined the route of a narrow road as it followed the banks of a stream flowing west, into the sunset. At dusk, the air in this part of Chagang took on a purity that made the light a river of memories. All the more reason I was surprised when the captain grunted and crumpled to the ground.

Nothing happened for what seemed a long time. Then a lanky man wearing a sharkskin suit and huge running shoes stood up from behind a row of bushes, brushed off his trousers, and walked slowly toward me. Even in the fading light, I could see he was very much a Chinese policeman. There was no mistaking the haircut or the way he moved. Somebody had once been shocked to find Chinese where he didn't expect them to be in Korea, not far from here. I knew how that felt.

The captain was on his back, completely still, with a pretty big hole in his head. That seemed strange, because the man walking toward me wasn't carrying a weapon, not where I could see one, anyway. Nobody else was in sight, but I presented a good target, so I picked out a place to fall down in a hurry if the bushes started moving.

"We know who you are, Inspector," the man said when he was close enough to be heard without shouting.

"I take it that's a good thing." I nodded at the captain's body. "If you'd waited for a moment, I would have introduced you to my colleague."

"Him we know. He's responsible for the deaths of two of my men. He was supposedly working for me, only I knew he wasn't. I warned him a few times. It didn't take. So, he's gone."

"Just like that."

"Just like that. And you, Inspector, I understand you are about to do funny things in funny places. Funny things happen to people in such cases."

"What are you talking about?"

"You don't know? I'm talking about your trip to Macau. You aren't welcome there. I can't guarantee your well-being if you go."

"Who the hell are you to be telling me where I can go and where I can't go?"

"Just someone trying to pass along a little friendly advice."

"Friendly advice? Since when is a hole in the head friendly advice?"

"When it isn't your head."

I don't react well when people standing next to me are shot. "Maybe on your own soil you can hand out advice. But this land, here, on this side of that river, isn't yours, or perhaps you need to check a modern map. The weather may come from your side. The wind may blow from that direction most of the time. But that's about all. The sun doesn't rise there, the sky doesn't start there, and I don't have to put up with your threats while you're standing in my country." It was a long speech, maybe a little provocative under the circumstances. I looked down at the captain. The hole in his head wasn't getting any smaller.

The Chinese policeman gave me a slow, ancient, imperial smile. "Keep it up, Inspector." He started to walk back to the bushes where he'd first appeared, then stopped and looked over his shoulder. "The captain didn't listen to me," he shouted. "Think about it." He disappeared from view, but I wasn't inclined to find out where he went.

3

The next day, well before dawn, I put gas in the car and drove like a madman back to Pyongyang. When I got to the compound, I slowed down; I made it a point to move up the walkway in a manner that wouldn't excite the tank gunners. Even though the door to Kim's office was ajar, I knocked. The first time it had been a good move to go in unannounced. I didn't think it was smart to make that sort of thing a habit, especially because as far as Kim knew, the captain and I were still on the border.

"Yes, Inspector, can I help you?" Kim had his back to the door, studying the old maps on the wall behind his desk. Apparently, he did know I wasn't still in Chagang.

"What's this about?"

"You mean your meeting with the Great Han up on the border? We'd all be better off if you didn't talk to strangers." He turned slowly to face me.

"I didn't have much choice, actually. He was hard to ignore. You already knew he'd be there?"

"In a manner of speaking."

"Who is he? He put a hole in your captain's head, or did you already know that, too?"

There was a slight pause, maybe an intake of breath. "I repeat, dealing with strange Chinese isn't wise."

"All Chinese are strange."

"Good, Inspector, at last we agree on something."

"How am I supposed to stay away from Chinese if I go to Macau?"

The face went several shades of red. "Who said you're going to Macau?"

"The Great Han. He didn't seem in any doubt that you were sending me. He emphasized that I'd better not go."

Kim picked up the phone. "I want a meeting in my office in fifteen minutes."

"Back to the previous question, how am I supposed to stay away from Chinese if I go to Macau? Or hadn't you thought of that?"

Kim was writing a note. "There you mingle; here you don't."

"How is it that the Great Han knows what you're going to do before you do it? Or shouldn't I ask?"

"That's what we're going to find out, Inspector, as soon as you leave."

"You going to cancel the trip? I don't even have a suitcase." I also didn't plan to go. There was nothing I wanted to see in Macau.

Driving to the border with the captain had been different. While I was in the windowless room reading that file, I'd felt a switch flip on somewhere inside me. It had been years since I'd looked at a file, traced connections, put together stray bits of information to see if they fit. I hadn't realized how much I'd missed it. But the image of the hole in the captain's head was enough to convince me that nostalgia for operations wasn't healthy.

"Cancel? Why should I? It's not as if we've lost the element of surprise. Pang—that's the Great Han's name—would know as soon as you passed through Macau immigration anyway. He's a colonel, and therefore impressed with himself. If it pleases him to think he has inside information on my plans, so much the better. It will give him more time to trip over his own big feet. We're not going to cancel anything. We just need to be careful, that's all. You, especially, need to take precautions."

"No, I don't, because I'm not going."

"In Macau, the Chinese will pitch you; almost certainly they'll make you an offer to work for them, as if they don't already have enough of your people on their payroll. They'll use anything and everything—a woman, money, a long-lost family member, maybe even an appeal to your sense of culture and history. Tell them to get lost. Can you do that for me?"

"Macau," I said. "It's a den of vice. People disappear."

"Are you worried? After all of these years in the police, putting your life on the line for the citizens of Pyongyang, do I detect concern about personal safety? Come on, Inspector; you're too old to fear the future. What have you got to lose anymore? Besides, I'm your friend, remember? Why would I send you on a trip if it was going to end badly?"

"The Chinese say, 'If we have one more friend, we have one more door.' I don't need any new doors at this point in my life, especially if I don't know where they lead."

"So, you want to back out. Fine, we can deal with that." He

reached for the phone. "If you're concerned about your safety . . ." He dialed a number. "I'll get someone else."

This was not a matter of pride. Anyone could see he thought he could shame me into going. It would have to be shame, because there was nothing else pushing me, nothing but a speck of curiosity about what this was about. I wasn't working for him; I wasn't working for anyone. Besides, the trees would still be on the mountain when I got back. They weren't going anywhere. "I didn't say you should get someone else. I said people disappear in Macau. I take it that's what I'm supposed to do, find someone who disappeared there."

Major Kim put down the phone. The face tiptoed around appearing cagey. "Not exactly."

"What, exactly?"

"On the one hand you might say that a woman disappeared."

Faint alarm bells rang. This wasn't a road I wanted to go down. "Been there, done that. I like women I can see. If they disappear, I can't see them."

"Only, she didn't actually disappear. It's more like she disintegrated. Or maybe you could say disarticulated. Since most people can't do something like that to themselves, by themselves, we're interested."

"Someone hacked her up, and you want me to put the pieces back together again."

"Not exactly." I felt that flutter in my stomach, the one that means my head hasn't caught up with what the rest of me already realizes is a reason to turn around and go the other way. "The Macau police think they can identify who did it." Kim said this slowly.

"Then, you must want them to think otherwise." I paused. "Is this the 'little problem' you mentioned the first night we talked?"

Kim raised his chin a millimeter.

"You're not thinking of setting me up, are you? Having me

met at planeside by a team of Macau detectives who will take me to a dark room and beat me for a week until I confess?"

"This woman showed up in pieces, Inspector, over two weeks ago. You have nothing to confess. The whole time you've been either on your mountaintop or under my control. How could you have strangled her, chopped her up in the bathtub of a suite in the Grand Lisboa Hotel, carried a matched set of luggage through the lobby at seven A.M. after eating a breakfast of tea and rice congee, and dumped the larger suitcase, the red four-wheeler, in the harbor where it floated for a full day before being picked up by the police who had been tipped off by a Japanese reporter waiting at the scene with a camera crew?"

"I never liked congee."

"Unassailable proof of innocence. Find something equally airtight for the person whom the Macau police are unjustly accusing."

"You want me to make it clear to the police that they are barking up the wrong tree, still assuming you are not setting me up. Still assuming that I'll actually go."

"Go to Macau, Inspector. Put the police on the proper scent. Get them off the wrong tree, as you put it. Above all, stop worrying. What enjoyment is there in life if every angle has to be covered? You might even have fun in Macau."

No, I would not. There was nothing about this picture that pointed to fun. "Your friend Pang advised me not to go. He sounded serious. Not to dwell on the point, but he killed the captain with one shot in bad light."

"Go; find what needs to be found. Clarify what needs clarification. Wipe clean whatever window seems befogged to you. My only advice: Stay away from willowy Chinese girls, from full-bodied Portuguese tarts, and from whatever else they throw in your path. Then, mission complete, we'll drive you in style back to your mountain, where you can saw boards until the end of time. What could be simpler?"

"One thing."

"What?"

"You haven't told me who didn't do it." It was the sort of thing I never wanted to say but did anyway.

"That's not your concern."

"Maybe not, but I'd like to know. Call it professional curiosity."

"Go downstairs to the second floor to pick up your tickets and passport. The ticket should be for the day after tomorrow. They'll have some travel money for you, too. Don't waste it; we'll need an accounting. It will probably take you an hour to get everything done. When you're finished down there, come back up here."

The passport had a ten-year-old photograph of me, but the clerk said it was close enough. It was a South Korean passport, which got under my skin. The travel money was practically nothing; the clerk said I was lucky to get as much as I did and if I played my cards right in Macau maybe I could turn it into a neat little pile. When I went back upstairs, there was a small man with an expensive haircut in a black shirt and black tie sitting in the green chair across from Kim. They stopped talking when I walked in.

"That will be all," Kim said to the man, who stood up and left without acknowledging me as he brushed by. He had on expensive cologne, a lot of it.

"Who is your thuggish friend who gets the good chair?" I waved away a perfumed nimbus.

"Just someone who thinks the northeast is his territory to dispense." Kim was looking through a small notebook.

"Oh, really? Of course, you set him straight. He understands it's not his and it's not yours, either."

"You got the passport?"

"I assume he isn't part of your operation."

"What are you talking about?"

"His shoes cost more than you make in six months. He's

been drinking. Even his cologne bath couldn't cover the alcohol. Your discipline can't be that bad. Besides, he is Chinese."

Kim looked up, momentarily amused.

"I'm wondering, though, why you were so tense when he was here? He doesn't look the type to have a hold on you. Still, your eyes have taken on that worried cast."

"Worried?" Kim blinked, twice. "No, Inspector. I may have braced myself, that's all. Zhao is not someone with whom you have a casual conversation."

"So, why the sudden silence when I walked in? What's he to me? You wouldn't have left the door open like that if you didn't want to make sure that we brushed antennae."

"Let's put it this way: If Zhao is in a good mood, he can be your patron, even your protector, in faraway places. He'll supply your needs and embellish your wants, beyond what you've got in that little envelope of travel money you're holding. He can also put you in touch with the right people in Macau. His access to the influential is exceeded only by his bank accounts."

"This, as you say, is if he is in a good mood. If not?"

"If not, he has a pet rat who can remove your lungs and use them to stuff the pillows of the orphans he's had a hand in creating. Zhao believes grief is a bad thing, a burden on society, so if he murders a husband, he makes sure to murder the wife."

"I have no wife."

"No one to grieve for you? Then the man's work is simplified."

"I'd rather this Zhao stick to enlarging my wants."

"'Embellish,' Inspector. I said 'embellish.'"

"Another friend, another door?"

"You'll have to ask him yourself. It's not my job to read his mind. We coexist, that's all."

"You can't arrest him?"

Kim smiled. I began recording a series of variables in my head—corners of the mouth, forehead, eye crinkling. This was the first entry, so there was no basis for comparison, but on the face of it, I thought it could go down as "wan."

"No, Inspector, I can't arrest him, not if I want to keep breathing. Unlike you, I do have a wife—a wife and two children."

"What about the Great Han? Can't he do something? Surely he doesn't approve of someone like Zhao."

"I guess you could say the Great Han prefers to keep breathing, too."

4

I went back to the hotel to think things over. It still wasn't too late to tell Kim to find someone else to go to Macau. I had made it a point never to get involved with gangsters while I was in the Ministry, because I knew it would be nothing but a headache. There was a tiny section in a dark office in the headquarters building that dealt with all gangs—Chinese, Japanese, Russian, and whatever else the wind blew across the borders. Gangsters were tough people, very smooth for the most part, and for the most part deadly. That was only half the problem. The rest of the problem—and the most difficult part—came from the fact that other entities, various central committee departments, military groups, special services, and we never knew for sure what else, loved to run operations using foreign gangs. We were never informed ahead of time. If we got in the way of an operation, we were in trouble. It took a lot of careful footwork to stay clear of something you didn't know existed. One hot summer, a Japanese gang tried to set up shop in my sector. It wasn't a big operation, but I was against letting them hang around, so I complained through channels. Channels told me to mind my business. It turned out a couple of the gang members were working for a foreign intelligence service and weren't very discreet about it, so after a few months the whole operation was shut down and moved to the east coast.

Around six o'clock, Kim called and asked if I wanted to go out for dinner. "Sure," I said. Either he was working overtime to cultivate me or he was seriously isolated in his own machinery. The girl in the red dress met us at the door, only this time she was wearing blue. "Blue is definitely your color," I told her.

She tossed her head. "This way," she said to Major Kim, and led us back to the triangular table.

Michael had the night off. We were waited on by Bruce, who had the same austere smile. I figured they handed them out in the kitchen, along with the white jackets.

Even before the drinks arrived, I got to the point. "Forget about it." That was as direct as I knew how to be. "I'm not going to Macau or anywhere else, except back to the mountain."

Kim was looking at the menu. "The quail looks good," he said.

"I'm not about to get back into all of this running around. Consider me a candle with nothing left to burn. No flame, all consumed. Look around, Major. Look. Look for heaven's sake!" I tried to keep my voice down. I wasn't sure what I wanted him to look at.

"Oh, Christ." He put down the menu. "You're wallowing like a pig in self-pity, Inspector. You sound like you're about to start singing an anthem to regret. A life wasted, wrong turns taken. Don't, please. Keep it to yourself."

"Look to the future, is that it? Let the past fall away. And where will it fall? In what peaceful graveyard do we bury the past?"

"Graveyard? More probably, a garbage dump in your case. You'd better hope all the years you spent in service of this mob can be recycled. Is there a great universal machine that takes old time and makes it new? How should I know? And why should I care? We're not here to compare philosophy notes. I'm supposed to throw a rope across this pathetic chasm of a country. I don't look down. I don't notice if there are rotting corpses or rivers of gold. Makes no difference. They want a rope so they can build a bridge from here to there. It starts with a rope. That's you, Inspector. That's you."

I shook my head. "Don't bet on it."

5

The next afternoon, I went downstairs to complain about my phone. It was blinking, and it wouldn't stop.

"That means you have messages," said the clerk. With his wrist extended just so, he indicated the button on the phone that meant messages. "You push this and your mailbox will tell you what messages you have. We'll make it easy. I'll push the button; you listen," he said. The message said I was to stand under the canopy at the front door at 1:00 P.M. It was almost one, so I started out the door. The man with the long stare had been at the far end of the counter, watching me, the whole time.

"Do we know each other?" I walked over to him. "Because if we don't, you're getting on my nerves."

He shrugged, a gesture with no impact on a stare.

I went outside, and a minute later a black car appeared.

A little man jumped out from the passenger side and opened the rear door. "In," he said. "Now."

I got in. The same man who had been in Kim's office was sitting in the shadows. He had switched cologne. The new stuff seemed to destroy oxygen and possibly affected the light as well. I'd never seen the backseat of a car so dark. It was like taking a drive in a black hole. That was not a comforting thought, and I started to sweat. The door slammed shut. Now all of the light from the outside was gone. I could see Zhao, dimly, but I couldn't see my own body. When I held up my hands, they weren't there.

"A nice illusion, Inspector. It gives people a sense of disquiet—who is here and who is not? Well, life is transitory, like pleasure."

"We have business?" Maybe it was only an illusion, but for some reason I had no trouble seeing Zhao's eyes. He was looking at me with unrelenting dislike. A stare may be unnerving, but it is basically passive. This look was launching a thousand poison-tipped arrows. "Or are we going to discuss Aristotle?"

The driver accelerated around a curve, and the car jumped ahead. We might have been preparing to take off, for all I knew.

"Some of the roads around here aren't all that good." I felt around for a seat belt. "Your driver might want to take it easy."

"Don't worry about the roads, Inspector, or belting yourself in. These are the least of your concerns."

"In that case, let me go to the obvious question: What are the most of my concerns?"

Zhao laughed. He might have been a panther sitting on a branch above the forest floor, licking his paws and laughing. His eyes were embers; his teeth shone; his hair was sleek. For the first time I could make out what he was wearing. Black, all black—black sweater, black trousers, black shoes. They should have been invisible in the darkness.

"The most immediate of your concerns is simply how to stay alive." The focus dissolved from his eyes. "I don't mean right now. You're in no danger at the moment. But next month, next year." He sighed. "Who can tell, the times are so unstable. In such times, we need to be under—"

The car swerved violently to the left. I was thrown against the door, but Zhao didn't move.

"You see, Inspector? This is exactly what I was saying. In unstable times, you need something secure, something you can hold on to."

"And why do you think the times are unstable?" They must have removed the seat belt on my side, because I couldn't find it. "Maybe there's nothing wrong with the times."

"Yes, that's right. Exactly right. As usual, you're on the mark.

That's what people have told me: 'Inspector O is a man who can see through the fog.' Can you actually do that?"

"Fog is not a problem."

"No? And what is?"

"Bullshit is the problem. You're wasting my time, Zhao. Get to the point." I didn't think I wanted him as a lifelong friend, so there wasn't much to lose by being blunt. He wanted to scare me, rough me up mentally. So far, it wasn't working.

Zhao's lids dropped, and for a moment I thought he was dying. Sleek and dangerous one moment, dying the next. Not all that unusual, especially for a gangster. He opened his eyes again slowly. "You plan to go to Macau. I don't think that is wise."

"Not wise."

"What happens in Macau isn't your business."

"Everyone seems to have a great deal of interest in this trip. Major Kim thinks it quite important that I go. So does Colonel Pang, as a matter of fact." That was not strictly true, but it seemed to me that Zhao wasn't a stickler for honesty. He and Pang apparently didn't get along; I needed to know exactly how bad their relations were. It took less than a heartbeat to find out.

"If I were you, I would stay as far away from that bastard Pang as I possibly could. People like him are a deadly disease, and you don't want to catch it."

"Anything else? I like my advice in a big bag so I can keep it all in one place. When advice comes in dribs and drabs, it can get mislaid, you know what I mean?"

" "Here's something for your bag, then." The window on my side opened. "Take a good look, Inspector. This is my territory now."

"What is it about you people? This is not your country. It's not yours, never has been, never will be—not now, not ever."

Zhao cocked his head, the first sign I had that he was really paying attention. "Down, boy, I said 'territory,' not 'country.' I

don't need your ragtag nation. But I'm serious about my territory. What's mine is mine. Do I make myself clear? And no one
takes it away from me. Not Pang, not your brothers in the South.
And especially not you."

Something clicked. "You and Kim share a dangerous mis-
conception. You both think my ragtag nation has already collapsed. You seem to think you can move in at this point to bite
chunks off the carcass."

"I don't think." Zhao lit a cigarette. His eyes reflected the
glow. They became yellow and luminous, bright spotlights in the
black. "Thinking is all about assumptions, and perceptions, and
convictions. To think is to assume rationality, and that can be
very fatal. I act on instinct." Again, the panther, outwardly in
repose, his head resting against the back of the seat, but every
muscle alert, every nerve primed. "Yes, your country is a corpse.
And you only have a few weeks, maybe a month, to decide whether
to die with it or to get away. I can give you a comfortable new
existence, a new life. I have money, friends, a place where you
can enjoy life for the years you have left."

"And what should I do to earn this reward of rebirth?"

"Do nothing, nothing at all. It's an ancient principle, Taoist,
not exactly in its pure form, of course. I have adapted it slightly.
But the core remains intact."

"The essence of the concept is effortlessness, Zhao, not 'do
nothing.' Give oneself up to the flow of the universe, become in
perfect harmony with Righteousness. That is not 'nothing,' but
everything."

"No!" He sat up suddenly. I saw the driver wince and turn
his head, which told me that the conversation was being piped
into the front. It also told me that the driver was missing part of
his left ear. "No! I'm not going to get into a philosophical duel
with you. I've given you a choice. Get out of my way or get run
over. That's it. That's your choice. At the moment you're in my
way. Very much in my way."

"I'll take my chances." The panther didn't want me to go to Macau. That made it simple. I was going.

The car pulled over. The door opened and the little man leaned inside. "Out," he said. "Now."

"You should learn to speak in complete sentences," I said to him before he climbed into the front seat and slammed the door. I waved, but as far as I could tell, no one waved back.

6

That evening, Colonel Pang met me near the Taedong River. He left a message at the front desk that he would be across from the monument at dusk and that perhaps we should try getting acquainted under better circumstances than we had the first time. Kim obviously didn't like him, and neither did Zhao. If the enemy of my enemy was my friend, that seemed to go double for Pang. I decided it was worth finding out what was on his mind.

"I'm sorry you got mixed up with Zhao," he said. "I should have warned you."

"Do you have a free pass across the border? How did you get here?"

"The border isn't much of problem these days, Inspector. You could go out and come back all without a passport if you wanted to."

"I'd rather not get my shoes wet." I could see that he had two bodyguards with him. One was about ten meters ahead; the other was the same distance behind. "Are we going to hold the entire meeting here, or should we walk a little, to give the SSD teams some exercise?"

"Either way. I like rivers. They are unambiguous dividing points. There is nothing uncertain about where you stand in relation to a river. You're either on this side or that. Borders shift around; rivers are usually more permanent. Don't look now, but up ahead on that bench is one of Zhao's men. It's his number three, a real viper. From what the coroner in Shenyang tells me, he spits poison in the eyes of his victims."

"Why, I don't know, but a lot of people seem to want to be helpful these days, giving me warnings. Let me return the favor. You ought to know—if someone hasn't made this clear already—that Zhao is not going to throw you a birthday party this year."

Pang moved his head and put his finger on a scar that went vertically down the left side of his throat. "This was not from a love bite, Inspector. The key point to understand at the moment is that Zhao doesn't want us cooperating."

"We're not."

"Zhao doesn't know that. No one who sees us walking together at sunset along the river would know that." Pang smiled at me. A person might think it was a pleasant smile. A person might even forget about the hole in the captain's head.

"How do you suppose that Zhao knows that I am going to Macau?"

"Zhao knows a great deal. That shouldn't surprise you, Inspector."

"Who told him?"

"He goes into a lot of offices during the course of a day, as you know."

"True, it could have been Major Kim, but it could as easily have been you. You knew about it even before I did."

"Why would I want to tell Zhao anything?"

"That's what I'm wondering."

"Good, keep wondering." As we passed the viper, Pang smiled again—well this side of pleasant—and said something in a Chinese dialect that threw hatchets. The security man in front of us had stopped and watched closely, his right hand in his jacket pocket. "I mentioned that I'd heard about his mother and turtles. I don't think he liked it." Pang looked at his watch. "I have an hour or two to kill, Inspector; would you care to join me for a drink? Don't worry. I don't shoot people at close range. There's no challenge to it."

"In that case," I said, "I accept."

Pang ran up a flight of stone steps that led away from the river. At the top of the steps a car waited, its engine running. "There's a place north of the city, not very far away. We'll be back at the hotel before anyone misses you. Please, get in."

7

As Pang promised, we ended up north of the city. For a moment, I thought we were heading to the airport—which suggested I might be going to Beijing in a box—but we turned off onto a dirt road and drove for about twenty minutes before stopping outside a compound lit with strings of electric lanterns. Through the gate, I could see a pond with four Chinese maple trees around it. Chinese maples are showy and overly delicate. The leaves take a lot of time deciding whether to end up as scarlet or yellow. A few had cut short the agony and dropped into the pond. Off to one side of the compound was a one-story building with no windows and a large radio antenna on the roof. A guard stood in front of the door. He was Chinese, carried a Chinese rifle, and didn't seem to like me looking at him.

"You might say this is an embassy annex, Inspector. We can have drinks over there." Pang pointed across a miniature brook with a tiny bridge. "We'll sit on the pavilion and be serene. Maybe a poem will come to you."

We sat on mats, which my knees hated instantly. "All very lovely," I said. "I never knew there was an embassy annex here. I don't think my Ministry knew it, either." From the looks of it, this was newly built, and screamingly illegal.

"Of course, this is all fairly recent." Pang gestured to someone I couldn't see. "We've had the land for a long time." He gave me a bland look. "The current situation has called for a few adjustments in normal protocol. The paperwork always trails behind. I'm sure you've had the same experience." A woman came out of a low white building some distance from the pavilion. She put down two porcelain teacups and a pot in the shape of a bird. "We'll have tea," Pang said. "Would you like ginseng tea?"

"No, I can't stand it."

"A Korean who does not like ginseng tea? Can this be? Well, in that case, let me suggest something else. I can offer you very good tea from Zhejiang. I'm sure you'll appreciate it. General Su Dingfang drank the same tea from these very cups."

The woman had moved away to stand beside one of the maples. Beneath the lanterns, a smile danced across her lips as she saw Pang pour the tea into my cup.

"Let the tea set for a moment, Inspector. The fragrance builds beautifully if you wait."

I waited, but not for the tea. Su Dingfang was a T'ang Dynasty general who invaded Korea. He had the help of other Koreans, true enough. If these were his teacups, they were in remarkably good shape. Pang's had a tiny chip on the rim. The glaze on mine was cracked, but I would be, too, if I were thirteen hundred years old. Assuming these were actually General Su's teacups, what was Pang doing with them?

"If you like, Major Su over there could refresh your understanding of history." The woman nodded. "She is a descendent of the general. The teacups have been in her family all these years. They wouldn't be sitting here in front of us otherwise. It's quite an honor, don't you think?"

If I didn't get up in another minute, I would never stand again. I put my hand on the floor behind me and leaned back to relieve the pressure on my knees. "Don't tell me, the family thought it would be a filial gesture, returning the teacups to the general's old battlegrounds."

Pang rested his hand on the teapot. "They thought the cups

would bring the major good luck in her mission. And I am delighted to have her ancestor here with me."

"A long, long time ago, Colonel. Didn't you tell me that borders change? The border right now is down the middle of your beloved rivers. That's where it is going to stay."

"Don't misunderstand, Inspector; I'm not here to seize territory. But if some of your countrymen want assistance in resisting pressure from another kingdom, there is a long history of our making ourselves available. Didn't Baekche ask us for help? In fact, in recent years we've been happy to provide shelter for a number of generals from your army who thought it best to live on our side of the river for a while. Now? Well, now they have decided they might want to go home. And we quite agree. In any case, Chinese have been here before, and now they are here again." He picked up his teacup. "We are quite tolerant, you'll see."

"The Japanese have also been here before," I said, "but that doesn't mean we want them back."

"Surely, Inspector, you aren't comparing us to them."

"I know General Su was a great military leader." I bid farewell to my knees. It was hopeless. I would have to be wheeled around from now on. "I also seem to recall—and you or the major will correct me if I am mistaken—that he went home in defeat, having failed to take Pyongyang." I picked up my cup. It was very delicate. If I crushed it between my fingers, I would not be doing history any favors.

Pang sipped his tea. "All the better for Major Su to return and remedy that." He smiled. "You could be valuable to your people, Inspector. If you'd rather work with your brothers in the South, of course I understand. But I can tell you that there is no way that they will reclaim this entire peninsula. And anyway, do you think there is any chance that they will integrate you into their fat and happy world? That would set their economy back decades, depress their living standards, lower wages, siphon off capital, create a burden to support twenty-four million needy people—and your people are needy, Inspector. You cannot dispute that." He waited to see if I would respond.

I put the teacup down gently. "I can dispute anything," I said. "The question is, what good will it do?"

"Let me be blunt. We know that some of your southern brothers plan to set up a gangster state on your territory. They need it to make money, to hide money, to move money. Other people think such a state will be useful because it can become an ideal platform for operations of all sorts against my country. There used to be such places elsewhere—Macau, for example. But we've been shutting down Macau, inch by inch. It is very slow going. Ridding even that tiny island of corruption is not like washing your face. It's not simply dirt; it has become organic. The job might take several more years to finish, maybe even a decade. Meanwhile, it has already become uncomfortable enough that the big people, important people, are looking elsewhere. People like Zhao. People who give Major Kim his orders. And where do maggots go? To a rotting corpse."

"Should I start composing poetry now, or should we wait a few more minutes?"

Pang's expression hardened. "We won't let that take place on our border. We will never let events come to that. I told you not to go to Macau, but now I've changed my mind. Go; look around. It's better if you get some sense of what happens when corruption takes root. I don't mean the petty bribery that goes on everywhere; I mean the full-blown version that turns men rancid. If it doesn't sicken you, if you don't come back here and tell me that you will work with us, I will be surprised."

"And you do not like to be surprised."

"It's not that I don't like it. It's that I'm careful to make sure surprise doesn't touch my existence, in any way." His mood visibly improved. "Why don't I put on some music for us?"

"Chinese opera, perhaps?" I was not looking forward to that, but it seemed all too likely in the presence of General Su and his cups.

"Do you like Chinese opera, Inspector? I can't stand it. The spectacle is tolerable; at least the costumes are a distraction from the noise. But a recording? I wouldn't even want to saw boards to it." He must have realized his mistake immediately, because he reached in his pocket and pulled out a small, paper-thin piece of wood.

"I understand you are much attracted to trees. This is a piece of white birch, from a forest near Harbin. Mean anything to you?"

"As your research has obviously discovered, my father was born in Harbin." Pang had done his homework. This was his way of telling me that he could step into my life and rearrange it any time he wanted. He didn't care if I despised him for it, as long as I understood.

Major Su walked over and took away the teacups. Pang waited until she had disappeared inside the white building. "If you look carefully, you'll see that on the piece of wood is a phone number. The digits are quite small and rather faint, but you should have no trouble making them out. If you see or hear anything in Macau that has a bearing on the fate of your country, call me. Tell the person who answers that you owe me money. They will put you through to me immediately, any time night or day."

PART II

Chapter One

Major Kim had told me to make sure that the evidence in Macau pointed "elsewhere." When I asked what the evidence was, he told me that was for me to find out. When I asked how bad it was, he said very simply, "Bad."

"There wasn't time to set up your trip through the normal contacts," he said just before I left for the airport. "You may run into interference here and there. I'll keep doing what I can to smooth things out from this end, but mostly you are on your own."

"Do I have a number to call in case of a real emergency?"

"No." Kim spread his hands. "Nothing. It's not that sort of assignment. You'll have to deal with things as they come up."

"Do you know me if something goes wrong?"

"What do you think?"

"About the passport."

"What about the passport?"

"I need something else."

"You may as well get used to carrying ROK documents, Inspector. Besides, on such short notice, even if I wanted to, I couldn't come up with anything else. Don't worry; you won't die simply from handling it."

I wasn't worried about a dread illness. I was worried about the entry stamps—they didn't look right. If they don't look right, even for a moment, they get a second glance from Immigration. And if they got a second glance, it usually meant having to answer a lot of questions in a hot room. I had that happen in Copenhagen once, and I didn't plan to go through it again. Some Danes are very persistent. I could see Kim wasn't going to budge, though, so I moved on. People can be stubborn about passports, even phony ones. "What about emergency funds?"

"You have all you'll need."

"There's not very much in this little envelope."

"There never is. I don't have more to spare. Be thankful you have an airline ticket and a hotel reservation. If you pay anything out of pocket, you'll be reimbursed, though it takes forever."

"How about advice? That's free."

"Stay away from your own people in Macau. They're all over the place, and they won't know you're there. At least, they're not supposed to know. Don't wink or nod or give a secret handshake to anyone. Stay out of Korean restaurants. I don't know who stands where on what issue, and we don't want to find out the hard way."

"You mean they don't know what's going on here?"

Kim shrugged. "Hell, Inspector, I don't even know most of the time."

We laughed. Neither of us thought it was funny.

2

My plane landed in Hong Kong around five o'clock on a muggy afternoon. I waited around in the airport for a couple of hours until the ferry left for Macau. We pulled up to the dock around eight at night; it was so humid that the raindrops were sweating. The immigration officer was bored, but not so bored that he didn't look at every page in my passport. Then he did it again, this time flicking each page with a sharp click, letting me know he wasn't fooled one little bit by all the travel that never happened. Finally, he stamped it wearily, unwilling to make an issue of what he knew could not be easily dismissed. He handed it back, never looking at me, as one might not look at a bag of garbage dropped at the front door.

When I gave the cabdriver the piece of paper with the hotel's address, he studied it for a long time. "OK," he said finally. He shouted into his phone, and I heard laughter from the other end. We drove down a wide street lined with casinos, neon signs dancing and shouting and making a mess of the night. Finally, we turned onto a quiet street, went another block, and then turned again. The hotel was a hole-in-the-wall between two dark buildings that looked abandoned. There was lettering over the entrance, "Hotel Nam Lo," and a piece of poster board just inside the door with pictures of the rooms. They looked bleak. The front desk was up a flight of stairs that led to a lobby big enough for a person to turn around and go back downstairs to find another place. Kim had said I should be grateful that I had a hotel. He had never met the desk clerk. The clerk looked up and shouted at me in Cantonese. Years ago I learned that having to cope with too many tones in a language makes a person angry. Who wants to go through all that effort to say something that someone else can coast through in a monotone? I let him vent.

"Three nights!" he said at last, in Mandarin. Having to deal in only four tones seemed to calm him down. "You must really think you're something. For everyone else, the rooms are for a shorter time. A couple of hours, but not you! Must be some pills you got."

"Is there a problem with three days?"

"No problem, as long as you aren't doing something weird. I don't want police around."

"OK by me."

"Absolutely nothing with animals."

"Nothing with hooves."

He put on his glasses and gave me a hard look. "Pay in advance. Extra day for damages."

"Over my dead body."

"Might be. That's why you pay in advance."

The room was up another flight of stairs. It was exactly like the picture, small and grim. I edged in. There was space enough for a ratty chair and one lamp with a minibulb. The television didn't work; the phone made gurgling sounds when I accidentally knocked it off the hook.

Thumping noises came through the wall from the room next to mine, but nothing that sounded like an emergency. I wasn't tired; it wasn't that late yet. I knew I'd strangle myself if I stayed in the room for another minute, so I went for a walk. One block to the right of the hotel were buildings with pulsating signs; the block to the left was deserted, empty, almost completely dead. A couple of jewelry shops were open, but the clerks were dozing with their heads on the counters.

Climbing the stairs back to my room, I passed a young girl coming down—short skirt, white mesh stockings. She had green eyes; even in the dim light of the stairwell you couldn't have missed those eyes.

"Watch yourself," I said in Russian. "It's dark outside."

"You speak Russian." She paused on the step below mine and looked back up at me with her green eyes. She wasn't more than twenty.

"I speak Russian," I said. "Go home; go back to your family."

"In five months," she said. "Good night."

It was simple, I thought as the stairway swallowed her. When you're young, five months can solve everything.

3

The next day, as soon as I found the right person, I would be able to see what was bothering Kim. The problem was finding the right person. It was already warm by eight in the morning, with the promise of humidity breathing down my neck. Even so, the sky sparkled; the streets were noisy with buses and taxis and motorbikes. It felt like a different town from what I'd seen last night. Maybe it wouldn't be so bad after all.

Everybody I asked was polite, but no, it was not possible for them to interact with me on an official basis without express approval of the proper authority. And who would that be? It was impossible to reveal without the authorization of that excellent person. At last, I was told that if I went to the post office in Senado Square and asked at window five, there would be a message waiting. The square was not far away; the clerk at window five produced the message as if passing messages were her main job. I was to call a certain phone number before noon. It was nearly 11:55, and there wasn't a phone in the post office—a machine selling all manner of phone cards, yes, but an actual telephone? The clerk shrugged. I spotted four phones in the office behind her. No, she said, and closed her window, it was not possible for an unofficial person to use one of those official phones. Perhaps, I said, the clerk would be kind enough to point me in the general direction of a pay phone? She recited the directions: "Outside, turn right, go up the square—though it isn't really a square," she said, "more like a cardboard box that has collapsed at one end—past St. Dominic's, which is yellow and not easy to miss, bear right, turn left at the ice-cream shop, and there, about twenty-five meters on the right, will be two phones. Only one of them works, unless, as sometimes happens, neither does." She gave me a faraway smile. "One never knows."

I trotted on the path she indicated and found what she promised. The phone on the left had a dial tone. I threw in all manner of coins and was connected to a male voice. It was 11:59.

"Ah, Inspector, I've been wondering if you had decided to go home."

"The idea occurred to me." I had no idea who I was talking to, which put me at a disadvantage, because the person on the other end seemed to know me. "We might have saved time if you had left this number at my hotel."

"But we did; we did! The old man at the front desk didn't give it to you?"

"He did not."

"In that case, where did you get the number?"

"At the post office."

"Indeed!"

"Perhaps we should meet, assuming you are the excellent person who can help me."

"God helps those who help themselves, Inspector." It was possible that Kim had told this man to expect me. Or Pang. Or even Zhao. The passport didn't list my title, and for purposes of this trip I was a diamond salesman, which I had put down on the immigration card. "But I do what I can. It might be wise if we continued our conversation in my office."

"And where would that be?"

"The location is not well known."

"Perhaps you could tell me—quickly. I think I'm running out of coins."

"You are where?"

"Past St. Dominic's, and a few steps beyond the ice cream."

"There are two phones? The one on the right does not work?"

"Correct."

"Then we are very near to each other!"

"God's will," I said, only because I had a feeling it might get me somewhere.

"Unlikely. No, in this case I suspect it was the Ministry of State Security man who parks his van near the Lisboa at night to keep an eye on the Russian prostitutes and their clients. You talked to him?"

"I don't know who I talked to. The van was a trash heap."

"Yes, he loves pork buns. Buys them by the bagful."

"So, MSS is part of this?"

Laughter. "My goodness, how could they not be? Very well, you're within a few meters of a sign with an arrow pointing toward the ruins of St. Paul's. Head in that direction for another twenty meters. On your left will be a small shop, dark, and very crowded with machinery and tools and wood."

"Wood?"

"The sign painted over the doorway will say: 'Carpenteria.' It is a place where they make fine furniture and intricate wooden screens. As you'll see, it is really quite beautiful. My office is in the back. I'll let them know to expect you. They close at noon, so hurry."

4

There were no introductions. The man behind the desk pointed to a chair, checked his watch, and began to summarize from a folder that he held casually in one hand:

"A young man, very rich, with the violent temper that came from too much pressure and too much restraint, had taken a very pretty, very elegant, very expensive prostitute into his room. They'd ordered dinner, watched a movie, and then started to argue. She threw things. He strangled her. In a panic, he cut her up in the marble bathroom and put her in a four-wheeled suitcase. Then he took a shower, went to breakfast—coffee, no cream, one sugar—read the paper, told the Assistant Manager he needed a limo to the airport, settled the bill in Hong Kong dollars, and all at once changed his mind. He didn't want to go to the airport, he said. No, he needed a rental car, something with a big trunk, so he could drive around and see the sights before he left. He produced a map—which way was the harbor?" The man looked up to assure himself I was listening closely.

"About breakfast, no rice congee?"

"No, why should he have rice congee for breakfast?"

"Just wondering." Major Kim's story suddenly had holes.

The man studied me a moment and then continued, "Security has tapes from the surveillance cameras. A girl had gone into his room. She did not rappel down the side of the building from the thirty-fourth floor. A helicopter did not pluck her from the balcony; indeed, the room had no balcony, even though that was what the young man had requested. The girl never left, it was concluded by all who watched the tapes, not unless you counted the drops of blood on the carpet down the hallway to the elevator." The folder was closed and put on the desk. "His fingerprints are on the knife." The room was growing hot. A fan started up and blew the hot air into a corner. It also blew the folder off the desk. The man smiled. He was cool and collected, a nice-looking, gray-haired policeman, rather thin, with long-fingered hands that he used to emphasize various points he seemed to think I might otherwise miss. He wasn't what anyone would call rugged, and he had about him what can only be called an indescribable air. He didn't look Chinese to me; I would have said he was Portuguese.

"I don't know why rich people do it," he said, and his long fingers sliced the air, "but they often chop each other to pieces, like a plate of Portuguese chicken."

I decided this was my opportunity to throw in a few questions, not only to get some answers but also to test his technique. "Rich. Do we know that?"

"Very few street people take suites at five-star hotels." He smiled. "How did I do, Inspector? Passing grade?"

"So, you have a suspect, a rich male. You're not saying, but I assume he's Asian." There was no sense specifying where in Asia I meant if for some reason they didn't already have that. "If he was a Westerner, you wouldn't even be talking to me. And where is he now?"

"Don't know."

"He's left Macau?"

"Don't know."

"He's still in Macau?"

"Possibly."

" 'A change in pattern responses represents a break in the subject's concentration, which is useful to exploit.' That's from our training manual, if I recall correctly. Can you still remember yours?"

"Our manual said 'when the subject attempts to raise a new topic, it's a sign of stress.' Relax, Inspector; no one is going to bite you. And neither of us is a subject, as far as I know. Please, if you wish, assume our man is still in Macau. In fact, assume anything you want. Assumptions are fine. They are like bouquets of flowers, nice to have around. Or should I compare them to the bottled water in your hotel room? Compliments of the house."

There was no such thing in my hotel room. No bottle, no space for a bottle. "I assume you have a full file, something other than that folder that is on your desk." It was actually on the floor, the papers fluttering whenever the fan swept over them. Pointing that out seemed unnecessary.

"Of course I have a file. We exist on files. They are like vitamins, like oxygen, like red blood cells. Your department has another approach perhaps? Something more modern? If there is a way to the truth without files, I'd like to know what it is."

"We swim in paper, same as you." I surveyed the office. No computer. That was comforting. It meant not having to deal with references to nodes and links and regressions.

"You share your files with anyone who walks in the door, of course." He walked his fingers up to the edge of the desk and then let them jump off.

"Yes, that is our approach exactly. Files to the people." I smiled to demonstrate I was not going to be a burden on his day. "I assume you eat lunch?"

The man immediately stood up and buttoned his jacket. He had the figure of a bullfighter. "I do, as often as I can, though the limits of custom and of government regulation dictate I enjoy lunch only once a day. It is my favorite meal. Dinner has considerable freight attached to it. Breakfast is an evolutionary afterthought. But lunch! Just as the day is reaching full potential—the sun scorching, the air heavy, the restaurant cool, the dark glass along the front turning the outside into a dance of vivid color while the leaves of the ficus trees flutter in a breeze God grants only to them. And on the table, a glass of wine, a plate of chicken and rice, a freshly baked roll dozing on its own little blue plate. What could be wrong with life at such a moment?" He shook his head. "Do you favor ficus trees, Inspector?"

"I'd have to think about it." Actually, I found them despicable trees, twisted around themselves as if they were afraid of the sky. "Why do you ask?"

"There are so many of them in Macau. They are like people."

"Interesting thought."

"Look at them closely when you have some time. They grow apart and then together again."

"My grandfather thought chestnut trees were like people— old people and foreigners. He considered them cranky."

"Interesting thought."

"Let me buy you lunch, then."

He bowed, a little stiffly. "My name is Luís da Silva Mouzinho de Albuquerque." He paused and observed me through slightly narrowed eyes. "I notice you do not laugh. The name means nothing to you?"

"It's long, but I can't say it tickles me."

"Good. Some people smile when they hear it. Luís da Silva Mouzinho de Albuquerque existed long ago. He was a man of many facets, and had one of those tangled lives that great people in those days lived. He was no relation to me, none that I know of, but it amused my father, who was Macanese, to name me after this man. My mother, a Chinese woman of strong opinions, was not so amused. Worse, there was never room in the space provided for 'name' on all the applications necessary for one's journey through life. Believe me, it was not always a pleasure. It is also, I realize, not as easy to remember as 'O.' Please call me Luís." He extended his hand. "I appreciate your invitation. It is very kind of you, but I fear I can't accept. It would be against all regulations, in force and contemplated—part of our anti-corruption drive, our fourth in as many years. I cannot go into a casino unless in pursuit of a suspect, I cannot be in the presence of any gaming authority unless there are three other people present, no two of whom can know each other, and I cannot accept a meal if it means sitting down."

We shook hands warmly. "You have to remain on your feet when you eat?"

"Yes, if someone else buys the meal. Standing is less corrupting, apparently. I can nibble tiny sandwiches by the plateful. I can heap on lobster, eat caviar with a shovel. But only if I stand."

"Perhaps, Luís, there is a restaurant where we can stand at the bar?"

He bowed, with more grace than the first time. "I have heard of such a place. In fact," he said as he straightened his tie, "I have heard it is nearby."

"How did you know my name, incidentally?"

"This is Macau, Inspector."

5

The bartender was a woman with a neck as thick as her head. All the more surprising that she had a voice as sweet as the spring breeze across a field of wildflowers. She and Luís exchanged a few words in what I took to be Portuguese. It sounded like Russian, but it was too wet around the edges.

"If you heard her on the radio," Luís said in English to me, "you'd fall in love, as I already have." He kissed her hand. "This is Lulu," he said. "She can do no wrong."

Lulu blushed, which must have put a strain on her heart. "And what would Senhor Police Captain like to start off with?" she asked. The room was suddenly a meadow in the glories of May. Exactly as Luís had said, the ficus trees rustled in a breeze; the colors of the day flowed through the darkened glass of the long front window.

"A leg, my dear Lulu. Surrender it to me or I shall go mad." Luís' voice was low and dreamy.

Next to this woman, Luís appeared frail; the thought of her leg worried me. "I thought you had to remain standing," I said.

Lulu turned to me. "And you? What can I offer?" She leaned her arms on the bar top and began to remove my clothing with limpid eyes. "You prefer white meat, perhaps?"

I coughed politely. What a voice! It could make a man weak in the knees. "I'll have what Luís has," I rasped.

"Good, then it's settled." Luís looked around the bar. "I'll have a drumstick, and so will the Inspector. We'll hunt for the rest of the chicken another time, eh? Some wine, Lulu." He clapped me on the back. "See what I mean about lunch?"

6

"This is completely against regulations, Inspector, taking you to the crime scene." We were walking through the hotel lobby, a gargantuan, stomach-churning place not conceived for loitering or watching the passing parade. Whenever a parade did pass, it was into the open maw of the casino, where attendants in blazing orange coats kept the money moving in one direction. Most of the state security people positioned around the edges of the cavernous space were easy enough to spot. They might as well have been wearing signs. This wasn't the result of sloppiness or inattention. It was deliberate, designed to breed confidence in anyone looking to avoid the MSS. The principle at work was simple and well proven—confidence bred contempt, and contempt bred the tiny mistake that led, without exception or mercy, to a quick trial and then a bullet in the back of the head. Some of this effort was aimed at Chinese officials gambling with money they weren't supposed to have; some of it was a normal screen. You know there are insects, so you put up a net. Some of them you get before they come in the window; the rest you squash when the opportunity arises.

In truth, it didn't much matter how many security officers were standing around. Every employee and every hotel worked for them in one way or another, sooner or later. A few of those employees also worked for the triads. A few more fattened their paychecks by working for a foreign "friend" who didn't ask for much and then only once in a while but always had an extra envelope waiting for them. The old man at the Nam Lo's front desk probably worked part-time for all three. By now, each of his employers knew an unusual guest had checked in. Even if he had waited to tell them, the bored immigration official would have already raised a flag that all three would have noticed.

"The elevator is around the corner." Luís was several steps ahead of me. "Don't gawk, Inspector, or it will make you dizzy. Nothing in this lobby fits with anything, so everything seems to be whirling around and repelled by everything else. The place is an abomination, I agree."

The elevator took us smoothly to the thirty-fourth floor. As we stepped out, Luís took a key card from his pocket. "Room Thirty-four Twenty-seven, to the left. This is the executive preserve, but I don't know if there are any executives awake yet. In any case, we'll tread softly."

Treading proved to be no problem. The hallway carpet was thick and the walls were completely soundproofed. Every room would be an isolated world in the middle of nowhere. Luís paused at a door and read the number. "Don't touch anything; don't take notes; just look. Regulations."

"You have a lot of regulations, it seems."

"We do. That happens in warm climates, have you noticed?"

"But you don't follow them all."

Luís shrugged and opened the door. "I do what I can."

7

As soon as we stepped inside, I realized that the middle of nowhere was exactly what had been on the mind of the interior decorator. Room 3427 was a place where nothing led to nothing, shapes blurred, and colors blended, with the exception, perhaps, of one particularly noxious square chair, bloodred leather that looked about to leap screaming from the window. The living room was considerably longer than it was wide, which was perfect for an executive used to working in a tunnel. The bedroom was not much better, and because of the odd shape of the building it was a tunnel sliced by a large angled column necessary to bear the weight of the twenty floors above that hung out from the building in a series of steps. The effect was to remind anyone trying to sleep that their life was dependent on this column and that the construction company that put it up had no doubt scrimped on materials in order to pay off the building inspector who at this very moment was in the casino downstairs, one small step ahead of the MSS. Outside the bedroom window the view was obstructed by steel framing with no obvious purpose. It couldn't possibly be structural, I thought. If it was, I wanted to get to a lower floor right away. The column in the bedroom came up about a meter from the window, creating an isolated alcove so useless that not even the crazed decorator had been tempted to use it. An absurdly wide window ledge added the final touch, separating the room from any sense of connection with the rest of the planet and underlining the impression that the hotel might actually not even be part of the known universe.

Because the room was on the corner of the building, the bedroom had windows along two walls. Looking out from the window opposite the bed, I spotted bamboo. Even here, in such a humid place, I thought, it doesn't grow to thirty-four stories. "What is that?" I pointed.

Luís swam across the carpet. "It's what they call a sky garden, balconies that take advantage of all of the crisscrossing structural beams. This floor doesn't have any. I don't know if the architect had them in the original plans, or if they were an afterthought designed to squeeze out extra money from the guests. It is hard to tell."

"It looks to me that whoever might be lounging in the chaise down on that porch could probably see someone at this window."

"I suppose so. We haven't checked."

Haven't checked? What had they been doing for the last few weeks? "If one can see, presumably one can also hear, no?"

"Probably not. The glass is very thick. And the rooms, as you can tell, are completely soundproofed. The walls have baffling on them covered in what looks like leather. It's like living in a cow's stomach. Personally, I wouldn't pay the money."

"How much?"

"About eight thousand Macau dollars, maybe a thousand in real money, or ten of your super notes if you prefer."

"Where's the bathroom?"

"Can't you wait until we get downstairs?"

"I only want to look, Luís."

"Ah, well." He pointed. "It's tucked away nicely."

The carpet stopped and a marble floor announced the entrance to a small hall that bent around a corner to the bathroom—Jacuzzi, dry sauna, and separate toilet with its own television, which worked. Opposite the bathtub was a long window, again looking down on a porch attached to the floor below.

"A reckless bather could put on a nice show," I said. As I moved to the window, I tripped on a ledge at floor level—no doubt the Ur beam holding the whole place up.

"Not what your thousand-dollar toes want to find at three in the morning." Luís was searching along the side of the window. "There's a shade here somewhere, but it goes up and down electronically and the switch is the devil to locate. Most people probably don't bother with it."

"Let's go back to the living room." I limped into the tunnel and pointed out the window. A city the size of Macau is not spectacular much above the twentieth floor. The contours of the hills are lost, and the quaintness of the colonial buildings is impossible to distinguish without binoculars. Who wants to pay a thousand a night to look at the view through binoculars? "What is that? That tall wall with all the windows, at the top of what looks like a long stairway, what is it?"

"Those are the ruins of St. Paul's. You were practically there when you came to my office. You want to go see them?"

"A lot of stair-climbing to see ruins on a hot afternoon," I said.

"It is well to look up to God, Inspector."

"Perhaps," I said, "but I don't need a heart attack in the process." I pointed a little to the right. "And those ruins, next to Paul's?"

"The hilltop fort. The Portuguese built it in the early sixteen hundreds. It's a nice climb up the hill. The view from there is much better than from here, or it would be if this hotel were blown up. You probably can't make it out, but the Portuguese consulate is down in front of the fort, at the bottom of the hill. Interesting building, very colonial. Extremely yellow."

"Is there a room safe?"

"No, I think the Consul General keeps his valuables at home."

"I mean in this room."

"Of course." We walked over to the dressing area, more dark

wood, subdued lighting, muted colors. It was exactly the place to mourn the loss of a year's worth of bribes in a single game of baccarat. "The safe is in the top drawer of the dresser. Would you like to put something in for safekeeping?"

"No, thank you." I bounced up and down on my toes. "A suitcase full of body parts wouldn't have rolled very well on this carpet," I said.

"It was an expensive suitcase." Luís opened the drawer and touched some buttons on the safe. "I think they design them for all contingencies. Besides, the floor from the bathroom is marble and, as I told you, the body was butchered in the bathroom. Rolling from the bath to the front door would have been no problem."

"And the hallway carpet?"

"The rich are like you and me, Inspector, only smarter, more devious. They don't let carpeting stand in their way."

"Anything else I need to see, before you tell me what you left out in your first rendition of what was in that folder?"

"You have seen all. Shall we return to the living room to sit? You take the couch. I'll take the desk chair."

"And the red leather one?"

"I prefer to let it rest in peace."

8

"So, you intend to stay with this case. You have a dogged nature; that much is clear from the way you looked at Lulu."

It was hard not to look at Lulu. She occupied most of the field of vision. "I don't like the smell of things." I also didn't like the couch. The cushions were made of concrete.

Luís sighed. "All right, I have a few more things to tell you."

"You mean you have another version to unload?"

"Not entirely. Simply adding a layer of detail may prove to

you that there is no need for you to remain in Macau. It really is a click-clack case."

"Click-clack."

"Open and shut. File and forget. Up the chimney and out to sea." He pondered his next move. "We know what happened. We know who did it. The people who viewed the tapes see no crack for the daylight of doubt to enter. All we lack is a confession. Or rather, all we lack is a signature. The confession we have already written."

"Really? We tend to wait awhile to write it out."

"The murderer checked into the hotel at six thirty P.M. the ninth of October, a Sunday, under the name of Raoul Penza, having passed through Immigration ninety minutes earlier. He had arrived on the four P.M. ferry from Hong Kong, with a super-class ticket purchased at the ferry terminal earlier in the morning, around ten A.M. On the ferry, he refused the food tray with a gracious nod and dozed."

"Don't drown me in extraneous details, Luís. It takes ten minutes to get from the ferry terminal to here, but it took him an hour and a half. Surely, he didn't have to wait in line that long at Immigration. Perhaps it was even arranged so that he didn't have to wait in line at all." I paused; Luís filled the space with nothing but a blank stare. "He stopped somewhere?"

"That is our feeling as well."

"Meaning you have no idea where."

"Not yet. I can tell you it was not at one of the large casinos."

"The boys in the orange coats are sure of that?"

"They are."

"What about a small casino?"

"There are establishments, and then there are establishments. In any case, to resume, Senhor Penza was definitely downstairs in the lobby at six thirty P.M. He gave his home address as Residencia Julia Calle Six, Number Twenty-four, at Fourteenth Street, Isabelita, Santo Domingo."

"He wasn't preregistered?"

"No, he did not have a reservation. May I continue?"

"Claro, sim."

"You speak Portuguese like a Russian, Inspector." Luís thumbed through a small notebook. "There is such an address. In fact, there is also a Raoul Penza in Santo Domingo. He is a baker at a place called De la Casa Pain, and he has never applied for a passport. So right away, we know we have a little problem, wouldn't you agree?"

There it was again—the "little problem." I wasn't about to agree to anything. "Not to get off track, but I like to fill in the details as things move along. It saves time later. Who checked him in?"

"The desk clerk was an intelligent young woman, named Lilley Li." He turned the page of the notebook. "She is observant, good memory, single, witty, and lithe."

"One of us should propose."

"One of us should."

"And what does lithe Lilley remember?"

"Our man wanted a room overlooking the blessed ruins of St. Paul's. He was not looking for anything ostentatious—a kitchen, a bedroom, a bathroom with plenty of hot water, and a balcony. Lilley told him she could satisfy some of his needs."

"Lilley, darling," I said, "you should be more careful."

"She was, actually. She wisely pushed the signal for the Assistant Manager to appear."

"And he did?"

"When summoned, the self-important Winston Woo brushes off his striped pants, pulls straight his cutaway jacket, slicks back his oily hair, and sallies forth. He greets Senhor Penza with a cold smile." Again Luís turned the page—not hiding the fact that there were a few observations he did not wish to share as yet. "Young Penza nods to Lilley and says he is sure the hotel will do its best to accommodate his requirements."

"Not his wishes. His requirements. As if he is used to being obeyed."

"That is the word Lilley says he used, and Lilley would not lie."

"I'm not saying the girl lied, Luís. Perhaps she misremembered a detail here, a detail there. Witnesses do that."

The friendly air around Luís dissipated for a moment. "Not Lilley," he said in a tone that gave no quarter. "The girl is a bulldog with details." He flipped through the notebook, skipping over additional characteristics of the bulldog Lilley that I was not to know. "Ah, here! Our fellow signs up for five nights. He is very tired and hopes to rest. He is handsome and composed, does not appear nervous or ill at ease. He is unhurried, smiles at Lilley frequently. He melts her heart."

"Lilley said that?"

"She didn't have to, Inspector. I know her heart." Luís stands and looks out the window for a moment. "Our man asks for a safe-deposit box—a detail you inquired about, I seem to recall. Only then does Senhor Penza turn to Winston, whose smile, Lilley recalls, is fixed on his face like a week-old slice of mango." Pages turn in the notebook. "Yes, here is what I was looking for. The bell captain, an experienced source that pays attention whenever the Assistant Manager appears, notices that Penza has one suitcase, a Louis Vuitton. I told you it was expensive. More precisely, it was a Pegase 60."

"Not very big. A 70 would be better for body parts, but it only has two wheels. You told me the body was in a four-wheeler."

Luís whistled. "You know suitcases?"

"I've been around the block," I said modestly, and shifted back to business. "Our man gets settled. Then what? Goes out for dinner? Gambles? Comes back drunk and collapses on this uncomfortable couch?"

It is clear that Luís is annoyed that I have interrupted his fable. "None of the above. For three nights and three days, he does not leave his room. No movies. No room service. Nothing from the minibar. The DO NOT DISTURB sign is lit the whole time, so no maid service. No visitors."

"You know that? I mean, no visitors?"

"In this hotel, on this floor, they make it a point to know such things. His door never opened."

"He must have eaten something. Maybe he brought his own food. You could pack quite a meal in a Pegase 60."

"He had tea. In fact, he used all of the hotel tea bags along with two bottles of water."

"You said nothing from the minibar, I thought."

"These were not the fake Evians from the refrigerator. These were the tap water in the bottles kept on the shelf above the bar. The maid says that when she was finally allowed in on the fourth morning—Thursday—he had gone through all of the towels, even the little ones, but had not even rumpled the bedsheets. No one was ever in the bed as far as she could tell, and she can tell plenty. This maid has been around the block, as you put it."

"In sum, for three nights, he was a monk. No phone calls?"

"None."

"Maybe he used a cell phone."

"Maybe he tied a string to a soup can. Yes, or maybe he stood at the window and used semaphore flags to talk to a long-lost relative. Anything is possible, Inspector, in your world as in mine. But he did not use a cell phone, *inegavelmente*!" I figured that meant I wasn't supposed to ask how he knew, so I didn't. "Moreover, Senhor Penza left instructions with the front desk that he was not to be disturbed. I neglected to tell you that?"

"One of the details you skipped over. You merely mentioned that he said he was tired."

Luís gave me a charming smile. "There was a message left for him the first night, but they held it at the concierge's desk until he came back to earth. They wait for the DO NOT DISTURB light to go off before they deliver messages. They don't even slip them under the door. Some people are sensitive to the sound of paper on marble."

"Did he ever get the message?"

"Yes, he did. On the day he left."

"Is that why he got nervous, changed plans, wanted to rent a car?"

"One can speculate. Before you ask, the reason he didn't get it on the fourth day was that the concierge forgot to give it to him. Sad but true, a gap in the Great Wall of service. I'm told it has been plugged."

"Very convenient. Do we know who the concierge worked for?"

"You mean, other than the hotel? No, but we're looking into it."

"You know, of course, what the message said."

He scratched his head and looked in his notebook. " 'Hurry up, hurry up cows.' That was in English, incidentally."

"Any idea what it meant?"

"Furious research is underway."

"To review. So far, we have a Dominican monk drinking tea, sleeping on the floor or in the bath."

"With a forged passport."

"I said a monk, not an angel. On the next day, day four? No, wait a minute. Back to the message, how was it delivered to the hotel? Phone?"

"By messenger service. They said it was dropped off in the office around nine P.M. by a middle-aged woman, Asian, nothing special that they could recall. She wore a scarf of some sort. We're looking, but I don't think it will be a fruitful search. There are many such women."

"Well, they can't all be Lilley or Lulu, Luís."

"Alas."

"So, what we can assume is that someone knew the phony baker was in this hotel within a few hours of his registering."

"An assumption, but not a bad one." From his expression, it was clear he hadn't considered this before.

"Let's return to day four."

"He goes out early, smiles at everyone, gives a tip to the doorman. He doesn't come back until ten thirty at night."

"Where was he all day?"

"We're checking."

"It's been more than two weeks. Macau is a small place. You're still checking?"

"In the glory days, we followed people as regularly as you breathe, Inspector. In olden times, we had staff. Now, we only do it if there's a reason."

"And a forged passport isn't a reason?"

"It is, unless it isn't."

No sense in going through that door. "You would know if he went to a casino anytime on day four?"

"We would."

"He didn't."

"Again, none of the big ones. As I've suggested to you, those are well covered—staff, cameras, whatever. However, there are a few other places, more private. He might have been to one of those."

"But you don't think so."

"I have an open mind."

"Maybe he went to church and prayed all day? Maybe he left the island?"

"There is a single report of someone of his description arriving on the ferry from Hong Kong Airport, the last one of the evening."

"Very vague. No follow-up?"

"The ferry was unusually crowded. That Thursday night, a lot of people came in. Plus, the schedule had been disrupted; an earlier boat had engine problems, so they were pressed to overload the final one."

"Lucky it didn't capsize."

"Lucky."

"No record of him coming through Immigration? Shouldn't be hard to find a Dominican passport."

"He could have used more than one. People do, I hear." Again, the charming smile. "At eleven fifteen that night, he had a visitor."

"At last."

"A Russian."

"Tall." I didn't want it to be the girl I'd met coming down the stairs.

"Seemingly. Well dressed, wearing a coat and a hat and very, very good high heels. It was a chilly evening and had started to rain soon after he returned."

"You know this was a Russian because . . ."

"She spoke Russian."

"Someone heard her?"

"She was overheard, yes." Luís's eyes searched the room.

"You have her picture?"

"No. Well, yes, a passport picture was recovered. It had been in the water for several days."

"In the water. Something else you skipped over." Kim had mentioned it to me; Luís had not.

"You can imagine it was not in the best shape. We can restore it partially, mostly around the edges. We think someone may have scratched out the nose."

"How was this visit arranged? He called her?"

"No calls. Maybe he met her somewhere during the day and issued an invitation. Maybe they were old friends."

"I see. An old high-heeled friend waltzed through the lobby at eleven fifteen at night, took the elevator to the executive floor, and no one stopped her? Some security."

"There are other entrances, other ways. Not everyone wants it known they have such visitors. It could be a problem for some people, I suppose. Besides, eleven fifteen at night is like noon around here."

"And the next time she is seen, it is in a Pegase 60, or some suitcase, in pieces?"

"Almost." Luís rubbed his hands together until I thought his long fingers would burst into flames.

"There's more."

"Some."

Luís was not, I could tell from the look on his face, prepared to be much more forthcoming than that. Neither of us said anything, which defeated the purpose of all the soundproofing. Finally, I decided to jump in.

"I heard the woman showed up in pieces a week ago. That she was carried in a matched set of luggage through the hotel lobby at seven A.M., dumped in the harbor in a four-wheeler, a red Lancel which floated for a few days before being picked up by the police, who were tipped off by a Japanese camera crew waiting there to film the whole thing and ask a lot of embarrassing questions. True?"

All right, I added the detail about the Lancel. Major Kim had said the bigger suitcase was red, and I'd seen a red Lancel once at a train station in Paris being pulled along by a tall woman with long legs. You don't forget a suitcase like that. I figured it couldn't hurt to wave something specific in front of Luís. Maybe he would tell me I was wrong and let slip a few details. One thing I already knew—the bigger suitcase wasn't a Louis Vuitton, because Louis didn't want anything to do with four-wheelers. That wouldn't have stuck out, except Kim had told me that the murderer had carried out the body in a matched set of luggage. Luís hadn't mentioned anything like that. Something was beginning not to add up.

Luís seemed to be wondering about the addition, too. He looked puzzled. "I don't know where you got that, Inspector, but it's not even close."

"Which part do I have wrong?"

"This is an open investigation."

"I thought you said it was an open-and-shut case."

"We're still on the open part."

"One thing we haven't discussed—Penza. What's your interest in him?"

"He is a murderer, Inspector. Isn't that enough?"

"Yes, murder is usually more than enough. Apart from that, I mean. This case has odd crosscurrents. From what you say, there are a lot of questions still unanswered, and yet you already have a confession waiting to be signed. I have to wonder what's behind this. That a person has bad taste in hotel rooms isn't a crime, is it?" I stood up. "My best to Lulu."

Luís put the notebook back in his pocket. "If you get to De la Casa Pain, please give Senhor Penza my regards." We shook hands. "The elevator is to your left as you exit. Why don't you relax for a couple of days, take in a show? Go out to the Venetian. Everything there is first class. I know the manager." Luís looked up at the ceiling. "He is an old friend, from before the regulations."

"Old friends are like doors, isn't that what they say?" I nearly tripped on the hallway carpet on my way out.

Chapter Two

I was eating a plate of roast pork—overdone in the worst way—in a small restaurant on the first floor of the Lisboa when the Russian girl with green eyes walked in. She headed straight to my table.

"May I sit?"

"I'm all out of engraved invitations."

"You really shouldn't stay in the Nam Lo. It isn't proper for a man like you."

"A man like me."

"My boss doesn't want you there. He says it scares clients away."

"I know your boss?"

"You will meet him soon enough." Her phone rang; she answered reluctantly. "Da, da." She nodded at me. "Da."

"That was your boss."

"Yes, he told me to tell you he would see that you were out of the Nam Lo one way or another. I'm sorry." She shook her head sadly. "You don't know this man."

"Would you like some dinner? Anything but the pork."

She looked at the pictures on the menu and pointed at a bowl of noodles. "This is what I have mostly." She shrugged, the way a young person does, not much weighing on their shoulders. "One more time won't hurt."

"You come here often?"

"Every night before I . . . go to work."

"How about on your night off?"

She laughed so convincingly that it was almost impossible to find the pain. "What night off? I work seven days a week. It's part of the contract."

"You have a contract?"

"Oh course. That's why I'm here. At the end of six months, I get paid and go home. Only five months to go. I'm never coming back."

"There must be lots of Russian girls here."

She shrugged, this time without the innocence. "I'm not pretty enough for you?"

"You? You're the prettiest Russian girl I've ever seen. You're also very young. Why don't you go home?"

"Can't. Told you. I have a contract."

"You don't have to abide by it. It's not really legal."

"You're going to get me a passport, and a plane ticket, I suppose?"

"Forgive me for asking—how much do you have to make a night?"

"Ten thousand."

"How much an hour?"

"A thousand."

I did the math. "That's awful. What kind of place is this?"

She pointed to a line of young, well-dressed Chinese women walking up and down the hallway next to the restaurant. "Ask them."

"What is it, a fashion show?"

She laughed. "They are here to make love."

"The whole group? We're in a fancy hotel. Shouldn't they at least be outside, on the street?"

"We walk the streets. The Chinese girls don't have to. A guest picks out the one he likes. Some of the guests are old, so that way they don't have to use energy walking so far back to the room. It's a service, I guess. Respect for the elderly."

I looked at the girls. "What if I don't like any of them?"

"Then you eat noodles with me." She patted my hand. "Just get out of the Nam Lo, will you?"

2

At my hotel, there was a message waiting for me. The clerk handed it over without saying anything. He waited until I started up the stairs to my room.

"Russian guy nosing around. Wanted to know if you were still here."

"And you said?"

"I yelled at him in Hakka."

"You don't speak Russian?"

"I don't like Russians. Except the young ones." He licked his lips.

I walked back to the desk. "You touch her, I'll kill you. You understand that?"

He shrank back. "You can't scare me. I've got friends."

"I'll bet you have scabies, too."

When I got to my room, the door was slightly ajar. I walked calmly downstairs, took the clerk by the collar, and dragged him back upstairs. "See that?" I shoved his head into the door. "Do that again and I'll burn this place down."

"Hey!" He unleashed all twelve tones at me. "What was that about?"

"It's called negative reinforcement, and there's more where that came from."

"I'll call the cops, you touch me again."

"Go ahead; call the cops. Call MSS for all I care."

He rubbed the top of his head. "That's the last time I rent to a Korean," he said. "You people are crazy-mad, not to mention being murderers."

"Wait a minute." I grabbed his arm. "What do you know about murders?"

"Nothing." He grinned at me. "Not a thing."

After the clerk disappeared, I opened the message. All it said was: "Blue sky." Everyone seemed to be getting short messages these days, but this one shook me. It shook me up so much I sat down in the ratty chair next to the television. "Blue sky" was a code a chief inspector of mine had used as an emergency signal. But he was dead, shot years ago by Military Security in an incident that wasn't recorded anywhere and thus never happened. It couldn't be from him. I had never heard of spirits using code.

There was only one other person who might have known the code, and he had disappeared. His name was Kang. He'd been a deputy director of what was then known as the Investigations Department—the party's foreign intelligence arm. He had also been on the Military Security hit list, but they never got him. I may have been the last person to see him before he went into permanent hiding. A few people wanted to get in touch with him over the years, and they thought I knew how to do it. I didn't, and I never wanted to find out. Now this. "Blue sky," another way of saying: "Make contact at once." But where? How? I pushed the door shut and lay down on the bed. Simple, I thought. If Kang wants to contact me, he knows where I am. Let him take the next step.

From downstairs, I could hear the clerk yelling into the phone. Ah, the lullaby of Canton, I thought to myself, and fell asleep.

3

Next morning, I went in search of parks, meeting places, alleys, drop sites, anything I might find handy if Kang turned up. It also helped me to wander around, let all the half facts that Luís had thrown at me sift through my subconscious. If anything remained by the end of the day, any nuggets that didn't turn out to be pixie dust, I'd give them a second look. Meanwhile, I had a little pixie dust of my own to contend with. Major Kim had deliberately left out the most important part of the case—who was allegedly, or actually, involved. Normally, this didn't mean much. Guilt was relative; innocence, fleeting. The crime might be more important than the individual, the accusation more significant than the facts. If we were told to find a reason to clear someone, that's what we did. It wasn't healthy to inquire into the whats and whyfors.

The case that Kim wanted fixed wasn't fitting into a normal pattern, however. For starters, there was the passport. Not a lot of Koreans carried one from the Dominican Republic. Then there was the message to the nominal Senhor Penza—and the fact that it had been so conveniently overlooked until almost the last minute. Finally, Luís was holding out on me. I didn't expect him to dump everything in my lap, but I had the feeling he didn't want to say too much, not because I was from a foreign service but because he wasn't sure of his own footing. It wasn't a matter of personal trust. After all, he had shared Lulu with me almost from the start.

The old city had a lot of small, green parks mostly filled with ficus trees, pretty much as Luís had said. Most of the trees had short trunks. They branched off quickly, after only a meter or so. "Wood from a ficus is like a promise of love," my grandfather would say when I was a boy and he saw me watching girls as they walked past our house. "It doesn't take you very far." He had another warning—one he often used on holidays when the girls dressed up in bright *chima chogori* and strolled from one village to the next, eyes sparkling with fun. It was breathtaking, I thought, like a parade of flowers along our dusty road. "Go ahead; look," he'd say, standing beside me, his hand on my shoulder. "Look. They're like shiny leaves. Did you ever see a tree worth a damn that needed shiny leaves? Well, did you, boy?"

Near the post office, up a pleasant street called Travessa de S. Domingos, I came upon a square with a fountain in the middle and a large ficus spilling shade onto a bench. On two sides the square was enclosed by a low wall of blue and white tiles. It seemed like a good place to get out of the sun and even held some promise for a meeting with Kang, if things came to that. No one else was around, so I took the bench beneath the tree.

A few minutes later, Luís walked into the square. He threw a couple of coins into the fountain and sat down beside me. "You keep up a brutal pace in this heat," he said. "You should slow down a little. Good thing you found this shade. I was about to drop." He took out a handkerchief and mopped his forehead.

"I thought we had finished our business."

"So did I. But then a friend of mine asked me to find you."

"A suite has opened up at the Venetian?"

"Better." He stood up again and looked over the wall behind us at the street below. "Nobody here but us chickens. Or us people who eat chickens." He studied his watch. "Lunchtime rolls around again, thank God, and not a moment too soon. In a short while, we'll have visitors. Whenever I go out, MSS tags along at a respectable distance. They think I'm helping someone launder a lot of money. Me!" He laughed until the tears streamed down his face. "I can't even wash my own shirts." His shirt was white and crisp, except where drops of laughter glistened down the front. "Listen closely," he said, once he pulled himself together. "Remember that fort we saw from the hotel room? The one on top of the hill? That's where you must meet my friend."

"I'm inclined not to trust anyone, especially people I've never met."

"This is different. You'll find out why soon enough."

I didn't even try to stop from appearing skeptical.

"I don't want you to go into this in a state of disbelief, Inspector; it's bad operational practice. That's what our manual emphasized repeatedly. Yours did, too, I imagine. Tell me, what's the matter?"

"Pretty exposed, that location, isn't it?"

"So! You are a cautious man, Inspector. This caution is impressive. Perhaps where you live it is essential. Here in Macau, however, it can be fatal. The fort is a good choice; I'm sure of it. There's only one way in. If you're followed, it will be obvious."

"Only one way in is fine. It's the only one way out that worries me. Even if I'm not followed, what about people already in place?"

"You mean MSS? They pulled their surveillance a few years ago. It wasn't worth their time, they said. Anyway, it's a very steep climb up there. My people don't cover it at all." He shrugged when I didn't reply. "All right, some security goes up a couple of times a month to make sure the fort is still there. They aren't due again for another week, and they stick to a regular schedule. They're afraid what they might find if they go to random visits."

"We won't bump into five other operations by five other organizations? The British have friends, the Americans, the French, maybe the Singaporeans. How can you be sure that no one else knows the place is wide open, that it isn't being watched?"

"Who says it isn't being watched?"

"Aha."

"This will work. I know it will because we've never done it before, so there's no pattern and absolutely no trail. They might catch on if we did it more than once, but we won't. Think of it as a onetime pad."

"Maybe some rough edges, though? The first time always has

rough edges, a few things someone forgets to consider, minor details—the sort that can get a person killed."

"None, no minor details, simple as rain. Just listen. You go up to the fort at nine A.M. tomorrow. It's still cool enough then so you won't give yourself heatstroke climbing that hill. Take a bottle of water with you, to be safe. Look a little touristy; you know the drill."

"The place will be deserted at that hour?"

"Deserted? Good God, no. There will be squads of old ladies using it for exercise, a couple of tape players blaring that music they need to stand on one leg and sweat. Sometimes they practice with fans; other times it's with swords. Don't walk too close or you could lose something. Your main interest is the front wall and the nineteen cannons that line it."

"Nineteen."

"Three main groups—five, nine, and five."

"That's nineteen."

"Face the front of the fort. You will see that there are two bulwarks—left and right. This is very common fort architecture for the period."

"I'll take your word."

"Each bulwark has five cannons. For the sake of convenience, we'll number those in the left bulwark one through five."

"One through five."

"Good. Now, forget they're there. You actually start counting with the sixth cannon. As you face the Grand Lisboa, and you can't miss it because the damned thing blots out the rest of God's creation, cannon number six will be the first one on your left along the wall. Use that as an anchor point in your mind; get yourself oriented."

"Should I close my eyes to imagine this?"

"As you wish. But you don't want to focus on the left side yet. You want to stroll over to the right bulwark to look for the go, no-go signals. If any of them are missing—any of them—back off."

"How many altogether?" My memory is normally good, but humidity does funny things with the circuits.

Luís looked up at the sky and counted silently. "Three." He nodded to himself. "Three. The first and second are in the right bulwark, where you will find that two of the cannons face the front."

I reached for my pen. "Can I write any of this down? Cannons to the left of them, cannons to the right of them. Maybe a diagram would help."

"No notes. Just listen. The cannon on the extreme right has the symbol of a crown stamped into the top of the barrel, fairly near the touchhole. I'm supposed to tell you *not* to touch that hole. I wasn't told why; I just pass it on. The next cannon over, to the left, has no crown on the barrel. Perhaps it did not get a royal blessing. Purchased in bulk, maybe. Instead of a crown, it has a diamond filled with a cross. Are you following?"

"Got it."

"Any questions about the cannons?"

"No. Should there be?"

"Trying to cover all the bases, that's all. If there's something about a cannon that you aren't sure of, speak up."

"Listen, Koreans invented cannons. I know them like the back of my hand."

"Really? I thought that the Chinese invented them."

"That," I said, "happens all the time. We invent something, and the Chinese take credit for it."

Luís nodded thoughtfully. "Further up, toward the muzzle, you will find the letter *M* stamped into the barrel. At the bottom of each of the letter's two main vertical strokes are little feet or platforms." He drew me a quick sketch on his palm, then spit in his hand and rubbed it off. "If the operation is proceeding, both feet on that *M* will be filled with a sort of putty. It won't fall out. The stamp itself is pretty deep. Even if you can't see the putty, you'll be able to tell it's there by running your finger over the letter. People do that all the time, God knows why, so no one will pay attention to you. Anyway, the old ladies don't use the right bulwark, feng shui problems possibly, so I doubt anyone will be standing around."

"Next."

"A half meter or so to the left of the cannon with the *M* is a round porthole through the stone wall. You can look out through it—that's what every other tourist has done for the last century. Then another half meter to the left is a triangular storage shed set into the corner of the bulwark. It has a blue metal door, locked with a padlock. I don't know what's in there, and I don't know why they lock it. There are three steps leading up to the door. Each step consists of five or six stones, irregularly shaped, and set in old mortar. On the middle step, on the right side as you face it, is a loose stone. If it's missing or out of place, you go home and forget we had this conversation."

"What if the groundskeeper knocks that stone out of place when he steps on it? Or some small boy decides to throw it at his sister?"

"Won't happen."

"*Inegavelmente!*"

"Your Portuguese still sounds like Russian." He shook his head. "To get to the heart of the matter. If the first two signals are positive, you move out of the right bulwark and go to cannon number nine—that's in the center of the front wall. Well, off center, actually. It has a number stamped on the top of the barrel—twenty-five–one–nine. On the left side, on the gun carriage itself, the number sixteen-three-eighteen is stamped along the top bar. Next to the 'eighteen' will be a leaf, a shiny one."

This, I thought to myself, is definitely fate.

"Only it won't really be a leaf, though it's pretty convincing.

Palm it. Then stroll along the wall, looking at the rest of the cannons, with dreams of history in your eyes."

"Why don't I simply get the leaf and be done with it?"

"This is Macau, Inspector. If we were in Hong Kong, we'd do it differently, dress up in suits and carry briefcases. Here we work with old cannons. Don't worry; we're almost done; let me go over a few background notes. Two people will be setting the first two signs. Neither knows about the other. They'll set the signals an hour apart, and then only when they receive a go-ahead from someone I have never met. The two that set the signals are completely undetectable, believe me."

"Old ladies with swords, practically invisible."

Luís tugged at his collar; the tree had decided to move its shade elsewhere, and we were now sitting squarely in the sun. "The first signal is to indicate whether things are proceeding. The second is to alert you if you've been followed into the fort."

"I can't figure out by myself if I'm being followed on a deserted street up a hill early in the morning?"

"I'm sure you're quite good, Inspector, but you have to admit, there might be people who are better. Let's not take a chance, shall we?"

"And the pseudoleaf? Where does that get us?"

"Ah, sweet mystery of life. It will have a number on it—two digits. If they are both even, you go to the bench directly behind cannon number seven. Not the stone bench, the one with wooden slats."

"Some operational significance?"

"It's more comfortable."

"What if both numbers are odd?"

"Then you go down the hill, slowly so as not to twist an ankle, and come back to this pleasant little square. You'll get further instructions."

"And if it's one even, one odd?"

"Then it's not our leaf. Jump over the wall if you have to and get out of there in a hurry."

A two-man team prowled up to the fountain. One of them reached in and fished out a few coins. Luís snorted. "They want to make sure I didn't throw money in that I'm not supposed to have." He stood up and gave me a slight bow. "A pleasure talking with you, senhor," he said in a loud voice. "Please give my regards to each of your adorable wives." As he went by the fountain, he threw in a fistful of coins.

4

The hill was gentle at first but became very steep very quickly. The sidewalk was barely wide enough for one person. The street had room for only a single car, and it was one-way going down, so at least no one in an automobile could follow me up. Everything was close and damp with humidity. The air was cool and smelled of rotting leaves; the light was still soft, the morning light that came from the sea. By the time I made it to the top, I was out of breath and sweating. Charming of the Portuguese military to pick a place so hard to reach, I thought, and fumbled with the bottle of water I had bought in the old city so far below. The troops must have cursed every morning they panted up this hill. Any enemy commander storming the place would have decided to break for lunch halfway there.

The fort itself would have been brutally hot, on an open hilltop perilously close to the southern sun, but for the shade of a few trees. From the looks of them, they were a century or more old, and had grown to enormous girth with limbs to match. If Lulu were to come back as a tree, I thought, she would be one of these. Clashing tapes of Chinese music occupied competing squads of old women standing, as Luís had said, on one leg and flipping fans open with the cracks of gunshots. Nineteen cannons sat silent along the front, prepared to blast away at the looming monster of the hotel, if only some Portuguese gunnery officer long in his grave would rise again to give the order.

On cannon number seventeen (counting from the left, including the five in the left bulwark) the feet on the *M* are filled. One green light. I stop and gaze out the porthole in the wall. I could see history from there, imagine Portuguese ships in the harbor, except it is impossible to see the harbor because of the hotel. I search in my pockets for matches to set off the cannons. On to the blue door of the triangular shed and the steps that lead to it, all in good order. It would take me only an hour or so to touch up that mortar. I'd mention it to Luís if I saw him again.

Each cannon gets a pat on its fat bottom as I pass. I smile at an old man who is leaning against cannon number thirteen, watching his perspiring wife exercise the hell out of a patch of grass. The ninth cannon, as promised, is numbered 25-1-9. It's unlikely anyone would move these beasts around, but I stand back and do a recount anyway. It's the ninth from the left, the third cannon from number six, which, as I think Luís said, was the first on the left along the front.

There is no danger of this operation being compromised; nothing this confusing could ever be compromised. Even if the whole thing was leaked, it would take hours to untangle the feet and the steps and the diamonds stamped with crosses. This does not have the feel of anything Kang would plan. He favored simplicity—one cannon and out. The humidity is climbing. I wonder if a person can drown standing on top of a hill on such a humid day. Why did I trust Luís again? He has a complicated existence. There is no reason he should tell me the truth about anything. I palm the leaf—and it is a reasonable imitation of a shiny leaf. The only problem, I see instantly, is that this one has been made to resemble a leaf in May and here we are in October. I walk over to the wall and glance at my hand. The number, ink already bleeding away, is 20.

Twenty? What is that? Is zero even or odd? The day is becoming too hot to worry. I go to the bench in the shade and sit, gazing at the Grand Lisboa. The shape of the building defies description. It is either a gigantic mutant flower feeding on laundered money, or a horrendous arrow from the bow of an angry god who came to earth for some fun and lost a pile playing five-card stud. My concentration is broken by someone who blocks the view. He looks like the man leaning on number thirteen, could even be his twin brother, but with shorter hair. This man has a newspaper under one arm, a small book in his left hand. He sits down and points at the tree next to us. "What do you suppose that is?"

"It's a ficus," I say. "An old one, maybe four hundred years. Some Portuguese missionary must have planted it." Anyone could have planted it. It could have planted itself for all I know. It is very hot, and the Grand Lisboa appears to be dancing.

"There's a plaque on the tree."

"Yes, but it's in Portuguese."

"Oh, you aren't from Macau? I could have sworn I'd seen you somewhere. At the Venetian, perhaps, taking in a show?"

I let my eyes roam around the fort. The only person not on one leg is leaning against number thirteen.

The man beside me is humming. He puts the book on the bench between us. "It doesn't bother me at all," he sings in a soft, high voice.

I take a sip of warm water from the bottle. What the deuce is that supposed to mean? "Yeah, me, neither," I say.

He smiles and hums a few more bars. "Gaaz-ing at the sky." He looks up through the leaves. "Going to be a pretty day. Puffy white clouds."

That rings a bell. I nod. "Blue sky." Wherever this is going, we are just about there.

"Too bad about your uncle."

All at once, this isn't the conversation I expected. I don't have an uncle.

"Well," he says finally. He walks away, holding the book. The newspaper is on the bench. I sit for a couple of minutes, wondering whether this is a trap. I don't trust Luís, but he doesn't seem to be the type to put me in a trap, I am pretty sure, almost sure. Still, that leaves a number of candidates. Pang didn't really want me to be here, despite what he said. Zhao hadn't tried to be devious; he had been absolutely explicit. The old man on thirteen has moved down to number eleven. He watches. It isn't a trap, I decide, so I pick up the newspaper and skim the front page. Then I fold the paper under my arm and walk slowly down the stairs to the hill, and slowly down the hill to a bakery for a cup of coffee. This wasn't the best handoff I'd ever seen, I think to myself, but apparently it was good enough for Macau.

5

When I got back to the Nam Lo, the clerk was hurrying down the stairs. He pressed himself against the wall. "Nobody touched your room; don't worry," he said. "I was cleaning up the one down the hall, the one your girlfriend uses."

"Out of my way," I said. "I lost a suitcase full of money at the casino and I don't want to talk."

This seemed to cheer him up, because he said something using only six tones.

The room looked untouched. I closed the door, put the ratty chair against it, and opened the newspaper on the bed. Taped on page 3 was an airline ticket for tomorrow to Prague, though not nonstop. That meant changing planes, risking delays. Why Prague? I got a funny feeling. I'd been there once before, long ago. There was a return ticket, but it was for Shanghai. That did me no good; there were no flights from Shanghai to Pyongyang. That meant I was going to have to change the routing at the airport in Prague, with a lot of unnecessary questions from the ticket agent about why I didn't book it that way to begin with. There would also be careful study of my identification, which meant the visa stamps would get attention. The ticket wasn't in my name. It wasn't in the name that was on my South Korean passport, either, but that was all right because on page 5 of the newspaper was an envelope with a Dominican passport inside. It had a better picture of me than the one Kim's people had used. My name was Ricardo, and I was fifty-four years old, which was fine. That knocked almost fifteen years off the wear and tear on my body. The age on a fake passport might not be an elixir of youth, but it helps.

I went downstairs and gave the room clerk a sad look. "My uncle died. I have to leave a day early."

"Sure," he said. "It's a curse. Whenever people have to leave early, they kill off an uncle. Never an aunt."

"I'll be back."

"You get charged for the full stay. It's policy." He pointed at a sign behind him on the wall.

"That's an explanation of the fire exits, in Chinese."

"Say, you're one smart Korean, aren't you?" He let loose a few long sentences in Hakka.

"OK, I get it," I said. "I pay for the day I'm not here, and you pocket the money."

"Any complaints, fill out the form in the desk in your room."

"There isn't a desk in my room."

"Really? Well, you can use one of the forms over there." He pointed at a few dirty pieces of paper on the counter.

"Where do I put it when I'm done?"

He grinned.

"I'll tell you what I need. I need a train ticket for tomorrow."

"In case you haven't noticed, Macau is practically an island. No trains."

"Yeah, I figured that out. But you must have travel agents that can make arrangements. I've seen one or two luggage stores, and that means people travel; if people travel, they have tickets, and they must get them somewhere."

"Depends. Where you going?" He gave me the canny look of a man calculating how much he could get for selling the same information to three buyers.

"Shanghai, to pay my respects to my uncle, who ran a noodle shop there. Then to Beijing to see my aged mother, who lives with her sister in one of those new villas near the Kempinski. You know it? Then on to Yanji. Yanji is lousy with Koreans, in case you didn't know."

"Right."

"Can you get me the tickets?"

"No, but I can tell you where to go."

"A ticket office."

"If you knew, why did you ask?" He was already reaching for the phone.

6

That night I went back to the restaurant where the Chinese girls ate before they went to work in the hallway. The Russian girl was sitting in the same corner.

"Hi," I said. "Can I sit?"

"Sit." She smiled up at me. "Yes, sit."

"You're here again." I scanned the menu. "You want something beside noodles and orange juice?"

She shook her head. "It's good. You want some?"

"Nah, I never eat the night before I travel."

"You leaving? Changing hotels? That's good. You don't want to be at the Nam Lo."

"I'm going to Shanghai. My uncle died." Might as well put

the story out in more than one place, though I felt bad using her.

"Sorry." She shrugged. "You're a nice man. I will miss you."

"And you're a nice girl with beautiful eyes. I wish you'd go home."

"I can't. I have a contract."

"Can I ask you a question?"

"I already told you, a thousand dollars."

"How many other girls does your boss control?"

"You want someone else?" She looked hurt. "All right. There are eight girls altogether. For a few days we were nine, but now it's back to eight again."

"Someone went home?"

"Who knows? We never got a good look at her. She was older than the rest of us, showed up suddenly. My boss put her in the Nam Lo for one night. I don't even think she was there the whole time. She didn't work, that's for sure, and then she was gone. I saw her from the back, just briefly. She was blond. When she left, my boss told me to clean out the room she had been in. There was a small suitcase full of clothes and a razor. Otherwise, it was as if she hadn't been there."

"But she had been there."

"Yes, but the room didn't feel right. It didn't smell right."

I stood up to go. "Maybe I'll see you again."

She stood and kissed me lightly on the cheek. "Make sure it's before April. My contract is up then, and I'm never coming back."

7

I had time on my hands, money in my pocket, and things on my list. The first thing I did was stop one of the girls walking up and down the hall.

"Where are the best pork buns in town?" The girl was carrying a black patent-leather bag with matching shoes. I figured if anyone knew about pork buns, she would.

"Fifteen hundred," she said.

"Maybe later," I said. "Right now, I need pork buns, the best. When you go out for pork buns, where do you and your friends go?"

She called over one of her co-workers, frilly white blouse and her hair done up in a tight bun. Very fetching, but not what I needed. The two spoke between themselves for a moment.

"You want both? Twenty-five." The black bag swung provocatively.

"Listen," I said. "When I need to kill myself, I'll call you first. Meantime . . ."

"I know," she said, "pork buns. Rua da Barra, not far. It's a place called Mama Nhi's. Pretty good."

An older girl walked up. "Keep it moving," she said, and looked at me. "Either buy or don't buy."

8

Mama Nhi didn't have a box, but she did have a big shopping bag.

"Fill it up?" She put her hands on her hips. "That's one hell of a lot of grease. You planning to sell the stuff? Tell me; I can get you more."

9

I opened the door of the van. "These are for you," I said. "Maybe we can talk."

10

The next morning, I was at the luggage store in the Lisboa when it opened. None of the suitcases looked big enough for a body, not even for one of the skinny models waving from the photographs in the window.

"I need something large." I smiled. "Let's say I wanted to go on a trip. Let's say for laughs I wanted to go in my own suitcase. You got anything?"

The clerk's eyes opened for a flicker. "This is the biggest we have." She went behind the counter and pulled out a Louis Vuitton, a two-wheeler.

"Nice," I said. "But cramped. How about a Lancel? How about red?"

She shook her head. "Too bad. I sold the last one a few weeks ago."

"Is that so? You remember whom you sold it to?"

"Sure. Some Russian woman, thin, very careful with the makeup. How come all the interest in red Lancels all of a sudden?"

All of a sudden, she said. I took a chance. "Luís was in last night?"

She shrugged. "You browse. Take your time." She went back behind the counter. "I'm not going anywhere."

I pretended to look around. So, Luís hadn't followed the suitcase angle before. We all had blind spots. His were baggage and balconies. Senhor Penza hadn't come with a red Lancel. A Russian woman had bought one and ended up floating in it a few days later. Luís hadn't realized that before. He did now. It didn't fit in my puzzle. Maybe it fit in his.

"This red suitcase you sold to the nice tourist lady, it had four wheels?"

"What if it did?"

"Lancel doesn't make four-wheelers, not elegant enough. I checked. Yours must have been a fake."

"So sue me."

I picked up a carry-on. "How much is this?"

"Eight thousand Hong Kong. Too small for you. You'd have to cut off your legs."

Chapter Three

The immigration official in the Prague airport looked at my passport and then at me. Then he looked back at the passport—the fatal second glance. "You have taken an odd routing."

The tickets had taken me from Hong Kong to Shanghai, then to Madrid, and then back to Prague. "Miles," I said. "I have a lot of them. A few more and I get a free trip to Copenhagen."

The immigration official looked closely at one page. He held it up in the booth for me to see through the glass. "You've already been to Copenhagen."

"Sure I have. And I want to go back." I winked. "If you know what I mean."

"Don't disturb the peace here in Prague." He stamped the passport and handed it back to me. "We aren't like the Danes."

From the airport I took a taxi to the hotel where I'd stayed the only other time I'd been in Prague. It was a little more frayed than it had been back then, but so was I. The day was cool but clear, so I decided to take a tram to the river, walk across the bridge, and wander around. Kang—or somebody—went to a lot of trouble to get me here; they could go to a little more trouble if they wanted to find me.

An old man with a hat got on at the next stop. He sat in the seat behind me.

"Long time, Inspector."

It was Kang. The voice was older, but it was still tough.

"Don't turn around. We're getting off soon." He spoke in Russian. None of the other passengers looked up. The tram swayed around a corner and then stopped. "This is it," he said. "Walk with me."

2

We climbed the stairs to an apartment house that looked like the one next to it, and the one next to that. They all looked the same. The door opened before Kang could put his key in the lock.

"Christ on a cloud, Inspector! You haven't changed."

"Neither have you, Richie." The stick figure in the doorway was nothing like the man I'd met in this city fifteen years ago. That man had been burly, self-assured, filling the safe house with his presence. This man was wasting away. He was dying. I searched for something to say. "You still have that little silver tape recorder you used last time we saw each other? It didn't work very well. I'll bet half of what I told you was lost."

"Maybe, but we don't use that stuff anymore. We read brain waves." He shook my hand. His grip was fragile like one of Colonel Pang's ancient cups. "Come in and have some tea. I can't remember—with milk or without?"

Another man stepped into the room. I try not to be judgmental, but he was Russian in the worst way. Put together from ugly discards, and none the happier for it. He stood next to Richie.

"Kulov here is my batman. Kulov, meet the Inspector."

Kulov extended a meaty hand. "A pleasure, I'm sure," he said in a low, cultured voice.

A tremor of pain passed over Richie's face. Kulov watched silently until it passed. "Next time," he said, "you'll take the pill when I give it to you. Sit on the sofa. I'll bring the tea."

Richie sat down. "Kulov is not full of sympathy. That's all right; sympathy is the last thing I need. Maybe a week at the baths would do some good. What do you think, Kang?"

Kang was on a stool that looked like it had been shoved into the corner as an afterthought. "How about trying some food now and then? That might help, too."

"Food I need even less than sympathy." Richie put his head back and closed his eyes. "So, Comrade O. Glad you made it. We weren't sure you'd come. Welcome back to Prague." He meant to smile, but there was nothing left, just the prospect of the void.

They must have pulled Richie from his deathbed for this. Did they think it would make me more comfortable, being welcomed by a near corpse? For some reason, they decided that they needed him to take the lead, even though there was no doubt that this was Kang's meeting. "How did you know I was in the Nam Lo?"

"It's a cinch you weren't at the Lisboa. How did you like it in Macau? I was there once, about thirty years ago."

"It's all right. They could use a few chestnut trees."

"Did you happen to get to the maritime museum?"

"It wasn't on my itinerary."

"There used to be a good restaurant in the neighborhood. Past a street called Rua da Barra. I never drove, so I never knew how to get there exactly. Just wondering if it's still in business. Maybe I'll go back one of these days." That didn't ring hollow; it didn't ring at all.

"You called me halfway around the world to ask about restaurants?"

Richie started to laugh, but then he coughed. "It's over, Inspector. All done, finally done. Time to choose. That's why we called you halfway around the world." He coughed again, a long, painful, desperate effort for air. "Kang said we should give you a choice." Kang and I waited while Richie caught his breath. Kulov brought a glass of water from the kitchen. Richie waved him away. "Get me some whiskey, you bastard." The Russian put the glass down on a table and disappeared into the kitchen.

I turned to Kang. "And you? Where have you been all these years?" The odds were he would never tell me, but it never hurt to ask. Sometimes even a short answer led somewhere. Not this time.

"Here." Silverware rattled in the kitchen. "And there." A tiny bit of irony arced over Kang's lips. Richie closed his eyes and smiled.

"Here and there," I said. Those were the boundaries. Near and far. Up and down. It was a mystery to me why I had even bothered to ask. "I always figured you got clear that night in Manpo when the shooting stopped. Your name came up a few times afterward; then people stopped asking." The door had closed and been permanently sealed. There was never a warning to drop the subject; there didn't have to be. The word was out that Kang had been shot, eliminated. Anyone who thought otherwise knew not to raise their doubts. "Richie here was particularly concerned about you. I had to tell him you were dead. I didn't think you'd mind."

"Mind? Why would I mind? I only did what anyone can do, Inspector." Kang gave me that look, the same one he'd used in the old days—the bear watching the rabbit.

"And what is it that anyone can do?"

"Accept fate."

This made me laugh. "Fate. I would never have guessed that was your style. What do we call it that I'm here with you and Richie? Fate?"

Kang went over to a low cabinet with a decanter on it. He poured a glass of whiskey and handed it to Richie. "Have a glass, Inspector? Calm your nerves."

"What makes you think I'm nervous?"

This time it was Kang who laughed. "You were always nervous, Inspector. You're a bundle of nerves, though you pretend not to be. Something like that never changes."

"Things change. I'm older."

"Good for you. So am I. So is Richie, here. The only ones who aren't older, I guess you'd say they're dead." That also didn't ring.

Richie raised his glass. "There are a lot of them, for sure. All the best ones are on the other side." He sipped the whiskey, then broke out coughing. When he stopped, his eyes were unfocused, as if they weren't seeing anything anymore. "That's a comforting thought," he said to nobody. "I wonder if they'll recognize me."

Kang moved to the window and pulled the curtain back slightly. "Walk around the city for a few days, Inspector. Go up to the castle, maybe, down to the Old Town. Take your time going through the paintings on the Charles Bridge."

"Am I looking for anything?"

"No, you're taking in the sights, that's all."

"How long?"

"Two days."

"Forget it. If I don't get back to Pyongyang right away, they'll wonder where I've been. I can't afford that."

Nothing. Richie didn't cough. The sounds of silverware being polished stopped.

Kang continued as if I hadn't said anything. "Day three, you go to the main square in the Old Town."

"There won't be a day three. What makes you think I'm going to hang around? Waiting is a bad idea. It's always a mistake. Things go wrong; threads unravel where you didn't even know there were threads. It happens tomorrow, or it doesn't happen."

"You sit on the edge of the fountain; make sure the town hall is on your right." Either Kang's hearing was getting bad or I was mumbling. "Can you remember the layout of the square from your last visit? If you don't, get over there and walk around. Take it easy. Amble. If you think someone is on your tail, let them stick. Don't do anything fancy. Just walk."

"Sure, I'm a piece of bait. That's me, Inspector O—bait-for-hire. Just send a plane ticket and book a room at a crummy hotel. Other people rent out as assassins, not me. I'm a little fish; want to see me dance on the hook?"

"The square, Inspector. Do you remember the layout?"

Hopeless! The man had no sense of give-and-take. Of course I remembered the square. The image of those buildings came back to me as perfectly as if I'd seen them yesterday. Maybe I couldn't remember where I put my keys anymore, but my memory of meeting places was still good, better than good. Someone once told me I had a sense of location like a homing pigeon. I could never figure out if that was a compliment. "You want me facing south. Coincidence, I suppose."

Kang let the curtain fall back. "Nothing is coincidence." He turned around and looked at me. "From here on out, there is no such thing."

Richie drained the rest of the whiskey. "That's better." He took a deep breath. "Forget the baths."

"Right, you just sit here and drink." Kang refilled the empty glass. He turned back to me. "I thought it would be a nice touch, Inspector, using the square as part of the plan. Ironic, don't you think?"

"Sure, a little irony is good. This plan of yours—I take it you want a meeting in front of Kafka's house."

"You've got to admit, it's funny. You and Kafka."

"A barrel of monkeys, him and me." I remembered what the doctor had said. "Any special time?"

"Four o'clock. A crowd gathers to watch the clock strike in the town hall tower. The police in the square focus on the crowd for pickpockets. The shadows are getting longer by then. You'll have a few minutes for the contact. It won't be me, incidentally."

Suddenly, this plan was more and more interesting. "Anyone special, or anyone but you?"

"Don't worry; you'll know."

"No recognition signal? No shoelace untied? A copy of *The Trial* carried in the left hand, maybe?"

"Nothing. You won't need it."

"Right, I won't need it. I have no needs. I am a piece of straw adrift on the wind currents of time."

A groan came from the kitchen.

"Then what?" I said. "Someone walks up, hands me a white envelope, and I buy a villa along the Dalmatian coast for persons as yet unnamed?"

"If everything works out, you'll be taken to me, at which point we can have a long meeting. There are things we have to talk about."

"None that I know of. Look, Kang, I'm here right now. Why wait? My ears are good today; who knows about tomorrow? At our age, parts are falling off every day. You have something to say? I'm listening."

"You were in Macau. You've been rubbing shoulders with a Major Kim in Pyongyang. Should I go on?"

Kang knew Kim? This did not sound right; it gave off that odd buzzing sound that meant a wire was overheating. So, all right, maybe I'd stay an extra day or two. I could come up with something as an alibi. Planes were always delayed. I could tell Kim I'd been quarantined in Macau with bird flu. The last place Kim would figure I'd go would be Prague. Or maybe it wasn't; maybe that was why Kang wanted me walking around for a couple of days.

"We'll meet if things work, you said. What if they don't?" Kang knew what the question meant; it meant I had bought into his plan, whatever the hell it was. He had the grace not to smirk in victory.

"If things don't work, there's a Korean restaurant over toward the Jewish Quarter, not far off the square. Go in and get something to eat. The *mandu* is good. Then take a plane home, get back to your mountain, and stay there. If you hear shots and cries for mercy, ignore them."

"I'm sorry about your daughter, Kang. There was no time that night to tell you I was sorry."

Kang turned away.

"Well," said Richie, "I think we've done enough damage for one evening. Good night, all." He struggled to his feet. "Kulov! See the man out!"

3

I should have left the next morning. Kang wanted me to tell him about Macau, which meant he must know what happened there. Maybe he was even involved with the murder. If he was still angry about his daughter, maybe he'd been plotting an assassination all these years as revenge. He also knew about Major Kim, and that meant Kang had a good idea what was going on in Pyongyang. If he knew what was going on in Pyongyang, he had sources of information. And if he had sources of information, he had money.

Instead of leaving, I walked around the city, asking myself questions and chasing answers. If Major Kim was right and the game was over, we were in for years of heartache. I hadn't been kidding with Kim about chopping wood and hauling water; he hadn't been kidding about my shining his boots. Pyongyang would be razed, dug up, rearranged, subdivided. Streets would be repaved, memorials toppled, factories put under new management and made to produce. Food would come into the markets, goods into the stores, rations brought back, prices controlled, intelligence files pored over, people taken away in the night. The rest of the country would barely get a taste of the new money for a long time. When Kim told me that the camps would stay, I knew everything I needed to know about what the next ten years would be like.

Kim said he wanted a smooth transition. He wasn't going to get it. If nothing else, the Chinese were not going to let it happen. Colonel Pang had made that very clear. There was also some sort of homegrown opposition stirring, and Kim didn't seem to have a hammer he could bring down on it. The longer he waited, the stronger the opposition would get. Even so, they needed a rallying point. I didn't see one—unless that's what Kang was working to create. Contacting me in Macau and getting me to Prague was not a major feat, but it took money and a pretty good network. We were back to money. Funds weren't so hard to get, if you knew where to look. A network was more difficult. That took time to build. How long had it been in place? I could probably date its origins precisely—to that night in Manpo when Kang's daughter was taken away. No one ever knew what happened to her. Maybe Kang knew. Maybe that's why he refused to forget.

On the afternoon of the third day, I wandered into the main square just past three o'clock. I wanted to see who moved into position before they spotted me. At first I hung back, drifting along the southern edge. A police van was parked near the fountain in the center. Compounds had ponds; squares had fountains—it was a law of nature.

Two uniformed police were talking to an Asian who was gesturing broadly the way people do when they don't know the language. He reached for his wallet, which made them nervous. They both stepped back. Unless this was designed to be a distraction, it all looked absolutely routine. Not far from the police, sitting on the lip of the fountain, very relaxed and red-faced with liquor, were three Koreans wearing black cadre jackets. A Westerner edged over to them, pretending to be uninterested. One of the men looked at him sharply; then all three stood up and walked away. Seconds later, another Korean, gray haired and bent in a shabby raincoat, shuffled after them. He kept turning his head from side to side like a mechanical toy. None of them gave any sign that they were looking for something special. But the whole thing made me uneasy. Too damn many Koreans in one place all of a sudden.

I moved around to the opposite side of the square, trying to find a place where I could watch but not be noticed. A cloud went across the sun, and the scene suddenly didn't look so friendly anymore. The fountain lost its appeal; the old buildings lost their gracious air and became angry. Then the sun came out again, and everything went back to normal. A woman moved out of the shadows and stood beside me.

"Hello, Cousin," she said in perfect English. She was studying a map and facing away, so I couldn't see much of her features. From the way her clothes fit and the strands of gray in her hair, she looked about fifty, well dressed but nothing flashy, a canvas bag over her shoulder, comfortable shoes. Then she turned to face me, and I got a good look at her. "Kafka lived over there for a while." She pointed and flashed a diamond ring. It caught the sun and burned a hole in my heart. This was the same woman Li and I had seen in Pyongyang in front of the hotel, getting into the car. It was the same woman who had trailed the golden thread. "He went to school right here." She turned sidewise to look at the building behind us. I don't know if she had Chinese blood or Tartar blood or the blood of Mongol princes in her veins. She was Korean, gorgeously so. This was exactly like Kang, to have such perfection in reserve for a meeting in plain view. Anyone watching would fixate on her. I might as well be a Styrofoam cup.

"I thought the meeting was four o'clock," I said.

"Change of plans. You're here; I'm here. No harm done. Let's be flexible."

"I don't have a cousin."

"Tough luck for you. No uncles, no cousins."

Someone had a very good network. "Well, it's your lead. I'm just hanging around hoping this doesn't work, so I can have the dumplings."

She laughed softly and looked across the square at something. "It appears we have liftoff."

Everything about her English was perfect—the cadence, the rhythm, the ease with which the lips found the perfect word. If I closed my eyes, I'd think she was a blonde with blue eyes.

"Let's walk," she said. "Engage in animated conversation. Put your arm around my shoulder. If we're not cousins, we're old friends. We have a lot to catch up on. How have you been?"

"A life squandered until thirty seconds ago. Which way do we walk?"

She made a show of taking my hand. "There's an old house in an area called the Karlin section, not far, just around the bend in the river. That's where we'll end up. It's nice in its own way. Some people find it drab, not quaint enough, but it's quiet. If you want, we can stop for coffee before we get there. The coffee is better on the other side of the river than it is here, though, so we may have to walk a little. Then we can sit and relax. Anyone who is interested will think we are chatting gaily about old times."

"No chance of going to the Korean restaurant?"

"You're in Prague, my friend. Try something new." She kissed my cheek. "You never know what might be good unless you try."

We crossed a bridge, took a streetcar, walked in narrow, winding streets. After a while, we climbed a steep hill, up a flight of stone stairs that led to more narrow streets. The café where we finally stopped was nearly empty. A few locals sat by themselves, smoking. We found a table in a corner, away from the window. She took the seat facing the door.

"Good thing we stopped," I said. "Those hills are killers. What if I had a heart attack?"

"Sorry, I thought you'd like the exertion, give you a chance to get your blood pumping." She leaned toward me. "Isn't that what old friends do? Get each other's blood moving?"

"Whatever you're thinking, don't." She was right, my heart

was pumping, and not from the stairs. "I'm not in the mood, and I doubt if I'm in shape."

"Well, well. Why don't we stop at a pharmacy and get you some of those pills."

"Aren't we off track a little? I don't think Kang set up this meeting for us to play the sultan and the harem."

"It may have crossed his mind. Kang has a strange sense of mission sometimes. But you're right. Business is business. Let's have a cup of coffee and a pastry. You're not too far gone for pastry, I hope."

4

She looked at her watch several times while we sat and talked.

"That's a good way to spoil a friendship," I said. "Love dies where deadlines loom."

"Cute," she said. "But we have a schedule to keep. Drink your coffee and shut up." She licked the sugar from the pastry off her lips.

She paid the bill, and we stepped out the door into the brilliant end of a golden autumn afternoon. The schedule seemed to have gone away. We walked slowly, not saying much. I was about to edge into something endearing when we came upon a stretch of lawn across from an old palace already deep in shadow.

"You ever notice that?" I dumped the endearments and knelt to run my hand across the grass.

"The palace? Looks like a cold place, too austere for me. I'd never want to get out of bed in December. Do you like to stay in bed in December, Inspector?"

"I meant the color of the grass. There is nothing in the world sadder than green, green grass on an autumn afternoon. Trees, crops in the field, animals—everything else alive knows this is the season to prepare for the worst. But grass? Hoping against hope that the sunshine won't ever go away. Or maybe too dumb to realize what is coming. It gives me chills just to look at it."

"Why?"

"Too many memories of when I was the same way."

The woman leaned down so that her face was even with mine, and very close. "Don't bring up anything like that when you talk to Kang. Don't talk about disappointment. Don't rake over memories. He has a job to do, and he can't lose focus now."

She gave me her hand and pulled me up. The light was fading. The buildings' shadows already buried the streets. "There's a car up ahead fifty meters on the left, a brown Škoda. Here are the keys. Go ahead and get in. I'll be behind you by about a minute."

"I don't think I should drive."

"Nor do I, Inspector. I'll take the wheel."

And drive she did. From the sound of it, the engine of the car seemed to have been worked on recently. There was no way of knowing if the brakes had received equal attention, because she never used them. I was not sure where we were going, but then again, I had no idea where we had been. Wherever we were headed, it was in a great hurry. I tried to fix a location in case I needed to find the spot later, but at that time of night one sixteenth-century building looks like another. The last time I was in Prague, it had been in winter. Everything had looked different then, in the gloom. We pulled up in front of a narrow three-story building with an elaborate doorway.

"Out," she said. "Ring the bell and if that doesn't work, knock politely. I've got errands to run. I'll see you later, old friend."

"Good thing we're not related."

"You react badly to pastry." She gunned the motor. "It's bad for your heart."

The front door opened before the sound of the bell had

faded. Richie stared out at me. He looked like hell. No, he looked like death itself.

"You better see a doctor, Richie."

"What for? He's not going to do anything for me." He coughed, doubled over. "Let's get inside; this cold air is bad for me. Everything is bad for me."

"Where's Kang?" I stepped in. The place was very tidy, very sterile. No one lived here.

"Kang's not here yet. You're early. Greta drives fast, doesn't she?"

"Greta? Is that her name?"

"Wonderful woman, well trained, very thoughtful. She looks after Kang like she was his daughter." He made a face. "Don't do that again, mentioning what happened."

"I know; I've been warned. He needs to stay focused."

"Who told you that? Greta?"

"What's her real name?

"Let's sit down. I can breathe better when I'm sitting."

We sat—Richie on the sofa, me in a pale yellow chair.

"Better? You want a glass of whiskey?" So, all right, no one was going to tell me Greta's real name. I'd ask Li. He clearly knew who she was. He'd stopped breathing when he saw her in the parking lot at the hotel in Pyongyang.

"We don't keep any alcohol here," Richie's eyes searched all the corners of the room. "In the other place, I can drink as much as I want. This is the safe house, and Kang doesn't like liquor in a safe house. He thinks of a safe house as a chapel or something."

"What was that charade in the square about?"

"Flushing quail."

"And?"

"Working with Greta is a pleasure." He coughed until his face turned red. "There isn't a quail around who can remember to keep his head down when she gets moving. You must have done a good job getting here from Macau. There's no one new in town that we can spot on your tail."

"You realize I can't hang around here for long. I'll have to get back to Pyongyang by the day after tomorrow at the latest. They're already wondering where I am."

A key turned in the front door, and Kang walked in carrying a paper bag. "I brought you something, Richie." He pulled out a bottle of whiskey. "Go easy on it, though. I don't want you passed out on the couch." He took off his hat and coat and threw them on the sofa. "Greetings, Inspector. Your day was good?"

"Nothing that I'd put in a logbook."

Kulov came out from the kitchen with a couple of glasses. He gave one to Richie and one to me. "Inspector." He nodded.

"You're not drinking?" I asked Kang.

Richie was pouring himself a triple. Kang grimaced. "I drink, but only sometimes, and this isn't one of them. Maybe you should wait until we're done, as well."

"Maybe I should." I put my glass on the floor. "Do we talk here, or is there someplace else where the walls don't have ears?"

"We're in Prague, Inspector, land of the free. And we're in a perfectly secure place, courtesy of Richie and friends. There is nothing here, not a single thing, that Richie hasn't personally approved; besides which, he controls all the on switches. Let's have our nice talk. How did you get along with Greta?"

"We're old acquaintances, it turns out."

"You saw her one time across a parking lot."

"Well informed, as always. You have your own spy satellite or what?" Apparently, not a satellite that could see into noodle shops.

"She saw you, too. That's how I knew you were in Pyong-yang, home from the hill."

"Greta . . . that's what we're going to call her?"

"That's right."

"Greta keeps you up to date on what's going on, I presume."

"It isn't like the old days, Inspector. Getting information in and out of Pyongyang is not nearly as difficult as it used to be.

For example, I know that Major Kim sent you to Macau on a mission he fully expected you to botch."

"And did I?"

"Not yet."

"Excellent, there's still time. You know Kim, I take it."

"Our paths have crossed."

"What's he doing in Pyongyang?"

"What he's doing there, what he says he's doing there, and what he thinks he's doing there are separate things."

"He thinks he is bossing people around. Me, for instance."

"That's good. Let him keep thinking that."

"He reminds me in some ways of that Military Security goon that wanted to kill you. His name was Kim, too."

"I know what his name was, Inspector." Kang paused. "He got promoted, I heard."

I waited to see if he would say anything else, but he let the subject drop.

Richie coughed. "I have a good idea: Let's rake over the most hellish coals we can find." He waved his glass at me. "Let's remember every failure, every bit of pain, everything that should have worked but didn't. Let not a single sleeping dog lie. Kick the shit out of every fucking one of them, how about that? Should I go first?" He finished the whiskey and banged the glass on the table. "God, what a bunch of stupid bastards I chose to die around."

Nobody said anything for a couple of minutes. Kulov made some noise in the kitchen, rattling silverware and slamming drawers.

Finally, someone had to break the silence. "SSD is up to something, by the way," I said.

Kang smiled at me. "Fine, let them think that nothing stands in their path."

"Kim says he's there to oversee a transition."

"Did you ask him from what to what?"

"We didn't get that far. We were only on the first date."

"German sugarplums are dancing in their heads, Inspector. They think we're going to fall on our knees and beg forgiveness for seventy years of sin, like the East Germans did."

"Are we?"

"You can if you want to. I have other ideas."

"So do the Chinese, apparently."

"They've got Kim worried?" There was a note of urgency in the question, not much, but I was weighing every word Kang used, measuring every inflection. The question could have been nothing, but the way Kang asked it told me this was something he really wanted to know. And that told me his network had a hole in it.

I thought over what Kim had said about the Chinese. The file I'd read in the windowless room had contained page after page about Chinese penetration into the country—agents operating under different sorts of cover, defectors being fed back in, agents of influence in the security services. "Worried," I said, "but not as much as I would have guessed. He thinks he has a handle on it."

"A handle. He has a handle on China. Mull that over a little. I'll be interested in what you conclude. And while you're at it, think about what you were doing in Macau."

"I was putting the Macau police off the scent. It's not like they had a click-clack case."

"Click-clack." Kang closed his eyes and thought a moment. "You were talking to Luís."

"You know Luís?"

"Luís helped me with a complicated funding issue some years ago."

"That's funny. He told me he couldn't even launder his shirts."

Kang smiled. "Luís knows more about laundering money than anyone alive or dead."

"Tell me that he's not MSS."

"Luís? Not anymore. He and discipline don't do well to-gether. They transferred him to the police, where they figured he couldn't do any harm."

"When I was in Pyongyang, someone told me I don't even know what I don't know."

"True."

"So, maybe you can tell me. What don't I know?"

Kang moved his coat and sat down on the sofa. "I'll give you the thirty-second version. Two years ago, the center, aging and unwell, decided that by 2017 he wanted to achieve a first-stage unity between the two Koreas." Kang turned around and yelled toward the kitchen, "Kulov, bring another glass and some of your awful vodka."

Kulov appeared with both items. He put them on the table in front of Kang, nodded to me, and returned to the kitchen.

Kang poured a few drops for himself and a few for me. "Ku-lov keeps the vodka hidden, but I know where it is. Cheers, In-spector."

"We were on first-stage unity."

"That year, as you realize, will mark the one hundred and fifth birthday of his father and his own seventy-fifth. The plan he has in mind, I'm told, is for a loose union, largely cosmetic but enough for him to be able to claim success in reuniting the 'bloodlines' of the Korean people, if not the territory. Last year, the two sides agreed to limited and quiet exchanges of person-nel, mostly in the field of internal security."

"Funny place to start," I said.

"It would be in the real world, but, as we know, this isn't the real world. So everyone decided that they wanted eyes and ears right where they could do the most good. Pyongyang sent two incompetents to Seoul from a department that shall remain name-less."

"And whom did Seoul send?"

"Its very best, also incompetent but well shod and well fed.

This exchange led to a lot of stumbling around for the better part of twelve months. Then, in March this year, the center had another health setback, serious enough to be confined to bed but not so serious that it was impossible to issue orders. I have my suspicions about who else is in the room when those orders are signed, but we can talk about that later. In any case, the South saw this development as a chance to replace its people with someone who actually knew what he was doing, could consolidate the gains, and could even—with a little luck—go on to the next phase. In pursuit of these goals, the incompetents were recalled and Major Kim was sent to Pyongyang in April. He had orders to proceed in all haste to achieve the consolidation part of the plan, and then to move with caution to explore the possibilities for next steps."

"How do you know so much about the South's plans?"

"Not everyone in the North is incompetent, Inspector. And Kim is not as smart as he thinks."

"All very interesting, but none of it explains why Kim sent me to Macau."

"It does, in a way. Consider: Officials in Pyongyang with even one eye open are already concerned about the drift of events, and have been searching for a rallying point, some sort of brake on what they recognize as dangerous, almost fatal South Korean inroads. To buy time, they have been urging that one of the center's sons be put in place immediately to ensure stability for an eventual transition. They gather all of this under the cloak of carrying out plans for the first stage of 'national unity.' That isn't what they want, of course, but it's the best they can hope for until they figure out something better."

Click. Clack. "Up the chimney and out to sea," I said. I nudged my glass nearer the bottle in hopes that Kang would pour more—a lot more. There was a leadership transition in the works? And a successor in play? And I figured in this exactly how? I had been brought down from the mountain to be thrown headfirst into a pit of snakes, big snakes, the sort of snakes that swallow full-grown deer and then burp with pleasure. My hands weren't shaking, but if Kang didn't fill the glass right away, I might not be able to hold it still. "That was the chosen son whose tracks I was sent to erase in Macau, wasn't it? Chopping up a prostitute can't be very good for a smooth transition." I remembered the room and its view. Nonchalance fled as reality knocked at the door. "No wonder Kim wanted me to get the evidence pointing somewhere else."

Kang waited a moment before letting a few drops fall into my glass. "You actually believed him?"

"I take it you mean that wasn't his intent."

"Oh, no, he really did want you to go through the motions. One of Kim's main tasks, though, is to accomplish exactly the opposite. He is supposed to make sure the son is so badly compromised that no one can possibly follow him. He must have wondered how to do that, until you crashed into view. Your appearance lets Kim claim that he's made every effort to save the successor's reputation, but due to the bad faith of the Chinese and the incompetence of a former North Korean policeman—the grandson of a Hero of the Republic no less—that has proved impossible. He discredits Beijing and the opposition in Pyongyang in one move. Brilliant."

"I didn't realize my skills were in such demand."

Kang screwed the top on the bottle. Vodka time was over.

"This leaves me with a question." I said. "Do you think the son did it? Murdered that prostitute in his hotel room?"

Richie coughed and fumbled with his glass. "How can you drink that potato water? Have a bit of this whiskey, why don't you?"

"The Chinese have become concerned," Kang ignored my question, "and concern has rapidly become alarm, at what the South is doing. Colonel Pang and his teacups are already moving to stop the process." Astounding, did Kang have Chinese maples on his payroll? "But the scent of blood is on the wind. Gangs from China and everywhere else see an opportunity to carve up the country into spheres of influence. For all I know, the Mafia has set up shop on Kwangbok Street."

"You forgot something."

"The opposition. Yes, meanwhile, there is a loose resistance building against outside efforts to seize on the situation. It isn't anything coordinated—yet."

"So I noticed. It sounds a lot like holly."

"Really?" Kang looked at Richie and smiled faintly. "Holly takes at least a couple of years to germinate after you put the seed in the ground, or so I've heard."

Richie sat up. He seemed better, energized somehow.

"Holly . . . ," Kang said. "Tough little tree. Refresh my memory, what kind of leaves does it have?"

"Leathery, spiny." I hesitated because I hated to give him what he wanted. "And glossy." What a son of a bitch he was, both of them were. "And you two want to talk me into joining this loose resistance, I suppose. It was you who pulled me back into this sewer from the beginning, wasn't it, from the moment that car stopped in front of my cabin. How you did it I don't yet know, but if I go back and look, I'm sure I'll find your paw prints."

Richie was staring at me intently.

"Sorry," I said, "but I don't have the time or the inclination to help."

"Is that so?" Richie had sunk back against the cushions. His voice was flat. "You went to Macau to help Kim."

"I didn't. I went to find out what is going on. Besides, I had to prove something to myself."

"That's fine," Kang said. "That's good. A little self-validation before the sheet is pulled over your face for the last time. While you're at it, you might consider whether you really want to be treated like dirt between the toes of China. Because that's what you'll end up being. The South Koreans will lose the game; the

Chinese will win. Seoul is a pack of fools. You want to join them? I wish you the best of luck."

Succumbing to imagery never leads anywhere good. On the other hand, the mental image of 10 billion Chinese toes did carry a certain weight. "What do you propose doing about it?"

"We don't need to fight the Chinese, Inspector. We don't even have to make them unhappy. We need them to think we are prepared to cooperate. It wouldn't take much. Colonel Pang is a reasonable man, as you've seen. It's too bad he's been marked to die."

"Pang? Marked to die?"

"That surprises you? Not by us. Kim and Zhao have apparently decided they need to get rid of him. Kim is under strict orders not to rile the Chinese, so he'll let Zhao and his viper do it."

"Kim and Zhao are cooperating in this?"

"Not only in this."

"What about Pang—I assume you've warned him?"

"Warned Pang? Why would I? He wouldn't warn me if he learned that I was on a list for elimination. And he won't warn you, either; don't fool yourself into thinking he will. He's very smooth."

"This is beginning to sound like a class reunion. Is there anyone involved in this whole thing that you don't know?"

"I haven't had much to do these past long years but go over my mistakes, pummel myself for all the missteps, and think ahead to this moment. Believe me, I've thought about it. I've examined every angle. I've run through all the options. I'm ready to do whatever is necessary. My only question at this point is: Are you?"

5

That night, Greta drove me back to my hotel.

"You don't like the brake pedal?" I said as we went through the gears.

"I'm saving it for someone special." She pulled into a spot near the castle, with a view of the city. "You're not as much of a coward as you pretend, are you, Inspector?"

"That depends." We weren't anywhere near my hotel.

"We went through a lot of trouble to bring you here."

"So I noticed. It might have been easier if you'd stayed in Macau long enough to talk to me there."

"I don't know what you mean."

"Sure you do. You go there to gamble, or just leave messages?"

"Macau is an interesting place," she said. "I'm sure you must have enjoyed your stay."

"Something went wrong; the message didn't get to him on time."

" 'For want of a nail,' isn't that what they say?"

"You must know why he wanted that room, that particular room."

She looked at her watch. "Deadlines loom, Inspector. Your hotel is at the bottom of the hill. It's not that long a walk, though the cobblestones can be murder in the dark. Maybe we'll see each other again."

Her car disappeared before the engine even made third gear. As I made my way down the hill, I looked for a phone. It seemed to me that I couldn't stand aside and let events take their course. If I knew Pang was targeted, he deserved to be warned. Yes, absolutely, I wanted him out of the country, back on his own side of the river. For that to happen, he didn't need to end up dead. Whatever he had done to the captain was between the two of them. This was different; it was between Pang and me.

"The colonel isn't here." The voice on the other end was clear and crisp. There was no crackling on the line. We could have been within a few blocks of each other. More likely, the voice was in Beijing, ready to route the call to Pang once a few details were cleared up—like who had dialed the number and why.

"Yeah, he isn't there. Never mind that. I need to talk to him, urgently." I was using a pay phone, and I didn't know how long I could talk. The woman who sold me the phone card in the tobacco store had been short-tempered. She was about to close for the night and didn't like it when I showed up. After I fumbled with the money, she muttered to her husband, grabbed the bills from my hand, and held up a few.

"What?" she said in Russian. "Tabak?"

It was the only Russian she knew, or all she would admit to knowing. I wanted the most expensive phone card she had, but judging by how she threw it on the counter, I wasn't too sure that was what I got.

"You need to talk to Pang urgently?" said the voice on the other end. "So do I. So do a lot of people."

I figured I knew what that meant. "Something happen?"

"You have a reason to know?" The voice became full of thorns. "Where are you calling from, anyway? Who told you how to access this system?"

"Maybe I owe him money, a lot of it."

A pause. "Well, invest it. Put it under your pillow." Another pause, longer this time. "Never mind; forget the pillow."

"He's dead?"

"You could say that. His lungs were next to him when he should have woke up this morning."

"Ah." It was all that came to my mind. I took a deep breath and hung up.

PART III

Chapter One

I didn't bother to tell Kang I was leaving. After a testy exchange at the airport with a clerk who insisted it was impossible to change the routing on my ticket, I booked the afternoon flight to Beijing and then caught a plane the next day to Pyongyang. When I walked in the door of the hotel, I was greeted with a loud shriek.

"Stay where you are!" A woman was shampooing the carpet, giving the fish a run for their money. "Don't move. It's wet. You'll leave footprints."

"Inspector?" The bird was on duty. "We didn't know where you were, and we were getting ready to move your things out of the room this afternoon, not that you have much there. Oh, and there's a message for you. It came about an hour ago."

The note was from Zhao. All it said was: "2." I went upstairs to wash my face and give Kim a call but decided to let him stew. When I came down again a little before two o'clock, the man who never blinked was standing at the front desk. He stared at me.

"I missed you," I said. "On the plane, I was trying to remember something my grandfather once told me. It's one of those things that if you think about too long, you can't remember. But as soon as you stop thinking about it, you remember. Maybe if you went away, I'd stop thinking about it and then it would pop into my head."

He didn't have much to say to that, so I went out in front. I only waited for a couple of minutes when the car pulled up. The little man went through his routine.

"Game time," said Zhao as soon as the door shut and we pulled away.

"What game would that be?"

"Ask Pang, why don't you." Zhao laughed his panther laugh. I saw the driver smile to himself.

"Is there a way we could talk, just between ourselves?" We could always get rid of his other ear, I thought. Why don't we do that?

Zhao pressed a button on the armrest. The driver frowned.

"Is that better?"

"Fine," I said.

"The last pieces are in place, and we are ready to put the machinery in motion. In case you hadn't figured it out, the Russians have the northeast. The Japs have everything on the east coast below Chongjin. And I have the west coast. I don't want anything to upset this arrangement."

"Pyongyang?"

Zhao appeared to consider this. "You want it? It's yours."

"No, thank you."

"Then stay out of the way."

"Like Pang?"

The panther's eyes looked sated. "Shall we mourn Colonel Pang, Inspector? Would you like a moment to grieve? It's not such a great loss, you know. He had orders to secure the entire northern half of your country. I don't think he would have tried to get everything all the way down to Kaesong, but one never knows what might happen in these situations. He was on the verge of sending in the stable of your sniveling defector generals he had been holding in reserve. They've been well treated, every need attended to. In return, they were going to help Pang stuff your country back under the imperial wing, exactly where the mandarins in Beijing think it belongs. Who can say? Pang might even have been appointed governor-general. I've saved you from that, and more."

"So far, I feel no stirrings of gratitude."

Zhao growled softly. "I told you not to go to Macau, but I know you went anyway. And then you disappeared. I don't like that, but I'll let it go this time if you give me what I want." There was sweat on Zhao's upper lip.

"And what would that be?"

"Keep an eye on Major Kim for me. He isn't your friend. He doesn't have your interests at heart. If he has his way, you'll be licking his boots."

"I doubt it. That would ruin the shine."

Zhao reached over and touched my chest. "We have a lot in common, Inspector. We both hate to be bossed around; we both want to preserve what is best about the old ways. And neither of us gives a damn about politics. This is the time when we need to work together." He pushed me back against the seat. "I know, you don't think that is possible. But I do. I think we are the perfect couple."

I slipped sideways. "You might be right," I said. "But I need some time to think it over. You see what I mean?" I put his hand in his lap.

Zhao moved away, his face twisted in rage. He stabbed the button on the armrest. "Pull over," he said. "Get this bastard out of my car."

We swerved to the side of the road. The little man jerked the door open. "Get the fuck out," he said. "Get the fuck out of the car right now."

"Very good," I said. "You've been studying."

"Take a deep breath." He grinned at me. "Go ahead, take a couple, while you're at it." He slammed the door, and the car sped away.

2

After getting out of the car, I went back to my hotel, hung the DO NOT DISTURB sign on my doorknob, and tried to sleep off the memory. At six o'clock, the doorbell rang.

"Room service."

"Go away. Look at the sign."

"That's for the room-cleaning staff. I'm not cleaning. I'm checking the minibar."

Sleep was impossible, so I had the hotel arrange for a taxi to take me to Kim's office. Under blazing lights, both tanks followed the taxi as soon as it emerged from the tunnel. The duty officer at the entrance to the building almost wouldn't let me in. I wasn't in the mood for barriers. I bared my fangs. Duty officers don't like trouble; it makes for work. He waved his pencil at the stairs. "Try not to have a heart attack on your way up."

"You don't look so good, Inspector. Did Zhao make a pass at you?" Major Kim stood up and walked around the desk to greet me.

"If you won't do something about Zhao, maybe I will." I sat down in the green chair.

Kim didn't seem pleased. "Zhao's a Chinese citizen. If something happens, our friends in Beijing will be unhappy. They will say we are endangering their countrymen, and that they must send in protection. They're waiting for an excuse. Stay away from him."

"Me stay away from him?" I laughed; it sounded like a cypress tree in a forest fire. "Zhao murdered Colonel Pang. *That* Beijing doesn't mind?"

"So, you know about Pang's demise. Word gets around, I guess." He pointed out the other chair where he wanted me to sit, the brown one. "Everything is calculus, Inspector, a matter of mathematics, of complex equations. For example, according to the etiquette of nations, Pang was not supposed to be here. He was here illegally, you might say, skipped the normal entry procedures, so his death has no standing. He was running operations that never officially existed, using people without faces to obtain results that were never written down. Zhao, on the other hand, is a legitimate businessman representing the best interests of his country. He has documents. And he has money."

"He rips out the lungs of people who get in his way."

"A businessman, like I said."

"He's an animal. Worse than that, actually."

"Yes, worse than that. And if you care to go to the east coast, I can introduce you to his Japanese counterpart. I won't list the body parts that are his focus."

"What about the Russian in the northeast?"

"Him we can handle, for the moment anyway. My big fear is that he will get himself eliminated and then we'll have to deal with someone who has more brains than muscle."

"Out of curiosity, how did Zhao get Pang?"

Kim studied my face, looking for clues. How much did I know? "Lack of attention, I guess. A momentary lapse, that's all it takes. You might say it was a surprise. He was lying in bed, listening to music on his earphones. Maybe dozing. When the killer left, the CD player was set on continuous loop. A macabre touch. It would probably have gone on forever if we hadn't broken the door down and found him there. The machine had been plugged into a wall socket. Him, too, as a matter of fact."

"Did you look to see what CD it was?"

Kim shook his head. "I didn't look, but from what I heard, it sounded like Chinese opera."

What a bunch of sadists. "He hated Chinese opera."

The television in the corner of Kim's office was on, and the 8:00 P.M. news was ending. Kim started to say something more, but I shushed him. The announcer read a report about "unfavorable days" due to "geophysical factors" and warned that those afflicted with high blood pressure or other maladies needed to take precautions on November 1, 4, 9, 12, and 15. I took a scrap of paper out of my pocket and made a note to myself.

"You don't believe that stuff, I hope, Inspector."

"No, but you'd better. It's what you told me to figure out."

"Which was what?"

"The SSD code. They're using the television, right under your nose."

"Impossible." Kim moved back to the safety of his side of the desk.

"Absolutely impossible. But they're doing it anyway. I worked on it while I was traveling. Something to pass the time."

"You only went to Macau."

"True, but even a short flight can sometimes seem long. At the end of every month, the television announces what days in the coming month are bad for health. It's a regular feature. No one thinks twice about it. Only old ladies pay attention, them and doting mothers."

"And?" The major finally sat down.

"And the bad-health days are apparently the days that are bad for *your* health, literally. Those are the days of the SSD operations, or maybe when they pass around the plans for the next set of moves. Go back and look at those dates. Take the first date in the series, and apply it to the announcement of the lectures at the Grand Study Hall each month. If the first unfavorable day is the third, for example, you look for lecture number three."

"Are you crazy? That's unbelievably complicated."

"No, it's pretty simple. Ask me when we have more time, I'll tell you about complicated operations."

"So, I look through the records, then what? What does it tell me?"

"That you'll have to figure out yourself. I didn't even try to get that far—too many possibilities. If I had to guess, I'd guess it's something about the lecture, or the lecturer, or the room where the lecture is being held."

"Or something else entirely."

"Could be. Meantime, you'd better hurry. The new series of lectures begins tomorrow."

"It's too simple. It's too complicated, and that's what makes it too simple. That's how everything is up here. Madness, pure madness." He gave me a wary look as he reached for the phone and pressed a button. "Get me the domestic radio transcripts for the last day of every month."

Television, too, I mouthed.

"Television, too," he said into the phone. "I want everything here in thirty minutes. . . . What? Go back six months; no, wait, go back a year." He hung up. "You're sure about this? Not pulling my string?"

"When I do that, you'll know."

A half hour later, a man brought in a folder. "You want it, you got it."

"Sit." Kim waved the man into one of the plastic chairs near the wall.

I stood up to leave. "No, you stay, too, Inspector."

Kim went through the transcripts. He used a pencil to make marks here and there, but mostly he bit on the end of it.

"You can get lead poisoning that way," I said.

"You can get lead poisoning from a bullet, too. Only I don't think anyone in the Grand Study Hall will be armed tomorrow. Let's hope not, because no one on our team will be. I'm not handing out firearms until I know who is doing what to whom." He looked at the transcripts again. "I don't know if I see a pattern or not. Cracking codes is not part of my job description."

"You're supposed to be in Paris, eating fine food and recruiting college girls."

"Don't remind me." He put the transcripts to one side. "I hope you don't have a picnic already planned for tomorrow, Inspector."

"Not at all. As a matter of fact, I think I'm coming down with the flu."

"Well, drink plenty of fluids tonight, because you lead the team tomorrow afternoon to the lectures to find out what is going on. There isn't time for a long investigation, so we might have to jump from gathering facts to shooting people in a hurry."

I coughed. "With what? You said no firearms."

"Not tomorrow. Maybe the day after that."

"Ever have the flu that makes your joints ache? That's what I've got. Most likely, I'm in the most contagious period right now."

"Tough for you and your joints."

"We'd better be careful. It could be the start of a pandemic. Maybe I picked up something in Macau eating monkey parts. Wouldn't that be something?"

"Forget it, Inspector; I'm not giving you sick leave tomorrow. I don't care if you infect the whole country."

I coughed in Kim's direction. "How can I lead a team I've never met? It's not even assembled yet. We need at least a couple of days to get to know each other's quirks."

"Your quirks alone could take years to explain. Besides, a team of strangers doesn't bother me. I'm not worried about people not knowing each other. I'll go through the files tonight, and we'll notify the ones we pick at the last minute. It's much better that no one has an inkling about this operation until the last possible minute. If the first they know about it is when they get to my office at the crack of dawn tomorrow, there's no chance someone will mention it to someone else on the phone. That should cut the possibility of SSD picking up a reference to the plans to zero. You," he pointed to the man who had brought in the files, "shut up if you know what's good for you. And you," he turned to me, "I know won't talk to anyone. You don't have anyone to talk to." He looked at his watch. "Get some rest. I don't

want you falling asleep during the lectures. See you in the morning, early. Think about the operation overnight while you fever-
ishly toss and turn. There will be a car in the usual place, at four
A.M. If the night clerk asks where you're going so early, tell him
you have a business meeting with an Egyptian investor. Everyone thinks the Egyptians are crazy anyway."

"I'm not on your payroll, Major. Don't forget that." My joints
really were aching. I sneezed twice on the way out.

3

Not counting Kim, there were four of us standing around the
table pretending to be awake. Dawn wasn't for another hour,
and it was raining hard. The others were already there when I
came through the door. That made me uneasy. I don't like walking into a group that has already bonded. If this hadn't been
about SSD, I would have stayed in the hotel and sipped tea all
day. There was a stand on Yonggwang Street not far from the
hotel where they sold special tea. The doorman said he could get
it brought to my door if I was too sick to walk over there, but it
would cost me. To deliver a cup of tea? I told him to forget it.

"This is Inspector O," Kim said to the group. "It's his operation. You follow his orders. If you don't, you'll live to regret it.
Or maybe you won't live that long. Don't try pushing the envelope." Kim turned to me. "You know these guys?"

I looked at each one of them carefully. "No. All from where?"

"What do you care?" Kim said. "They're here, and I picked
them. That's what matters." This was going to be an unpleasant
morning all around. My joints ached, my head ached, and Kim
was a pain in the ass.

"Their pedigrees don't interest me," I said. "I really don't care
if they're all hicks from the hills of Kangwon. I need to know
what organization spawned them. Training differs; skills differ;

operating philosophies differ. In some organizations, they're taught to duck behind a woman if shooting starts."

"You kidding me?" Kim sounded alarmed. "Up here? I thought you people chewed barbed wire for snacks. Who teaches ducking?"

"That would be SSD." I watched the other three. Two of them smiled. I smiled back. It was the third one, the one who smirked, who worried me.

"Well, go ahead; introduce yourselves. You," Kim pointed at a short man, "tell the Inspector something about yourself. Not much, just enough to give him a sense of who you are. Then the rest of you do likewise. For the next few days, maybe longer, you'll be like brothers."

"Maybe some of us don't get along with our brothers." The man from SSD looked at me. "Isn't that right, Inspector?"

"Off to a good start," I said.

The short man shook his head. "You want me to talk or not?"

"Sure I do; go ahead." So the SSD man knew who I was; he knew that my brother and I didn't get along. He probably knew plenty more. As far as I was concerned, this operation had died before it got out the door.

"You listening?" The short man raised his voice a notch. "Because if you're not interested, I'd as soon save my breath."

"You're right. I'm all of a sudden uninterested. It's better if no one knows anyone else. Instead, we'll use the time to go over the operation." I didn't have a clue what Kim thought we were going to do. Not that it mattered. "There are lectures today at the Grand Study Hall. The first one starts at one P.M. Lecture Room Six. We go in and sit."

"What are we looking for?" The SSD man took out a notebook.

"No notes!" Kim nearly leaped across the table. "You listen, that's all."

"Actually," I said, "that is the interesting part of this whole thing. We don't know what we're looking for. Most of the time, the lectures start at four o'clock. Someone needed this one earlier, and we need to figure out why the hurry."

"Can we take notes when we get in the room, or what?"

"On the lecture? Sure." I looked at the list from the radio. "If you're interested in 'the application of technology to take care of the boiler water and heat net supplementary water through the separate lime softening method,' or how about 'the relevance of nanotechnology to self-replicating systems'? I don't know for sure which one of those we'll get."

The short man looked glum. "How long do we have to sit there?"

"Until you're so bored you think you're about to die. Then pinch your bottom and sit some more."

"I don't like this," said the other man, the one who hadn't opened his mouth until now. "We get called in here the day of an operation and then find out no one knows anything about what we're doing."

Kim moved around the table and pushed the man so hard he almost fell over. "No one asked you for your opinion, did they? When someone asks, maybe then you can whine. Until then, you do as you're told." He turned to the other two. "Same goes for you. I thought that's what you people did best, followed orders. If you can't do that, there's not much left, is there? All right, get out of here. There's a room down the hall where you can sit around and complain. I've got a few things to go over with Inspector O."

After the three of them left, Kim picked up the phone. "Get Li in here."

4

Li stood at the door. "You wanted me?"

"Yeah, come on in. Tell the Inspector what we found out last night."

"We were going through your file again. There was a piece of paper tucked away that said someone heard you had a stroke."

"Not so."

"It says your health is not very good."

"I'm fine. Better than fine."

"What was it, then? Something scared you off the mountain into a doctor's office last year. That's not like you."

"It was nothing. Well, maybe it was something. A sign, an omen."

"That's what the doctor said?"

"In his own way. He said everybody dies eventually."

"A doctor said that?" Kim threw up his hands. "I could have told you the same thing. Li could have told you. Some doctor you have. Who needs to hear that from a doctor?"

"How much longer you have?" Li looked a little unsure of how that sounded. "I mean, do you need a glass of water or something?"

"I'm perfectly fine, in the pink of health. Better than either of you, I'll bet. And you want to know why? When I realized what had happened, I had this sense of ecstasy. I was in my cabin on the mountain, looking out the window at the trees, when all of a sudden my brain shook. And then I got weak; not just weak, it was beyond that, the other side of weak. It was like going through the secret door in the floor of our house when I was young."

"It sounds like you were stunned, kind of in shock or something. The driver said the ceiling in your place looked kind of low. Maybe you hit your head." Li was trying to be helpful. This was the Li I remembered from a long time ago, when we first worked together.

"Shock? No, I'd say it was the opposite of shock. Maybe revelation. In that instant, I realized that I wasn't doomed to wind down like an old clock. I could go all at once, in a moment that I controlled. Not controlled consciously, of course, but something deeper, older, a self within, one that knew more, had seen more, like starlight passing through the earth, a speck of dust on the way to the other side of nowhere, everywhere, boundless."

"Careful, you're getting out of breath, O. Sit down. I think you might be hyperventilating." Kim moved the green chair closer.

"I don't need a chair." My eyes must have had a strange gleam in them. Kim looked frightened, as if he wasn't sure who I was. "Don't you get it? It means I'm not on a leash. No one owns me."

"Good. Forget the leash and sit. I'll get you a glass of water." He turned to Li. "Do we have a physician around here?"

"Don't bother," I said. "It's only a power surge in the system. I get a little boost of energy once in a while, nothing to worry about." I felt my blood pressure dropping back to normal. "It's like stepping on the gas when the transmission is in neutral, that's all. Probably helps clean the carburetor."

"Don't pay attention to him," Li said. "Mechanical things are not his specialty."

"Cancel your operation, Kim. The guy with the smirk is from SSD; I'm sure of it."

"We now classify people according to their smirks?" Kim's face ran through a dozen expressions. "What about these?"

"You think I'm kidding? If we're lucky, they'll leave us twiddling our thumbs and move things to another time. If they really want to make a point, they'll do something ugly."

5

The lecture hall was deserted when we walked in. It wasn't a big room—maybe twenty chairs—and it was going to be harder to blend in if we ended up with only a lecturer, my team, and three or four SSD operatives. Kim refused to cancel the operation. He said I was afflicted with a fear of shadows, that it was a result of my living too long in a warped environment. That left us at the mercy of SSD. In the best case, SSD might send only one person, but I had a feeling there would be what we always called belts of security—the key agents, then a team watching them, then a team watching *them*. The Ministry never worked that way, but SSD was in the business of shooting ghosts, or at least tracking them. They needed a lot of people to do that.

I had assumed the room would also have a few students, several academics, a couple of bureaucrats desperately trying to learn new vocabulary that would help them keep their jobs, and the inevitable party types taking notes on what was said and who was there. It was beginning to look like my assumptions were wrong. At 1:10 there was no lecturer and still no one else in the hall. The short man leaned over to me.

"Maybe we're in the wrong room."

"You have inside information?" I said. "Maybe you know something the rest of us don't?"

He sat back and let a faint frown settle around his mouth. The man from SSD had closed his eyes and was resting comfortably. The third man, the one who didn't say much, was looking at his hands.

The room was still empty at 1:20 when the door opened. "The lecture has been canceled for unavoidable reasons." A young woman walked to the front of the room. "We have another group coming in at one thirty, so you'll have to leave."

"When was it canceled?" I looked at the man from SSD.

The short man was on his feet. "And why didn't someone bother to come in and tell us before? We've been sitting here waiting. Do you think that's all we have to do?"

"I don't know what all you have to do. I do know you'll have to get out of this room."

"Is it OK if he stays through the next meeting?" I pointed at the man from SSD.

"And why would it be OK if he stayed?" she asked.

"Because he's dead."

6

"Who knew?" I was sitting in a chair—not the green one, which had been moved to the other side of the room—in front of Kim's desk while he chewed on pencils. "You could certainly argue that it was a day bad for *somebody's* health."

"I don't think he just keeled over."

"He didn't keel over. He didn't even slump. He was sitting up."

"How did they do it?"

"How did who do what? I don't have any idea what happened to him. All I know is that he sat down at one o'clock and by one twenty he wasn't going anywhere."

"They must have killed him." Kim looked worried. "Why would they do that? He must have known something that he wasn't supposed to know. Either that or he had plans to jump ship and they needed to stop him."

"I doubt either one of those. I also doubt that SSD killed him. They don't do that to their own people. It's very bad for morale."

"Maybe you were wrong. Maybe he wasn't one of theirs."

"Then whose was he?"

"I don't know. It was in his file, but the file is gone."

"Gone. Mislaid, I suppose."

"Files do disappear sometimes, Inspector. This is a secure facility. I don't think anyone here made off with it." Kim was looking more worried by the second. The more he said out loud all of the reasons everything was all right, the more he realized that things were starting to go bad. "We'll have to do an autopsy. That will tell us the cause of death. The police can take it from there."

"The police? You really don't understand this place yet, do you? The police won't have anything to do with a dead SSD agent."

"They won't? Then who will investigate?"

"That's a good question, Major. If he died of a heart attack, everyone will breathe a sigh of relief, because a big red check can go in the box on the file that says: 'No Further Investigation Necessary.' If his heart stopped for unexplained reasons, no one will answer the phone when you call."

"What do we do? Forget it happened?"

"No, you keep it in mind at all times."

"Was it a threat?"

"Against you? Not likely. They're not going to threaten you. They aren't sure who is going to come out on top. What if you emerge as top dog? They don't want to be on your bad side."

"They want to be on my good side. Then why murder that agent?"

"Fair enough: Why murder that agent? It could be they need you to keep some distance. Remember I told you to call off the operation? Actually, I don't think they meant to kill their man to make that point. I think they meant to kill someone else."

"You?"

"Could be. The question is, why?"

"Don't they realize that killing you wouldn't have mattered to me?"

"That helps."

"They must think you're working for me."

"Or something." It could be that. More likely, they got wind of my meeting with Kang in Prague.

7

Finally, I decided to ask the major. The man in the lobby, the one who stared at nothing but always seemed to watch as I walked in and out of the hotel, was there every day. The clerk said he'd been away for a weekend while I was traveling, but he was back on his chair the day before I returned. Who was he?

"Him?" Kim was glancing over a report. He made a notation

in the margin, put a big star next to one passage, and turned the page over. "We don't know who he is. Your people say they've never heard of him and have no records. Should I believe them?"

"My people? You mean the Ministry? They might not have any records, but someone sure as hell knows who he is. Anonymity is not a hallmark of what we have built here all of these years, believe me. Why not bring him in?"

"You worried? You want a personal bodyguard? The man is just staring, Inspector."

"I was only letting you know, that's all. If he's one of yours, call him off, would you? It's unnerving."

"I told you, he's not one of mine. Maybe he belongs to Zhao. His people don't have much going on in their heads, so they tend to stare. That's not your biggest problem right now."

"I take it that means you can't bring him in. I thought you were in charge."

"In charge? What an idea! I'm hanging on for dear life, Inspector. An admission of weakness that I probably shouldn't make to you, but you might as well know where things stand. There is no cooperation, only a sullen quiet when I walk into the room. What do you think is going on? You seemed to understand the situation with SSD. What else can you tell me?"

"How would I know?"

"How would you know, that's exactly my question. Incidentally, I was told this morning that we lost track of you in Macau for several days. Why?"

"If you thought I was going to let that madman Zhao follow me around, you're crazy. If you could keep tabs on me, so could he. I took some precautions. Nothing elaborate."

Kim was suddenly alert. "What makes you think Zhao was in Macau?"

"Nothing. I just wasn't taking any chances. I told you, I took some precautions, that's all."

"Like taking an airplane out of Macau?"

"I certainly wasn't going to buy a train ticket to Beijing."

"The idea is starting to bounce around, Inspector, that you aren't on our side, that you are on the wrong side, in fact. That's not good." Kim walked over to a large cabinet and turned a switch on the side. "You're not bothered by white noise, I trust. Now no one will hear our conversation. I hope you don't have a transmitter in your shoe or anything."

"I did, but it gave me bunions, so I threw it away."

"Here's your dilemma. You don't mind if I speak frankly?"

"I wish you would."

"This place," he looked around the room, but it was clear he meant the gesture to be interpreted more broadly, "is gone. Frankly, all that holds it up is the fear in my capital that a collapse will be disastrous for us. Believe me, people are shaking in their Guccis."

"I think you're wrong. A bigger real dilemma is that if you move too soon, or the wrong way, the Chinese won't sit still."

"Thank you for your advice, Inspector, but I read the same file you did. We're handling the Chinese, and we don't have any new openings for policy advisors. I'll tell you if we do."

"Money, that's your problem. It makes your world go round. You're afraid of making history for fear of losing money. Here, we rely on power. So why would people with power in this city agree to fall into your lap? Purely for money? I find that hard to believe. This group has no desire to spend the rest of its days on the Riviera."

"Not money, Inspector, loss of nerve. It happens—not often, but it happens. That's all it takes. Someone wakes up one morning, looks in the mirror, and can't see anything familiar. It's contagious. The result is extreme loss of self-confidence on a grand scale. I think it might be connected with the same gene that causes animals to stampede."

"No, that gene doesn't exist here. Maybe somewhere else. India, for example. Not here."

"You don't think so? You don't think the whole structure could crack, from basement to penthouse? The whole rotten lie? It was a lie, O; you know that. You always knew that."

"You're going to find this hard to understand, Kim, but it wasn't a lie. That word can't cover how tens of millions of people lived their lives for nearly seventy years. We had something to believe in, a way to order existence. Maybe people didn't have much, most of them had very little, but for practically all of those years they felt they belonged to something. Not so long ago, we used to be friendly to each other; young people stood up and gave their seats to the elderly. There was a simplicity in who we thought we were. We even had hope for the future."

"That's what innocence is, Inspector, hope."

"You southerners lost it along the way, and now we have, too."

Kim looked about to say something but changed his mind. He gestured for me to continue.

"You think your skirts are clean, rid of the camps you used to have. But I notice you're not rushing to close the ones up here. Too complicated, you think. You'd rather draw up a list of particulars, crimes against humanity after the fact. Maybe you already have. Maybe that's one of the lists on your desk."

"And you, Inspector? How did you fit into this idyllic society?"

"I lived according to the prevailing myth, that's all. Everyone lives by myths. Prettied up, they're called truths—basic truths, natural truths, self-evident truths." None of this sociopolitical pabulum was worth a damn. All that mattered was that I was not going to give Kim the pleasure of seeing me admit that my entire existence had been wrong. Never in a thousand years, I thought to myself—not now, not ever—will you see me grovel. "What I knew or thought a year ago is beside the point. The problem is today. Even if the past was a lie, what am I supposed to replace it with? Another lie? All that's necessary is to pull the old one out and put a new one in, like a circuit board? Your lies have more diodes. I suppose they work faster, more color and noise."

"What you replace your empty past with, Inspector, is your business. I'm giving you something different. I'm giving you a choice. Think about it. You choose, and that becomes your fate. Whatever years you have left, it's all in your hands. Can you handle that? Can you make a decision on your own, without someone telling you which way to go?"

Kang had wanted me to choose. Now Kim wanted the same thing, only he couldn't help being nasty about it. People who know the truth are that way. "And what if I don't want to make a choice?"

"Dead. Very simply, dead. We'll shoot you. In fact, I'll do it myself. We'll make it something dramatic, something that will send a message to the others. 'What a waste,' they'll say as they cluck their tongues. 'O had a choice to live, and he chose to die. Too bad.'"

"Maybe that will turn out to be your worst nightmare. What if I end up being a martyr?"

Kim's smile told me the thought had already occurred to him. "You aren't martyr material, Inspector. You have no cause; no one will rally around anything you have ever said, or been, or imagined. It will be as if you stepped off a cliff for no reason."

"I could choose to go back to my mountain, fade away, not cause you any trouble. What's wrong with that?"

"Not possible. We can't have you on the fence. It would be a bad precedent, and we're dealing with a period right now when setting precedent takes priority over normal considerations of right and wrong. I may not accomplish much in the next couple of months, but one thing I will get done and that is to establish precedents."

"So you'd rather eliminate me. Nothing personal, simply setting precedent."

"Look, O, here's a list." He pulled a paper from the folder. "See the names with the check marks next to them? They're with us."

"The familiar name list. I'm not on it, I hope. It seems an unstable place to be. You keep fiddling with the order. These are the ones you're propping up, I assume." I glanced at the list. Nobody I'd want to have drinks with. "You don't pick your friends all that carefully as far as I can see."

"I'm not picking them; they're picking me. They come knocking on the door in the dead of night, promising to deliver whole sections of the country, army units, security files, whatever I want."

"They have probably done the same with the Chinese." Most of the names were of people used to landing on their feet.

"I don't care whose tummy they are rubbing, as long as they realize they can't afford to ignore me. We need a quiet transition, as seamless and unremarkable as we can make it. Nobody raises his head, nobody gets hurt. This is a list of what we like to call our guides, people who know where the paths are, and where they lead. If these are the right paths, and everyone cooperates, all that happens is that the sign in the front window changes. 'Under new management.'"

"The immaculate omelet, made without breaking a single egg. I don't think so."

"You don't think so. I don't think so, either, but that's what the plan calls for. If you ask me, there's no chance things will stick to the script, and when they don't, we have to go to plan B."

"Always plan B. Why not start there?"

"You won't like it. Trust me, no one will like it."

"Tell me honestly, Major. Do you really think you can blow the whistle, point to the scoreboard, and convince twenty-three million people that you've won the game?"

"I don't know why anyone would believe it, but I'm telling you it's already happened. It doesn't matter what the people at the bottom think. They'll do as they're told. But the ones at the top, they can see what has happened. I'm not going to spend a lot of time analyzing the causes. The fact is, I've never seen so many whipped dogs in my life."

"Is that so?"

"You saw that group at the table the first night. If I shift my chair, they wet themselves. They're not cooperative, but they are resigned."

"Good. In that case, you have probably already looked into how many of your army divisions are going to have to stay for the next hundred years to keep all the dogs in line. Do you think you're going to pacify the whole country? Go up to the mountains in Chagang sometime and tell me that. Try driving a tank through hills and dales of Yanggang. How long do you think the railroads will last? Will you guard every tunnel and every bridge?"

"It's *one* country, for the love of God, O."

"Of course! You're a Christian. I should have guessed."

"That's not relevant."

"Oh, no? You expect me to think that your heart doesn't race when you look around and think of the possibilities for converts."

"Be serious. Are you with us or against us? I don't have time to kick this ball around."

"I know, I know; you are on a tight schedule. Only I don't think you realize yet what is going on outside the bubble of this compound."

"Let me try inserting something you may find interesting. Your grandmother was a Christian."

"Is that so?" Pang did his homework. Kim did his homework. Pretty soon, I'd have a nice genealogy chart to hang in my house.

"She was educated at a Methodist school in Haeju. That's where she grew up, wasn't it?"

"You seem to have the file on my grandmother. You tell me."

"I thought you knew."

"Fascinating, all fascinating. And it means what? I'm next in line to be Pope?"

"The Pope isn't a Methodist."

"What a coincidence. Neither am I."

"Look, O, you may not believe it, you may not like it, but the biggest change either of us will ever see is already here. Not on the doorstep, not in the wings. It is here, now. In a year, this rump state of yours will not exist. Understood?"

"Within a year, I get to bring in the tray with your breakfast."

"Maybe."

"And my friends? What happens to them?"

"Depends who they are." Kim picked up his pencil. "Who are they?"

"And my world?"

"Your world? I should think you'd be happy to see it disappear. Besides, the new one won't be so bad."

"Is it already on display at the hotel? I get headaches."

Kim put all the papers in a neat pile. "Things have been quiet up to now. But we go into phase two soon. I need a decision from you. Help me make it smooth, or I guarantee you won't live to see the end of it. That's the way it is going to be."

"More threats. That's the sum total of what you have in your fancy knapsack." Kim's eyes dared me to keep going down that path. I decided it was time to try a new tack. I didn't have a lot of options at the moment; I might as well try purring. "You'll keep Zhao off my back?"

"He won't come near you." The response was automatic, almost as if he was hypnotized. Zhao was a fixation. It was clear to me that nothing worried Kim as much as, nothing blotted out more light or consumed more oxygen than, his fear of Zhao. He didn't control the gangster, and it scared the hell out of him.

"You're going to protect me sort of like you protected Captain Sim."

"Sim was working against me, Inspector. I let Pang have him. In fact, I told Pang where he'd be."

"Don't try that with me. There's a key difference. Sim was one of yours. He didn't know which way was up around here. I do."

"Are you bargaining with me? Because you don't have any leverage, Inspector. None. Not a tiny bit, not a sliver. None."

"Keep believing in angels if it makes you sleep any better." Purring was hard work. I'd have to practice.

8

The next day, I stayed in my hotel. The phone rang; I didn't answer it. A note came under the door; I didn't open it. When the maid came to make up the room around ten o'clock, I went downstairs and stopped at the front desk. The man of a thousand stares was waiting in the lobby. He had on a striped shirt. It accentuated his thinness. He made Luís look like a water buffalo.

The desk clerk looked annoyed. "Who is that guy? He won't talk to anyone. He just stands around, staring at nothing. I've put up with him long enough. I've had it. End of the line."

"It only looks like he's staring at nothing. Actually, he has wide-angle vision, sort of like a walleye pike. If you pay attention, you'll see his eyes move independently."

"Yeah, sure. And my fingers dance the rumba on Thursdays. He looks like a friend of yours. He only showed up when you did, as I recall. When you go away, so does he. He's like a wart. Get rid of him before I call security."

The only person I liked less than the staring man was this clerk. "That probably won't do any good. He works for them, or somebody like them. What harm is he doing, standing there?"

"It makes the guests nervous."

"I'm your only guest. Do I look nervous?"

"Why did you come down here? You're not the chatty type."

"It gets lonely up there in the room. Besides, I thought you might give me some help."

"You, I don't help. The word is out to keep a healthy distance from you for now."

"Why's that?"

He looked at his watch. "Listen, I'm busy. I've got to call a girl. Two girls, actually. You don't mind? Come down again sometime, we'll talk more." He turned away.

The man in the lobby stared at him. "That's it," said the clerk. "I don't care if his eyes are diamond studs, I'm calling the security boys."

9

It was a little past eleven o'clock when I arrived at Kim's compound. My name must have been put on an approved list, because the tanks ignored me as I hurried up the walk.

"I've been away from home for weeks already." I was at the window looking into the courtyard. "If I'm going to stay here any longer, I've got to go home to pick up some stuff."

"Why?" Major Kim was half-listening. "We can supply you with whatever you need. We've got more shirts if you need them."

"I'm not talking clothing."

"What then?"

"Wood. I didn't think I'd be here so long, so I didn't take more than a few pieces with me. It's autumn. Things get melancholy sometimes in the evening when I'm out walking. All these lights you've installed, they make it worse."

"Light makes it worse?"

"You're a creature of the wrong civilization, Major. The sun goes up; the sun goes down. That's natural. Light blazing at midnight is abnormal. It's unhealthy."

"So close your curtains. Get yourself some eyeshades. Put your head under your pillow. Think happy thoughts."

"Let me go home for a day, I'll pick up some wood, and then I'll be back."

"I don't think I can spare a driver. We're having some people coming in for inspections."

"I can drive myself. I still have a license. Or have you voided all of them?"

"It's for your safety. I don't want you on a mountain road by yourself."

"Afraid I'll decide to end it all?"

"No, afraid Zhao will decide to do it for you."

"Ah. I get it. Well, I can wait a day or two. Am I going to need a pass to get around my own country?"

Kim's phone rang. He stared at the button that had lit up and gave me a funny look. "Can I take this, Inspector?"

I stepped into the hall and closed the door, almost the whole way.

"Again?" Kim said. "I don't like it." A pause. "Then take care of it yourself." I closed the door completely. When Kim opened it, I was looking at the photographs on the wall.

"These look like plane trees in summer," I said. "See how they droop? It's a form of anger—passive resistance, isn't that what people call it? My grandfather used to say that lumber from plane trees should never be used to make a wedding chest."

"When can you be ready to leave?" Kim blocked the door. He wanted to get rid of me.

"How about in an hour? You found a driver?"

"Just wait in your hotel room. Someone will call. They'll ask if your TV is working or if the sound needs adjusting. Don't go with anyone else."

"You are one scared rabbit, Major. One day you're telling me you are about to take over; the next day you're peeking out from behind the curtains. Which is it?"

"Cautious, Inspector, cautious. No one ever lost a lung being cautious."

10

The call came at noon. The voice said, "I heard there was something wrong with the TV. The volume control or something."

"Yeah, something."

"Well, get it fixed, why don't you?"

"I'll be right down."

I was surprised to see who was waiting in the car. "You have more sage advice for me, Li?"

"Get in and close the door. We're going to have to drive like a house on fire to get there and back before dinner."

"Where have I heard that before? Never happen. I can cook something at my place. It won't be anything elaborate."

As soon as I closed the door, we were moving. Once we were out of the city, the colors of the harvest took over. "If you've got to die, autumn is best, my grandfather used to say." I thought about that as we sped past a checkpoint. "He was probably right."

"When did he die?"

"Summer."

"Can't exactly set the date, I guess. When it comes, it comes. Any season it wants. What do you think your grandfather meant?"

"What did he mean about anything? He used to talk about rhythms, about how things had to be aligned. He thought trees understood that better than any other living being. Not embodied it, *understood* it. On summer nights, when he was making benches for the village, he'd grumble at me, 'You've got to look at a tree, listen to it, see how it grew, before you know how to use the wood. These people just chop them down and cut them up. What sense is that? No wonder everything is ugly these days. And I'm not talking about just ugly to look at, you know what I mean, boy?'"

We drove for a while. I opened the window and let the wind rush in.

"Nice drive," I said. "The fields look pleased with themselves. The harvest must have been good this year, though I haven't heard anything."

"What would you know about harvests, O?"

"Hey, I know plenty. I grew up in the countryside, don't forget. My grandfather didn't like cities, not after the war, anyway. He said he wanted to smell earth that hadn't been pulverized by bombs."

"Who wouldn't? Do you mind closing your window? I start sneezing otherwise, this time of year."

I cranked up the window. "How is that you got assigned to watch me?"

"Meaning what?"

"I don't know. For some reason, I've been getting the impression you and Major Kim don't get along."

"Come on; you know me, O. I get along with everyone. That's my nature."

"So you're working for him?"

"I'm not working against him, if that's what you're getting at."

"He's very interested in loyalty, have you noticed? Doesn't like divided loyalties. He's after me to choose."

"And what do you tell him?"

"What did you tell him?"

"Me? I'm loyal as they come. Loyal as the day is long."

"It's autumn."

"Yeah, so?"

"So the days are getting shorter."

He laughed. "Maybe your grandfather was right; maybe autumn is the best time to die." When we got off the pavement onto the dirt road that led up the mountain to my house, he turned to me. "Watch how you choose, O."

"I'm always careful."

"That's good. But careful isn't enough anymore. You have to be right every time. Take your hands off the wheel for one second," the car hit a rut and careened off to the side, "and it could be all over."

"Watch where you're going," I said. "Other than handing out advice, what do you do all day?"

"Don't laugh, but I'm a chief inspector now. Surprised? They did a scrub of the chiefs after Kim got here, let several of them go, and moved up some of us who had been sitting around all these years. You probably could have made chief, too, if you hadn't been up on your mountain. What were you doing there for all those years?"

"Making wooden toys. You have to concentrate when you make toys. They've got to look simple. It's a lot of work, making something look simple."

"Is that so?"

"Like doing a 'scrub.' Sounds cleaner than a 'purge.' But that's what it is, a purge."

"I know what it is." He opened his window partway. "All of a sudden, it's stuffy in here, don't you think? That's my dilemma; I have to choose between stuffy air and my allergy."

"It's going to get cold pretty soon, a couple of weeks maybe. Then you won't have to worry."

"Yeah, I won't have to worry."

For the moment, the car was headed almost due east. The setting sun poured light across the fields in front of us.

"Did I tell you about the woman I met in Macau, the one whose voice sounded like wildflowers?"

"What kind?" Li lifted his head slightly. His nostrils flared, like an animal when it senses danger.

"You smell it, too? It must be from a wood fire," I said. "That's strange, because no one lives out here. The nearest village is behind us and the wind is blowing the wrong way." I put my head out the window to get a better look. There was a glow at the top of the mountain, my mountain. "You see that?"

Li stopped the car and peered out the windshield. Then he accelerated sharply, so the tires spun in the dirt before we jumped ahead. "I hope you didn't leave the stove on for all this time."

"I don't have a stove."

We tore up the road past the abandoned guard shack and hit the steepest part of the grade going so fast I thought we might flip over. We went around turn after turn, sliding close to the edge in places, brushing against the sides of the mountain in others, going at a reckless speed that seemed to be in slow motion, a dream speed, a horror film remembered years after. When we burst into the clearing, my house was gone. The roof had caved in, and the only wall left standing was pitched at a funny angle. The remains were still smoking. The tallest of the tall pines had been chopped down; it had fallen against an outcropping of rock. The next big wind would bring it down onto the road. Another car inched away as we drove up. It stopped when it came abreast of us, and the rear window rolled down.

"A total loss," Zhao's voice came out from inside. "A pity. I'd come up here to see if we could do business, and I find your house in flames."

"My grandfather's carpentry tools were in there, you Chinese bastard."

"Well, that's a loss, I'd say."

I got out and ran over to Zhao's car. "By the time I finish with you, you'll beg me to kill you." It wasn't clear what I was going to do next. I wasn't armed, and beating on the car with my fists didn't seem much of a follow-up.

Zhao moved closer to the window, so I could see him clearly. He stared at me for a moment; then the glass went up and the car drove away. Li got out on his side and watched as it made its way down the hill.

"Let's get out of here, O. We can come back tomorrow or the next day, after the place cools down. They must have used gasoline. It's going to stay hot for a while. You can feel it all the way over here."

"I'm not leaving until I go through the ashes."

"That's what they're counting on. They'll be back, and you'd better not be here when they are."

"Why? You think they can do any worse than this? Look at that tree. They cut it down. Can they do anything worse than that?"

"Yes."

"Go, if you want. I'm staying. Maybe I can find something that wasn't completely destroyed."

Li shook his head. "Have it your way, but first we need something to eat. We'll have to drive back to the nearest village, that's almost fifteen kilometers away, unless you know somewhere closer. Even there, they may not have anything to give us."

"You can drive all over the damned county. I'm staying. If Zhao comes back, I'll rip him to shreds."

"Easy, Inspector. You heard what he did to the Great Han. We don't want that to happen to you."

I started pulling away burned timbers. The ashes were still hot; in places a flame flared when it found a breath of oxygen. Li stood and watched. Finally, I touched a piece of metal. It scorched my fingers, but I didn't care, because I knew what it was—the old wood plane that my grandfather had given me fifty, no, sixty years ago.

"Look at this, Li." I pulled the plane from the wreckage. "My grandfather said it had been his father's and that he wanted to give it to his son. But that wasn't to be—he would always say that more to himself than to me. He hated to talk about what happened to his son, my father. Everyone lost someone in the war, so he didn't want to be seen as complaining. But he felt the loss deeper than anything I could imagine then. Even now, I don't think I can feel anything that deeply."

Li didn't say anything. He was listening the way people do when someone else reaches inside for the story that they never want to tell.

"It wasn't until I was older, maybe ten or twelve, that he went into any detail about how my parents had died. He had told us right away, my brother and me, that they were dead. The same night he found out, he sat us down and told us, but he hadn't gone into detail. We were too young, and he didn't know what words to use. So he waited. When he finally told me, he was sanding a piece of ash. It was from a tree that had crashed through a neighbor's house in a windstorm a few weeks before. The whole family had died. I still remember that storm."

Li was looking down the road. He was pale.

"Something wrong?"

"No, just thinking about the wind. I grew up on the coast. When the wind blew hard, the fishing boats couldn't go out. A few did, but they never came back." He blinked, and his face seemed to clear. "Before the storms would come in off the sea, I would wake up. Even at three in the morning, I would wake up. Maybe it was something about the air pressure; no one could figure it out. But I always knew when a storm was coming." He looked back down the road. "Always."

He seemed to have drifted somewhere else in his mind, so I left him alone and went back to digging through the remains of the house. There was nothing. The green vase with the cranes, the chest made for my grandmother, a small box of old photographs—all gone.

"You said something about an ash tree?" Li had moved so quietly that the sound of his voice startled me.

"I did. You know what one looks like?"

"Not if it smacked me in the face."

"You wouldn't want that. It's very hard wood. I nearly lost

my arm once because of it. The pain wouldn't go away for months. Still hurts sometimes. That's ash."

"So your grandfather had a piece of ash, and he was talking to you. That's where you left off."

"No, he wasn't talking to me so much as to the years that lay around us. That's what he said, sometimes—that the years don't pass; they don't disappear. They were still here, he'd say, invisible, infinitely thin piles of them, heaped in the corners of rooms. It was one of those things that he'd say that wasn't clear to me at the time. In winter, he'd often brood and tell me that the past was never gone; it was inside of us and all around. I wasn't to believe what people said, that on January first everything was new."

"You know, if I could come up with a single year that I wanted to keep, it would be nice. But there isn't one, not even one." Li pointed at what had been the front entrance to the house. "Every December thirty-first, I open the door at midnight, to let the old year out. Who taught me to do that, do you suppose? I can't remember." He looked into the smoking ruins. "Go ahead; keep looking for whatever there is to salvage. I'll watch the road. If I see a car, I'll whistle. We'll need to get out of here fast. Someone will take care of Zhao eventually; don't worry."

"I don't want 'someone' to take care of the son of a bitch. I'm going to do it myself."

"As soon as we get off this mountain, I've got to find a phone to call Kim. He won't be happy to hear about you and Zhao spitting at each other. He's afraid of Zhao. Everyone seems to be."

The words were barely out of his mouth when two big guys appeared from nowhere. They each took one of Li's arms and dragged him to the edge of the cliff. Then they threw him over. One of them watched for a few seconds before they both turned to me. They didn't say anything. What remained of the house made a sound, a painful sigh as the wood died for the last time. The sun dropped over the next hill, and in the darkness the wind picked up. I turned away and walked back to Li's car, expecting the whole time that they'd stop me, permanently. Li had left the keys in the ignition. That was how we used to do it, I thought, as I started the car and turned around to drive down the hill. We always left ourselves a way out. Only I was starting to think there wasn't one left.

Chapter Two

Let me get this straight. You were standing there. Two husky guys materialized, threw him over the cliff, and watched as you drove away." Kim swallowed hard but kept writing. "That's it? He didn't struggle, or yell? Big guy like Li, you're telling me when they grabbed him, he went limp?"

"Maybe he did. I think one of them jammed something into his neck. It was getting dark, and it happened pretty fast."

"You were a policeman for all those years, a trained observer, and you're not sure what you saw?"

"I was upset. They'd just burned down my house."

On the drive back, I'd gone over the whole thing ten times. There was no other conclusion. Kim must have known what Zhao was going to do. That's why he was hesitant to let me go home until he got that phone call. And Li? He didn't have to assign Li as the driver.

"*Your* house." Kim kept marking his list. "I didn't realize there was such attachment to material goods around here. I thought it had been squeezed out of you people."

"We don't wallow in it, if that's what you mean. But we don't go around destroying each other's property, either."

"That sounds like an accusation, Inspector, and I don't like it."

"Sorry, I'm still a little rattled." If someone had handed me a pistol, I would have shot him right there, point-blank. I wouldn't have even told him to look up. "Do you mind if I ask you a question? Why is it that people who work for you end up dead?"

That stopped him. He put the pencil down and sat back in his chair. Some people do that to show how relaxed they are, but sometimes it's a fighting stance. With Kim, my money was on the latter.

"You've admitted that you gave the captain to the Great Han. Then—I'm thinking out loud here—maybe you gave the Great Han to Zhao." That wasn't my insight, it was Kang's, but I could use it if I wanted. "Then, what do you know, Li gets shoved off a mountain."

"It's funny, Inspector. I was thinking that you're the common thread in all these deaths. You—not me."

"How do you figure that?"

"All of them were killed to make an impression on you."

"Well, good, we can stop now, because I'm impressed."

"Zhao wants you to work with him; that's clear. And he's trying to scare you away from working with me. Captain Sim was the first step."

"Really? I thought you said you arranged for Sim's execution."

"I did, but only because Zhao thought he was betraying us to the Chinese."

"Really? What does Zhao consider himself? A Druid?"

"He considers that his interests transcend the normal concerns in modern Beijing. He pretends not to care about tradition, but if you ask him after a few drinks, he'll tell you about his sick dreams. They take place in the imperial court. It seems he's always wearing an ermine robe with nothing underneath. Colonel Pang was very Chinese, and so, in his own way, is Zhao. I'm supposed to keep them all out of here, Inspector. I would have thought that was something you wanted, too."

"I bar the back door and you come marching in the front, is that it?"

"At the moment, to tell you the truth, I'm less concerned with who is at either door than who is already inside. What do you know about the opposition that's been scurrying around here? It's like listening to rats scamper across the ceiling at night."

"What did you expect? Sheep?"

"They need to understand, Inspector, that they have no chance of changing the course of history. I think somebody is filling their heads with bad ideas. You wouldn't know who that might be, would you? I'm afraid Li might have been talking to them."

"You killed him for that?"

Kim didn't respond, he didn't even register the question, but I knew he had heard it, and I knew he wouldn't forget. "And you, Inspector, you wouldn't be working for somebody else, would you? Because if you are, it won't take me too long to find out."

"Then what? Are you going to turn Zhao loose on me, too? You don't scare me, Major, because I don't have anything left to lose—nothing at all. The good die young. I missed the cutoff a while ago."

"Maybe you really are more useful dead than alive." Kang mused on that thought. His posture mused. The face fell to four types of musing. It seemed a shame to interrupt the show. I waited. He looked at me. "Should we test that theory?"

That did it. I wasn't a mouse he could bat back and forth between his paws. "You know your problem? You are convinced that you know this place, but you don't. You speak Korean, we speak Korean, and that makes you absolutely sure that you know what we think. But we don't think alike at all. With you, everything is hierarchy. You're in charge, and you need everybody else to salute and shut up. Maybe that works where you're from, but not here. If you're going to take over, you'd better get that through your head."

"Discipline is the essence of civilization, Inspector. It's the only way people know their place."

"Keep butting your head against that wall if you want."

"You don't like discipline? What about fear? That works almost as well, though apparently it breaks down after a while."

"Use whatever you think works. Don't blame me when it doesn't."

Kim's fist came down on the desk; several pencils jumped but landed again, I noticed, without his say-so. "I understand what I need to understand, Inspector. Nuances don't interest me. And you damn well better be clear on that."

It was a perfect moment to sit back in my chair and look relaxed. There was nothing to say. Whatever was going to happen was grinding its way along. I wasn't going to bet against Kim, but I wasn't going to help him, either.

2

At that moment, the radio in the office came alive. A flood of calls tumbled in all at once, they overwhelmed the system, and it fell silent. The last brief call made clear what had happened: "Gunfire . . . casualties . . ." Then the transmission stopped.

Kim was white-faced. He paced into the hallway, and when he stepped back into the room he slammed the door. "Now they've gone too far," he said. He picked up the phone. "Did you monitor that? I don't want to see it on the TV, I don't want to hear it on the radio news, and I don't want anything about this to get to Seoul. Not a word, not a whisper. I will personally beat to a pulp any son of a bitch who leaks this." He paused, listening. "Pull a team together and get to the scene. I don't care about the goddamned roads, you hear me? You find who did this and bring them in. If we don't make an example of them, it's all over." He hung up and turned to me. "You have any ideas?

Because if you do, I want to hear them. This was no bunch of old women pushing cops around at the market. These were your colleagues that were butchered. It was a Ministry of People's Security patrol, not a squad of goons. Just police, and now their brains are all over the street." He sat down behind the desk and broke a pencil.

"All we know is that the transmission cut off. I wouldn't jump to conclusions."

"You heard the reference to casualties, same as I did. Don't forget, you're the one who told me to go look at the mountains in Chagang. That's where this happened; that's where that patrol was assigned. Did you know it was in the works, Inspector? Have you heard whisperings on the wind that blows through this barren, pathetic Soprano state of yours? If you know something, you'd better tell me, because I promise you, this is going to stop, right now." He tightened his lips; that seemed to calm him. "If something like this happened before, how would your leadership have responded?"

"My leadership? I left five years ago, Major, and you know it. I'm not privy to their thinking, past or present. Ask them yourself."

"That's exactly what I intend to do. Why don't you come along? I'm sure they'll be interested in what you have to say."

"Me?" I wasn't about to get myself into those airless rooms trailing behind Major Kim. "No, thank you. Anyway, it won't do your case any good having me in tow. I'll diminish your stature. They were never crazy about me."

"I thought they liked your grandfather."

"They made him a Hero of the Revolution, but I am nobody. That was my goal in life, and I achieved it."

"I've decided to shorten your leash, Inspector. For the past few weeks, I've given you a lot of room to roam. I thought it would help you adjust to what is happening. I even entrusted you with a sensitive assignment as a way of our building confidence. It was an experiment. It had to be tried, but as of now, this minute, it's over. We're switching to something completely different, an approach advertised to be effective in breaking wild horses. Maybe it will work in your case, too. For the next week, two weeks, as long as I can spare the manpower, someone is going to be with you every second. If you move, they move. Go right, they'll be next to you. Go left, they'll be there waiting. I'm telling you this so you won't be tempted to do something stupid." Kim stood up and went to the door. A man appeared, the thin man. He stared at Kim, then turned his gaze on me.

"I thought you said you didn't know who he was."

"Since when do I owe you the truth?" Kim indicated the man should stand next to my chair. "This is your new friend," Kim said to me. "You and he will be inseparable. He's one of mine, but he knows this place pretty well."

I nodded at my new friend.

"You're plotting again, Inspector. Don't." Kim turned to the thin man. "Your instructions are bare-bones simple. Do not let him out of your sight. Not for a second. No excuses." He seemed to weigh what to say next. "None."

3

Once Kim left, the thin man took a seat across from me. That's when, out of the blue, it came to me.

"I've figured it out," I said. "People who stare are special. That's how my grandfather put it—special. He said if someone gave you a Baltic stare, it meant you would have good luck for a year. That was the term he used—'Baltic stare.' He didn't know why it was called that, but he had heard it when he was in Russia, and the name stuck. How about it? Let's have a real Baltic stare. I need some luck."

No response, an empty lighthouse on a windswept coast.

Well, I thought with some disappointment, might as well pick at the scab you have rather than the one you hoped to find. "Ever been to Estonia?"

He didn't react to that, either, and I wondered if we were going to have trouble communicating. As I was drawing a breath to repeat the question, he said evenly, "Why don't you just shut up? I'm not supposed to let you out of my sight, but that doesn't mean I have to listen."

"Right," I said. I closed my eyes for a minute or two. "What's a Soprano state? Kim used the term. You know what he meant?"

"Fuck off."

We lapsed into more silence. "How about Latvia?" I asked at last. "I was in Riga once. Talk about fog! I couldn't see my hand in front of my face." I held my hand up and opened my eyes. "No wonder people look like they're staring into nothing. The fog can do funny things with sound, too. Did you notice? It muffles everything. Even the train was delayed; they couldn't find the tracks. I was glad to leave, no offense."

"I'm not Latvian." The man glared at me. "Do I look Latvian to you? What the hell do I care if a Latvian train was delayed?"

"Well, Kim said you were one of his. But he uses that phrase so much it starts to lose any real content. Besides, there are still Koreans in Latvia; did you know that? Or there were a few years ago. Most likely Stalin put them there. He shuffled Koreans around a lot, like cards in a crazy deck. I'd guess they made their way back to the motherland by now. Did you come with them? It must have been an emotional moment, uniting again with the nation, women weeping, flags flying, and so forth. I guess they gave you some sort of welcome home money, compensation, pocket change so you could get around. Or am I wrong?"

As I spoke, the thin man was transformed before my eyes into a block of granite. How he willed his entire being into this unmovable, unresponsive mass was the sort of thing that might have intrigued me when I was still working in the Ministry. In those days, I often wondered how during interrogations people became inanimate without warning. It seemed to me it was a defense mechanism and my job was to find a way to break it down. Now, I could care less if he turned into the Taj Mahal.

In fact, I was never much taken with stones. Other kids would skip them in the pond, or throw them at birds. My grandfather thought rocks were a nuisance, a blight on the earth, and he infused me with the same worldview. He would not even let us have an inkstone in the house. He sharpened his axe on a whetstone only rarely, and then with an expression of obvious distaste. "Look at this," he'd say as the sparks flew. "When one hard thing meets another, you get nothing but sorrow."

"Diamonds are hard," I said to him once, wanting to see his reaction.

"So what if they are?" he countered. He was studying a piece of corkwood he'd found. "Damnedest wood," he said, holding it up to the light. "Might as well build something out of air."

"Diamonds, if you go back far enough," I said, "come from trees, ancient trees."

"I don't give a damn about ancient trees." He looked at me sharply. "Pigs eat corn that grows in the dirt. Do I eat dirt? Use your head."

"It was in a book; that's all."

"Listen, I'm telling you that we don't know about ancient trees any better than we know about ancient kings," he said. "What we know is this day, right now, and you," he pointed at me, but not with the ragged urgency that sometimes took hold of his being, "you are going to have to pay attention to each day as it comes. You'll have to pay attention more than I ever did. Don't let them tell you about the glory kingdoms of the past, old rotten trees that they want to make into diamonds. Did you ever see a tree that thought it was a diamond? Well, did you, boy?" There it was, the "they" my grandfather used on rare occasions, and only when we were alone. I never asked what he meant; I didn't have to.

"You and Major Kim work together long?" I stood up and ambled around the room. Eyes followed me, alert eyes, not of the fog-bound stare. "He and I haven't known each other long. Delightful man, wouldn't you say?"

"Sit down." The thin man got to his feet. "I don't want you standing or moving around. You're not going anywhere. Don't even think about it."

"You mean contemplate making a break? Are you kidding? I've got no reason to run. This is my territory; I'm perfectly comfortable here." I stopped in front of the maps on the wall. They were old, Yi Dynasty. "Interesting maps," I said. "My family is from here." I pointed at the northern border. "The village was pulverized during the war. It was on a mountaintop, not worth anything to anyone, but bombs came down anyway."

"Is that why you picked a mountaintop to go to?"

It stunned me for a moment. I hadn't ever thought about it. It never crossed my mind before. But there it was. A perfect stranger finds a key lying around and unlocks a door you've walked past how many times in the dark?

"Who knows?" I said, only I did know. I had been migrating, no different from a bird or a fish that goes upriver to complete the perfect circle. And I understood why. Once, only once in all those years, I found my grandfather drunk in his workshop. That had been a terrible shock to me. Because of his status as Hero of the Revolution, he was given a bottle of whiskey every year in April, not rice whiskey, but something from Scotland, a mark of his standing and the esteem in which he continued to be held. Mostly he shared the whiskey with others in our village, but he always kept some of the bottle for himself. This he nursed, took small sips on anniversaries that meant something to him—the day one of his friends was killed in the anti-Japanese struggle, the day my parents died in the war, the anniversary of the death of his young wife. He drank only to mark sadness. I noticed that, even though I was quite young. But on this occasion there was no anniversary. It was, for all I knew, a normal day. When I walked into the workshop, I found him—eyes bright, cheeks flushed. He sat carefully on a small bench, his back against the wall. With effort, he focused on me. When he finally spoke, his voice was clear: "What have we done?" Each word came out deliberately. He said it again, and this time his voice broke: "What have we done?"

Years later, very near the end, he said the same thing when I came to his room at the hospital to say good-bye. The shades were pulled and the room was dark, but his eyes were bright and his voice was surprisingly young. I had a little speech prepared in my head, but after I'd said a few words, I realized it was for me, not for him, so I stopped. He looked into my face for a long moment. After a while, he sighed. "What have we done?" They weren't his last words, but they were the last I heard him say.

That was the reason I turned in my resignation and retreated to the mountain.

"No," they had dismissed it out of hand when I first put in the request. "Impossible. You can't resign."

"You don't think so?" I said. "I'm through, and you can't do anything about it. If you arrest me, I'll be off the force anyway. It's all the same."

In the end, they let me leave Pyongyang, to "retire," but only after I signed an agreement that I would not have contact with anyone, no one, ever again without permission. In turn, they agreed never—ever—to call me back to any official duties. I worked on the language with great care so everything was covered, because given half a chance, they'd come up with something and say I'd missed a contingency. I made sure there were no exceptions. I never meant to come back to Pyongyang again.

There was no other way, because one morning as I woke, I

heard a voice, "What have we done?" When I sat up and looked around, there was no one. The voice was mine. And I knew it wasn't a question. It was an indictment.

4

The thin man and I drove around the city all the next morning. I asked him if he wanted to go up to the top of the Juche monument and stare at the city; he repeated what he'd already said about not having to listen to me. Finally, the radio in his car squawked and the dispatcher told him to drop me at Kim's compound.

"I'll be sitting right here waiting," he said as he parked in front. "Don't get any ideas about going out the back way. There is no back way."

Kim was in the lobby, chewing out a couple of pasty-faced guards.

"The last time, I'm telling you, this is the last time I'm going to warn you. If it happens again, you go home in a paper bag. You understand?"

They indicated that they did.

"Then get back to work, and this time do it right. If that bastard gets out of your sight one more time . . . it's a big black car, for the love of Pete! How can you lose it?"

I waved from the doorway. "If this is a bad time, I can come back."

"No, this is a good time. Come up to my office. I have something to show you."

As soon as he sat down, Kim started looking through the papers piled on his desk.

"I have some good information. The source is reliable. A good source is a good source; that's what I say." He didn't look like he was getting much sleep. The strain must be taking its toll. "What it tells us is that Zhao is getting paid by a foreign power, one other than China. I don't know which one, yet. But this source had it right, and this is a good source."

I knew what that meant right away. He had been ordered to break off relations with Zhao but wasn't sure how to go about that and still keep both of his lungs. He had to go slowly, build a case.

Kim was getting more agitated, going through the piles. He had some information on a piece of paper, and the piece of paper was somewhere on his desk. I knew Kim well enough by now to know that on any single day reality was formed from the pieces of paper in front of him. Change the papers, change the world.

"I don't trust a source unless I know him," I said, "and if I know him well enough, that always means there are reasons not to trust him."

"A good source is a good source, especially in this Soprano state of yours." He must have just come across the term, because he was trotting around with it like a dog carries a stick. "Where is that damned report?" A few papers dropped onto the floor. He looked at them as if they were part of a prison break. "It was right here. Isn't that always the case? If you don't want a file, it's always there. Never mind. This source works in Sinuiju, good access to the relatives of ranking officials." He paused. "Well educated. That's important in my book. It's all I can tell you." Finally, he looked up at me. "Sit, Inspector; why are you standing? It makes me nervous when you stand." His eyes searched the room. "Get yourself one of those black plastic chairs and bring it over here."

"A woman, isn't it?"

He raised his eyebrows.

"And this woman works where the wives of ranking officials drop by and chitter-chatter."

"So?"

"So, one place those wives like to go is the cosmetics factory, and it has nothing to do with vanity. There is a bootleg store attached to the factory, and they can get discounts there. They take boxes of the stuff home, and then resell it at prices that undercut the state stores."

"That's not my concern. I'm not worried about the black market right now. How did you figure out who the source was? Not that you did, but what made you guess so confidently?"

"Sinuiju, access to relatives, educated. People don't deal with male sources anywhere but Pyongyang. They figure any male still in the provinces—especially Sinuiju—isn't worth much. Once you're looking for female sources in Sinuiju with access to relatives of ranking officials, there are only a few places to consider. Most of those drop off the list if the source is educated. It could be in one of those fancy coffeehouses or the bar in the new hotel, but women don't go there to talk about Zhao. It has to be in a place where money is changing hands, someplace like a black-market store in a factory that is selling something people have become convinced they really need—like cosmetics. This particular factory makes a lot of one product, and I think you might want to buy it in bulk?"

"What's that?"

"Vanishing cream. You're going to need great quantities of it before this is all over."

"I'm not going to disappear, Inspector. Don't you understand yet? I'm here and I'm not leaving. What I stand for is not leaving. The past is being washed away. Whether you like it or not, I am the future."

It was very quiet. There was no air left in the office. It had all been consumed in a firestorm of righteousness.

"In that case, I'm going back to my mountain. When the future makes it up the road, I'll stand at attention and salute."

"Your house burned down. Very symbolic, isn't it?"

"What do you want, Kim? You keep trying to get me to say that everything I did for the past sixty-eight years was wrong, that everything was for nothing. Why do you need to hear it? Will it validate something, keep the planets in their orbits? Won't you be sure of your own beliefs until those words leave my mouth? Go ahead; hold your breath. You'll never hear me say it."

"But that's what you think, isn't it? That's why you resigned."

"What I think, Major, is mine. You don't get to use it as a brick in your shining castle."

5

I couldn't stay anymore; I was done trying to exist in the same city with Kim. I was done watching the jockeying and maneuvering and people being murdered for no reason other than because someone needed to stand on their bodies to see over the next hill. I couldn't stay, but I had nowhere to go. Nothing was far enough away. My cabin on the mountain was ashes; the hills of Chagang were in turmoil; the Amnok and the Tumen would soon run with blood. Even Lake Chon, high above everything, would weep.

I could leave completely. There was nothing holding me here. I looked out the window from my hotel room. This wasn't my city anymore. Pretty soon, it wouldn't even be my country. I had two shirts, three counting the one I was wearing. I still had the passport Kim had given me and some money left over from the trip. Not much, but it would be enough to get me to an embassy in Beijing. Richie's people, maybe. I'd ring the bell, they'd let me in, and that would be that.

That was the choice. That was my real choice. I watched the light sparkle off the waters of the Taedong. How many times had I crossed that river? "It's my choice," I said, and went to the mirror. Kim had insisted the issue was a loss of nerve, that peo-ple looked in a mirror and suddenly couldn't see anything familiar. I looked. "Well," I said, "you just made your choice. You're staying."

That felt fine. I was in the middle of the most complex, tangled mess I'd ever been in, and it was fine. I was staying, there was work to do, and if it was the last thing I ever did, I'd get it done. I opened the bureau drawer and found a piece of chestnut. Stubborn wood—maybe. Touchy and ill-tempered—maybe. But it was beautiful, lustrous, hard, calm in the storm. I put it in my pocket, sat down on the bed, and began to review everything I knew.

This was a complicated moment in time, and so the relationships among people were more complicated than usual, or maybe it was just that they carried more weight. My normal practice would have been to make a chart, a web showing who was connected to whom, and how. Kim, Pang, Zhao—separate, disparate, contending; joined, cooperating, unified. It could be one or another, or it could be all of them. That's what worried me most. It could be all of them, which would mean any move I made might be wrong. What had Li told me? These days you had to be right every time.

Even Kang might not be who I thought he was anymore. Kang, most of all, was a cipher, fitting everywhere and nowhere. He'd set up a meeting with someone who led me right back to him. He had me driven around the city with a beautiful woman who had been in Macau to do what? I turned out the light and lay down. Draw a chart, I thought.

6

When the phone woke me up the next morning, I had a better idea. Forget the chart. Focus on the murder in Macau. That's where the lines were converging. Kim had sent me there; Zhao had tried to warn me away; Kang had pulled me out; the woman with the golden thread had been there right when the murder took place. The one person who seemed to know something about what had really happened was Luís. But Luís wasn't going to give any more ground, not that I blamed him. To me, at least, he was pretending that he knew who the murderer was. I didn't think he actually knew, and from a couple of things he'd said, he seemed perfectly aware that the conclusions—and the confession—were running well ahead of the evidence.

It was an open-and-shut case of a petulant young man murdering a beautiful and expensive whore. Only it wasn't. At this point, it was still only open. As of right now, maybe no one other than the murderer and whoever paid him knew what had really happened. Why did I think someone had paid the murderer? Luís had put the motto over the gate: "This is Macau."

I listed everything Luís and I had discussed. When you looked at them on a list, the facts as Luís recounted them were very convincing. That is to say, each fact was convincing. The problem was, they didn't fit. I wouldn't say there were holes. They were more like joints on a piece of badly made furniture. They weren't tight. That's why tables wobbled.

The phone wouldn't stop ringing. "What?"

"Ah, good morning, Inspector. Can you hear me?" The connection wasn't bad; it was just that there were too many people listening in at the same time.

"Good morning, Luís. Funny you should call. I was just thinking of you. How is the weather in Macau? Pleasantly humid, no doubt." I could imagine the transcribers sitting up all of a sudden. They'd make a note—"WEATHER/MUST BE CODE." Let them spend their morning chasing that.

Luís laughed. "Lulu sends her regards." This time, I really could hear the scratching of pens—"LULU/NAME TRACE."

"Always nice to hear your voice, Luís. Anything special I can do for you?"

"I was thinking of taking a trip, Inspector. I've never been to your country, and am in need of fresh scenery. A bulldog is angry at me. Northeast Asians are different, very industrious, not like us tropical people. You know how it is."

"Yes, I know how it is." In the background, pens write furiously—"REPETITION/5 + 1."

"How would it be if I came for a visit? I don't mean to invite myself. If you're too busy, let me know and I'll figure out something else. Maybe I could go to Changchun or Harbin." Quick note—"LOCATION DATA."

"No, I'd be delighted to show you around. I assume here none of your rules and regulations apply, which means you can sit for your meals."

Luís laughed again. "Don't forget, I like thighs." A flurry of notes taken, pages torn off notepads and passed off for immediate action—"SEXUAL PREFERENCE/LEGS."

"I'm looking at a plane schedule. According to this, the next flight is tomorrow."

"What a coincidence. That's the one I'm on. Can you meet me at the airport? I'm very bad with airport security procedures."

"I'll be there. Have a good flight."

"Adeus, Inspector."

Two phones clicked off, then, after a sigh of relief, a third. Amazing. One of them must have been Kim's people. One of them was Zhao's. I could only guess about the third.

I gave things the rest of the morning to cool off. Then I called Kim.

"I'm tired of being chauffeured around, Major. I need a car."

"That takes paperwork, Inspector. Vehicles don't grow on trees." He laughed.

That afternoon, a note came under my door: "It's old, it runs, and it has a tracking device."

7

The next morning, there was no Luís at the airport. I watched as everyone came through the door and lined up at the immigration counters. Westerners, Koreans from Japan, a few Middle Easterners, an Indian family, a group of Chinese military officers, and a couple of South Korean businessmen. I hung around until they all had claimed their bags and gone through Customs.

"Waiting for someone?" Major Kim came up behind me.

"No. I enjoy standing in cold spaces and watching luggage ride on a conveyer belt." I turned around. "And you?"

"The police in Macau cabled us that a visitor was coming to follow up on the investigation, the one I ordered you to fix. Apparently, it's not fixed. They still haven't changed their theory about who committed the murder. You were supposed to get them looking for another suspect. They're not."

If what Kang had told me in Prague was the truth, then Kim was still playing his game. He was a lying bastard, pretending to want to shift the blame for the murder. Lying bastards are a dime a dozen, but he was toying with me, and that I didn't like. "Apparently, it's still not possible to tell police in another country how to conduct their business."

Kim scanned the empty terminal hall. "Shall we dance, Inspector?" He took my arm and guided me out the front door. We went past a short man pacing up and down at the edge of the parking lot, a Westerner with a hat pulled down over his eyes. Kim studied him for a moment, then turned back to me. "I don't know why your friend wasn't on the plane. You find out; you get hold of him; you fix this. Clear?" He tightened his grip on my arm. "Crystal clear?"

"Don't paw at me, Major." I shook off his hand. "It dilutes your authority. And it makes me stubborn."

Kim straightened the sleeve of my jacket and brushed it clean with elaborate care. "There, all better?" He took a step back. "There's only one reason I got you down from your mountaintop, O. Don't make me sorry I did it." His car pulled up. "I'd offer you a lift, but I know you have your own transport and things to do." Right before he closed the door, he leaned toward me. "Fix it," he said.

The man in the hat looked up and watched as the car drove away.

Chapter Three

As far as I was concerned, things had taken the turn on which all cases ultimately hinged. This was the "good things come to those who wait" approach to investigations. It was rarely favored by chief inspectors, but I had never wavered in my devotion to the creed. Wait long enough and something would turn up.

Luís, apparently, had that "something." He had something he wanted to tell me, and it must be important, because someone didn't want me to hear it. Kim was at me again to fix the case, or he kept saying that's what he wanted. He'd left it hanging long enough after my return to half-convince me that Kang had been telling the truth. Maybe Kim didn't want it fixed.

Meanwhile, SSD was still fooling around outside of Kim's authority. At this point, though, no more dead SSD operatives had turned up. Explaining the mistake that permanently turned off the lights of their operative in the lecture hall must have required a lot of fast thinking. Three police had been murdered in Chagang, in a tiny village where no one ever did anything before but nod and look the other way when officials from Pyongyang appeared. There were whispered rumors of incidents in other locations in the mountains on the east coast, but the facts were being tightly held.

I decided to drive around the city, over one of the bridges, and find the apartment house in my old neighborhood where I'd lived years ago. I turned down the street where I thought it should be, but most of one block of apartments had been leveled, and the road had been widened. There was new construction going up, nothing like what existed in the western part of the city. These were plain boxes with big painted numbers on their sides. One of them looked finished; the others still had cranes at the top. The street ended abruptly with a barrier. A traffic cop lounged against it. He held up his hand and frowned.

"You don't read so good? The sign back there said: 'No Traffic.'" He stuck his head into my car and checked the front seat. "That means you. Or do you drive wherever you want?"

A big black Mercedes nosed around the corner and blocked my way out. No one had been following me. I had no idea where this car came from. "What about him?" I said. The traffic cop pulled his head out and walked back. In the mirror, I saw a hand reach out from the front seat and give him an envelope. He put it in his big white hat and shuffled back to his resting place. A few seconds later, the car's back door opened. Zhao climbed out. There wasn't anywhere to go, so I turned off the engine, put my hands on the wheel and waited.

"I see we are both interested in the future, Inspector." Zhao stood a few feet away and looked up at the construction cranes. "These are ugly buildings, wouldn't you say? Pretty soon the whole city will look like this. Row after row of these boxes, just like in Beijing. It almost makes me pine for the Grand Lisboa."

"I warned you, Zhao, after what you did to my house."

"So you did. Why don't we take care of that later? Just stay in your car, both hands on the steering wheel, and pay attention. Right now, we have something else to discuss."

"Like what?"

"Sonnets from the Portuguese." He indicated the traffic cop should move farther away. "I have a note for you from Luís."

"You?"

"Luís and I have a long history, Inspector. I can't get rid of him, he can't get rid of me, and so we agreed to coexist. Nothing formal. It was only going to be temporary, but that was more than twenty years ago." Zhao handed me a folded piece of paper. "It was hard for him to write, but he wanted to make sure you got this."

I took the paper and put it beside me on the seat.

"Aren't you going to open it?"

"What happened to him, Zhao? Same thing you did to Li?"

"No, I told you. Luís and I have an understanding. In fact, we found we became extremely useful to one another after a while. He is the last person on earth I would want to harm."

"Don't," I said. "Don't try to sound sensitive. It would make a cat laugh."

Zhao looked at me, then at the apartments again, and then at the ground. "Read the note, Inspector. Then get rid of it. If Luís wants to set up another meeting, he'll let you know. Lulu will call in an emergency. Meanwhile, drive carefully." The door slammed; the black car backed up at high speed. Barely slowing, it spun around and disappeared down the road. As I turned the key in the ignition, the traffic cop appeared again. He was counting a small wad of bills and listening to the earpiece of his radio.

"The bastard never pays what he says he'll pay, Inspector. Can't we arrest someone like that?"

"I'm thinking about it."

"Well, think about it while driving. I just got a report that another car is headed in this direction, fast. You can turn into a dirt alley past that finished apartment building, go out the back way, and get on a road that will take you toward the river. Get moving."

"You're a funny guy." I put the car in reverse.

He shrugged. "I'll sell you to the highest bidder if I have to."

The worst of it was, I believed him.

2

The note Zhao handed me consisted of only one word: "Fotos." I read it several times when I got back to my hotel room. It might not really be from Luís, but something told me it was: intuition, I don't know what to call it. After a while, you decide you can't question everything all the time. I held the note up to the light, steamed it with steam from the shower, rubbed it with urine to make sure there wasn't something else on it. Nothing. I turned out the lights in the bathroom, filled the sink with water and soaked the paper before tearing it into tiny pieces, rolled them into a ball, soaked it again, then tore it into more pieces before swallowing half of them and flushing the other half down the toilet. It was a lot of work for one word, but I didn't have anything else to do, other than wonder what Luís meant.

Even though I had decided the note was from Luís, I went over again in my mind whether it was worth trusting Zhao. Intuition is good, but checking the doors and windows one more time never hurts. Obviously, it was crazy to trust Zhao. You might as well trust a python with your pet rabbit. But I wondered anyway. So what if he knew Lulu? I answered my own question: If he knew Lulu, he knew Luís. I was back to intuition.

So, where was Luís? The story line was simple. He wanted to see me with some information, but he didn't make it to Pyongyang. Somehow, he got a message to Zhao, and Zhao got the message to me. No, that wasn't the story line; this was: Luís had discovered that the open-and-shut case was more complicated. "Fotos." Photographs could make things very complicated. People saw what they thought they saw, not what was there. Worse, photographs could be doctored. Videotapes could be altered. Anything digital could be made to appear the opposite of what it was. An entire section in SSD did that full-time. Maybe I should go see someone in SSD. Someone thin, maybe.

3

"What makes you think I work for SSD? If I worked for SSD, would I work for Kim? Answer me that. Anyway, you and me have a score to settle. You disappeared, and Kim kicked my ass all the way down the hall. Something happened to that transmitter on your car. I knew you'd screw with it. You screwed with it, didn't you?"

"Me? Do I look like a mechanic?"

"Don't disappear again; I'm warning you, O. Stay close. If I spit, I want it to land on your shirt."

"Yeah, make your life easy. You really are from SSD, aren't you?"

The thin man grinned, the first time I'd seen him do that. "It's all about survival in these troubled times," he said. "And my money is on survival. Angles, everyone is playing the angles."

"No, not everyone. Some people are playing for keeps."

Early in the morning, before the mist lifted, we stood on the bank of the river, beneath a row of willow trees. One or two trailed their branches into the water, but the rest stood back. Willows look loose and sleepy; they aren't. "Don't let them fool you for a second." My grandfather would point to the willows when we went to the river to fish. "They're wide-awake and a step ahead," he'd say. "Nothing much gets past them."

The thin man picked up a rock and threw it into the water. It disappeared without a sound. "What about you, Inspector? What angles are you playing?" When he had anything to do with stone, he tended not to stare. Rock beats fog, I thought, that sort of thing.

"None. I'm done with playing angles."

"That's what you say. I hear different. I hear you're in the middle of it."

"Really? In the middle? Then I guess that's where you are, too. Right in the bull's-eye."

"What does that mean?" The thin man looked both ways, up and down the riverbank.

"You heard about Major Kim's deputy, I suppose."

"Maybe." He gave me a Baltic stare that would bring the city of Riga to its knees.

"His name was Sim. He was a captain. Friend of yours?"

The stare deepened. Latvia fell; Lithuania was next. I avoided meeting his eyes. "The captain was standing about as far from me as you are right now."

That did it. The stare dissipated. The thin man slid a few steps away. "So what? He was playing both sides."

"So, you knew him. And you know what he was doing. It sounds like angles to me."

"You want something, right? I can always tell."

"Of course, that's why I'm so sure you're in SSD. It's hard to fool your type. How long have you been working there?"

"Long time, too long, I'm thinking. Listen, if you get the idea you're leading me, forget it. I do interrogations, too, you know. I know how this works."

"Sure, you do. Probably good at it, am I right?" I didn't wait for an answer. I had my entrée to SSD, and if I had to pay him one more compliment I was going to throw up. "It's good for the circulation to get out in the fresh air like this, but I've got to hurry over to see Major Kim. I'll pull out first, but I'll drive so you can catch up. Spit whenever you feel like it."

"Thanks for nothing." He stripped a few leaves off one of the branches and put them in his mouth. "Sort of medicinal, you know? Good for headaches, that's what they say." He spit out the leaves. "Tastes like crap. Don't forget, keep close."

"Don't forget." I said it softly enough to make him slow down to catch my voice as he walked to his car. "Don't forget who's in the bull's-eye."

4

I kept my speed down. The thin man trailed by about thirty meters, which meant every time I went through an intersection I had to make sure he didn't get stuck on the other side. I pulled over once or twice to let him catch up and then decided to hell with it. He knew where I was going.

There was a line at the tunnel. The guard was looking closely at everyone's ID. Normally, the numbers on the plates would be enough, but not today. When I pulled up, the guard walked around the car. "You ought to get this thing cleaned, don't you think?" He wrote down the license number. "Or maybe you should junk it. Pull around the side, behind one of the tanks, will you? We don't want to drag down the tone of today's meeting."

"What meeting?"

The guard stepped back onto his platform. "Well, well, guess who wasn't invited. Move it; there's a line of cars behind you."

When I started down the hallway to Kim's office, a burly figure stepped in front of me. "Wait in the waiting room. That's what it's for."

"I need to talk to Major Kim."

"Good for you." He gave me a little push. "In the waiting room. We'll call you. Take a number or something."

Two men, well dressed but with worried faces, hurried past us and disappeared into Kim's office. "What if I told you I was with them?"

"Last time." He drew himself up to his full height. "The waiting room. Shut the door behind you; it'll be nice and cozy."

An hour later, the door opened and the burly man pointed a finger at me. "The major wants you in his office."

"The other meeting is over?"

"Let's not have a long conversation, all right? Major Kim says you're to get into his office. Do it."

I stood up and stretched. "How come everyone is giving orders all of a sudden? It's like all the imperatives are falling out of the bag at one time. You know, if you use them all up, there won't be any more to go around."

The burly man scowled. "You want me to tell you where I'm about to put an imperative?"

"Not necessary." I walked into the hall. "Leave it to my imagination."

The furniture in Kim's office had been shifted around so that there was room for ten or fifteen people to sit in a semicircle. They all looked at me when I walked in. I didn't recognize any of them. From the look of their shoes, it was a good bet that they were Kim's people.

"Good morning, Inspector." Kim was standing near the window at the back of the room. He pointed to the chair next to his desk, the brown one, and indicated I should sit down. "This is Inspector O, gentlemen. I've been telling you about him and about how busy he is. Fortunately, he can join us for a few minutes, is that right, Inspector?"

"Sure," I said. "I'm at your disposal."

"That's good, because we have some questions, and then we'll need your thoughts on a few ideas we've been discussing."

This struck me as a bad idea. I had nothing to say to this group. And they couldn't possibly have anything in their heads that I wanted to hear.

"These gentlemen are all aware of the case we've tried to resolve. You want to tell them your progress to date?"

A little clarity edged into my brain. This wasn't a group of Kim's subordinates. These were senior people, and they were nervous. Kim hadn't accomplished what he was supposed to accomplish, and they wanted to know why. Maybe this was connected with why Luís wanted to see me, to warn me.

"Progress has been slow because of the need for coordination between police forces with somewhat different procedures." A few heads nodded, but mostly I got blank stares, blank bordering on hostile. "Procedural delays are the price of doing business globally, as you know." Apparently, they did not know and, judging from their expressions, they did not care. What they wanted was some signs of progress because—it didn't take a genius to figure out—the case Major Kim told me to fix was very important to them. Very important. It was so important that this group had traveled all the way to Pyongyang to find out what was holding things up. If these were Kim's superiors, they must be under a lot of pressure. Good, now we understood where we all stood.

"Inspector?" A man in a blue suit stood up. He had a self-satisfied air about him, which instantly put my teeth on edge. "That is your title, isn't it? What do you inspect?" The others smiled. "Because if you can't do this job for us, we'll get someone who can. We're not going to carry you people on our backs, you know."

I looked at Kim, but he cut in before I could say anything. "This is a complicated situation, Inspector." His eyes pleaded with me not to articulate what he knew I was about to articulate. "Perhaps you could mention something about your trip to Macau and your discussions there. That would give the group some context."

The man in the blue suit was still standing. "I'll be succinct," I said, "because I know you all must be very busy." That seemed sufficient abasement on my part, because the man sat down and the others shifted happily in their chairs. "The Macau trip went very well. The authorities were completely cooperative. All records and files were opened for my inspection. We believe that the work can be wrapped up in a week or so, at most. We did encounter some procedural delays, which I noted to you, but those are behind us. I'm only waiting for a final report and for the intergovernmental agreement to be signed in order to wrap things up."

There was the deadly silence that comes when self-important people are at a sudden loss for words. Finally, a man sitting on the edge of his chair spoke up. "Did you just say something about an inter-governmental agreement?"

"Yes," I said. "Of course, you knew that my government has no agreement covering the transfer between police authorities of information pertaining to political, economic, or capital crimes. Simply a formality, naturally."

A wave of relief made its way around the semicircle.

"Once the papers are submitted for the agreement," I waved airily, "it only takes around eight months, a year at most, for the legal documents to be drawn up, signed, and ratified."

A deep silence ensued, very deep, deep enough to swallow a lot of careers.

"Well," I said. "I hope that answers all your questions." A couple of men looked up numbly, as if trying to remember how to swim.

5

"I should skin you alive for what you did this morning." Kim slammed his door so hard a map fell off the wall. "What treaty? You never mentioned a treaty to me."

"That's because I didn't know about it before. We have treaties with everyone, all sorts of treaties. The Foreign Ministry has a bureau that does nothing but treaties. When Macau became part of China, we had to redo all of our liaison agreements. You're going to have to deal with them, replace them, renegotiate them, or something. You can't just trash them."

"Says who?"

"They're legal. They're on paper. That makes them sacred, isn't that right?"

"I have news for you, Inspector. When your government goes out of business, everything it ever signed goes in the toilet."

"You wish. What happens is, everyone goes to court and

things are tied in knots for years. Meanwhile, though, my government is still in business, and its treaties remain in force. That's the law, comrade."

"Since when are you an international lawyer?"

"I'm not, and neither, obviously, are you. The fact is we don't have any exchange agreement with the Macau police on this particular issue. I checked."

"We keep circling around on this, O. How is that? I don't need any documents from Macau. I need you to fix a problem."

"'A little problem' is what you said. Only it isn't little. If it were little, Mr. Blue Suit wouldn't have been up here. If it were a little problem, we might be able to wiggle between the words. But it's big, a very big problem, and big problems fall under the heading of Treaties, Agreements, Memoranda of Understanding, and So Forth."

"Can you or can you not fix this problem? The man in the blue suit wasn't kidding. He'll get someone else to do the job, and he won't want people hanging around who are leftovers with a lot of information they shouldn't have."

"Tough guy."

"Not tough, thorough. He doesn't leave loose ends. He wasn't happy with what he heard today. He made that clear after you left." Kim picked up the map and put it back on the wall. "Funny how territory can be moved around, yet it always goes back to where it belongs. See what I mean?"

"It's crooked," I said. "Tilted to the right."

"You haven't told me, Inspector. I've been waiting patiently. But I'm not waiting anymore. Are you with me or against me? Your performance this morning was ambiguous. It raises questions. There can't be questions about loyalty. It's not possible."

Loyalty? Did the man actually think I was loyal to him? Or might ever be? "Is that how things are in your world, Major? Do you imagine that people here are going to line up, once you've raised your flag and sounded the trumpets to announce a new dynasty has swept aside the old? What are you going to do, have everyone sign oaths of allegiance? You don't have enough pens."

"They'll come along, as long as there aren't troublemakers stirring things up. The point is, it will be even smoother if they have someone at the top whom they can cheer and weep for, someone on the reviewing stand, waving as they march by. The lead on every newscast, the picture on the front page every day, the name that follows them around from the moment they wake up in the morning."

"If that's your idea of order, good luck." That was the problem I was supposed to fix. That was why Kim's assembled group was so anxious. They needed a shepherd for the sheep. It didn't matter what he had done or not done. The past was irrelevant when the future was about to blow down the walls.

Chapter Four

In the line standing at the front desk was a man whose wig was not straight. This was the sort of thing I used to focus on right away. These days, I might not have paid attention if not for the young woman on his arm. She was golden brown all over from what I could see, and I could see plenty. The fish on the carpet were goggle-eyed.

The bellboy was standing next to me. "My lucky day," he said. "Brazilians! Hot! Hot! Hot!" He wiggled his hips. The people in line turned to watch him. The golden one put out her arms and made a noise with her tongue. Then she laughed. The man in the crooked wig laughed. The desk clerk—busy collecting passports and giving out room keys—frowned in concentration, but the group laughed as it did the samba up the stairs.

"You want a list of their rooms?" The bellboy had loaded the luggage onto his cart and was pushing it toward the elevator. "You never know when one of them will get lonely. Beautiful people. Very hot."

"You fool around with tourists and you'll get a one-way ticket to a coal mine."

"These days? My, oh my, Inspector. You are a relic. We interact; that's the word. We interact globally. Boy, I'd like to interact with the Golden One. Why don't you have a drink with her friend later? Give us an hour or three." He winked at me as the elevator door closed.

I walked twelve floors up to my room and was sitting on the bed catching my breath, thinking about what Kim had told me, when an envelope came under my door. The note was on the hotel's stationery. "Drinks at 4:30?" No signature. At 4:15, I went down to the bar and made my way to the darkest corner, farthest from the door.

"You don't have any customers," I said to the bartender as I walked past him. "I'm not here."

"So what else is new?" he said. "Don't tell me, you just want to sit."

No one came in at 4:30. A few minutes later, a wig poked through the door. "This the bar?"

"It's not the bus station," said the bartender. "Have a drink?"

The rest of the man stepped inside and immediately was searching the corners of the room. "Sure," he said at last. I could tell from the way he moved that he'd seen me. "A bottle of vodka, if you please, senhor. And two glasses."

He sat down at the table next to mine. "Sorry to have kept you, Inspector."

"Not at all, Luís," I said. "I've been expecting you."

The bartender appeared. "Finnish vodka. The label came off the bottle, but I know it's Finnish." He put down the glasses. "Why don't you sit together? That way I don't have to wipe off two tables. I think there's another bottle somewhere if you finish this one, so go ahead and drink yourselves silly."

When we were alone again, Luís straightened his wig. "I love Brazilian girls, but they can be rough."

"Already? You just got here. Besides, I thought you were Portuguese."

"I am. But your consulate people were rejecting all Portuguese passports, wouldn't even take any extra money for the visa.

I figured it must be serious. That's why I didn't get here when I promised."

"I didn't realize you'd make the next flight. I was worried someone had come up behind you in a dark alley."

"Nothing so dramatic. I went back to the office, rummaged around in the bottom drawer of my desk, and came up with something from Brazil. I nearly forgot I had it."

"And the wig?"

"It wasn't what I would have chosen if I'd had more time. Work with what you have—that's what they teach us. It fit better in China. Something about the air here makes it slip."

"What have you got for me?"

"You want to talk now?"

"This is good, better than going for a walk. That only attracts flies. Don't worry about the bartender."

"All right. It's simple. Remember those security tapes I told you about? The ones taken in the hallway? I heard they were altered. New times put on. Who knows when that Russian girl was there? That's not all that was fixed, I bet."

"I think I know how to get something more on the tapes. But that still leaves a problem. Either he brought out a bleeding suitcase or he didn't. What difference does the time make?"

"Maybe it wasn't him that came out."

I thought about it. "Back up a second. Has anyone seen him in the meantime?"

"Not that I know of."

"Would you know?"

"I know people who would know."

"Has anyone heard from him?"

"Messages, I'm told. I haven't seen them. I haven't asked to see them. I prefer not to see them."

"Phone messages?"

"No."

"So they're written, these days maybe e-mail or whatever else they use. Birdsongs, I don't know. Anyone could be sending them in his name. In other words, he could be missing."

"Yes."

"OK, so he could be dead."

"Didn't I imply that?"

"New problem: Who wanted him dead?"

"We call that 'motive.'"

"The old rectification of names. Call it by its right name and it gets you most of the way you want to go. I call it someone-wanted-to-make-sure-he-was-out-of-the-way. I have my suspicions why they would want him on the sidelines. But dead?"

"Not just dead. Parked in a Louis Vuitton. I double-checked. They took out the hanger to make space."

"Kim's people, maybe. Pang's people. That bastard Zhao. All of them could have done it. Personally, I think it was Zhao. Something this sick, it's right up his alley."

"Maybe. Each of them had reasons to get rid of him. Each of them had reasons to keep him around."

"We call that motive."

2

"Everyone was supposed to believe that no one had a reason to kill him, that anyone who thought about it needed him alive. But late at night, when everything was quiet and the branches were brushing against the windows in the wind, it occurred to someone that if he was around, there was always a chance he might turn out to be brilliant. What then? What if instead of chaos they ended up with stability? Maybe even recovery? What if he turned out to be charismatic? Even 'capable' could be a problem. They couldn't risk the chance that a thirty-three-year-old might know what he was doing, might rally his forces and tell them to get out of his country."

"So, she killed him, and they killed her." Kang was sitting across from me in the restaurant on the second floor, except we had missed breakfast and so were picking at our lunch. "I needed him alive. Without him, we don't have anyone to hold the flag."

Kang had appeared that morning. There was a knock on my door at 10:00 A.M. and there he was.

"May I come in, Inspector?"

"Well, cut off my legs and call me Shorty."

Kang gave me a puzzled look.

"I saw it in a movie a long time ago. I think it indicates surprise in the American West. Come in, absolutely. It says in the hotel rules I'm allowed to have visitors until ten P.M. Here, let me take your bag."

Kang had a small nylon carry-on over his shoulder. "No, I'll keep it with me." He stepped inside and gave the room a careful once-over. "Nice place," he said. "You think we can get some tea?"

I went to the desk and retrieved the room service menu. "It says here we can. All I have to do is dial six." I dialed 6. "Yes, a pleasant good morning to you. . . . Yes, I slept well. . . . Yes, you can do something for me as a matter of fact. I would like two pots of tea." I paused. "I see. . . . Yes, it is after nine thirty. All right, two pots of coffee. Maybe some toast with strawberry jam as well? . . . Aha. I see. All right, blueberry will do fine. Thank you." I hung up. "Ten minutes, they said. Meanwhile, make yourself comfortable. Take a shower if you want. Don't mind the TV; they promised me the picture only goes one way."

The coffee showed up; the toast did not. I was a little concerned about talking in the room, but Kang said not to worry.

"Not to step where I'm not wanted," I said, "but how did you get in the country? I would have thought some sort of lookout had been issued for you."

"They don't even know for sure if I am still alive, Inspector. They have a collection of faded photographs and out-of-date descriptions. I could be anybody's grandfather. I'll bet my documents are better than yours. It was time to come back. I'll be out of your hair and set up in another part of town by the end of the day. Then we shall see what we shall see."

After a little more Delphic volleyball like this, by 11:30 we were both hungry. "Let's try the restaurant. I hear the soup is good."

3

"Maybe he's not dead; maybe we're still speculating," I said, though I only said it to make Kang feel better. It didn't make me feel any better. The armrest on my chair was loose. Fancy restaurant, gold-trimmed mirrors, gold-trimmed tables, and the damned gold-trimmed chairs were falling apart. The table wobbled, too; it was the sort of wobble that would only get worse if they didn't tighten the screws. I reached underneath to see if I could turn the ones on my side with the end of my spoon.

"No, I'm not speculating. I know Macau, Inspector. I used to do my banking there. It was hard not to bump into someone who would dispose of a body for the right fee. When the economy was bad, you could even get a rate for more than one body. He's gone; I'm sure of it. But I need to know what happened. That's the only way I can figure out where the solid ground is, and where the swamp. If we know who did it, and how, it may put us in a better position for the next move. Greta thinks you have a theory."

"Greta. You know, if you mix up the Roman letters for her name you get 'great.' How is Greta, by the way?"

"Busy." Another couple of words would have been polite, but he wasn't handing them out. "Now, tell me your theory. Don't worry with the political gloss. We'll treat this like a police matter."

"Nice try," I said. "But you know as well as I do that these strands wrap around each other. I can't separate the political from the criminal even in normal times—on this one, it is completely impossible."

"What a relief, Inspector. For once, I thought, you might actually do exactly as I asked, and that would mean we had both become boring old men. All right, we'll throw everything into the pot and see what we get."

"He arrived in Macau on Sunday night, the ninth of October, at five o'clock, but you already knew that. There is a gap between that time and when he showed up at the Grand Lisboa Hotel. That you may not have known. He wasn't preregistered, didn't even have a reservation. That suggests a last-minute move, or an effort to keep his travel as far as possible under the radar. I don't know where he was between the moment he put his feet on the soil of Macau and when he walked into the lobby. It might matter a lot, or it might not matter at all. If you ask me, it was the first time he had been out of the country in a while. Maybe he wanted to stretch his legs and gather his thoughts before the operation got underway."

I kept myself from staring into Kang's eyes. I knew they would tell me nothing. They would go from expressionless to dead, barren orbs in a frozen sky. It wouldn't even help to watch his hands. I'd learned the lesson sitting across from him fifteen years ago, and I never forgot. Kang was in complete control of his every gesture; if he needed a nervous tic, he could time it to the millisecond. If I wanted a reaction, the only thing to do was wait. I'd laid down the challenge to him—that I was pretty sure what had happened in Macau wasn't the result of an accident, that it was far worse than that, that it was a political assassination. I'd already told Greta that I suspected she had been in Macau to pass a message. Kang knew I was picking up the shards of a broken operation, but now I was challenging him directly to tell me the details, or at least a few of them.

"Maybe someone spotted him while he was walking around." Kang's voice was completely noncommittal. Then his cheek twitched. Astounding, I thought, right on schedule. "Maybe it was someone who wasn't supposed to know he was there."

"Could be."

"That wouldn't help if, as you say, he was involved in an operation."

"Listen, either we play this on level ground or we finish our lunch and go our separate ways. You know exactly what the operation was. I have my suspicions. You don't have to tell me if you don't want to, but please don't play dumb. It's annoying. After all these years, it's very annoying."

Kang nodded. "Let's put it to the side for now. Good enough?"

It wasn't nearly good enough, but it was clear that I wasn't going to get anything more on this from him, not yet, so there was no sense pouting. "I'll throw some more in the pot. You tell me when to stop. He arrived at the hotel at half past six. He wanted a very specific room. He gave the front desk a list of requirements, but that was chaff. There was only one thing he really cared about: It had to have a good view of the Portuguese fort on the hill. I think I know why. I think you do, too."

Kang made a sweeping gesture with his hand. "More for the side pile."

"He had one suitcase with him, a Louis Vuitton Pegase 60. That's a two-wheeler, good enough for a few days' travel if you don't care about wrinkling your suit. Not as good as the 70."

"Get on with it, O."

"He goes up to his room and locks himself in for three days. I think he was nervous. He wanted to be alone to think. Maybe he wasn't sure he was ready for what was coming. And he was waiting for a message. That's when he made the first mistake. He put on the DO NOT DISTURB light. He may not even have known he turned it on. The light switches in those rooms are a nightmare. They're like the control panel in an agent submarine. But the housekeeping staff had no way of knowing whether he did it by mistake or not. All they knew was that the light was on and that meant they were supposed to stay away."

"And they did?"

"Religiously. He waited for the message. By the second day, he began to worry when it didn't come. His stomach was in knots and he couldn't eat. He wanted to talk to someone, anyone, but he knew he couldn't do that because he wasn't supposed to tell anyone at all where he was. It was too dangerous. He was alone, without friends, without protection, for the first time in his life. His only hope was the message. That would be his lifeline. But the message didn't come."

"Why not? It was delivered." Kang bit off the last word. He knew he had gone too far. Or he wanted me to think he had.

"Yes, it was delivered. It showed up the first night, exactly according to plan. But the concierge held it. The DO NOT DISTURB light was on. The next morning, word came in that the message was to be 'misplaced' for another day or so. The concierge didn't ask why. He just put it in the bottom drawer. Once that happened, the trap was set."

The waiter came over to the table to see if we needed anything else. Kang waved him away.

I continued. "Almost as soon as our boy disappeared from Pyongyang, there was a frantic search. Alerts went out. He had to be found. And he was. I still don't know how. You said it could have been that someone saw him walking around. Maybe. Or maybe you have a problem in your organization."

"I can do without the free advice, Inspector. We'll leave it where you put it—he was found, and we don't yet know how. You said something about a trap."

"Once he was found, a decision was made to make sure he never came back. It was a quick decision, almost instantaneous. It was one of those things that came out of nowhere. No one thought about it. The opportunity was too good to pass up, not merely because it was a chance to eliminate him physically, but because his reputation—and everything he stood for—could be destroyed as well."

"Let's not deal in ciphers, Inspector. You think you know who made this nondecision. Throw that in the mix."

"You told me Major Kim wanted to destroy his reputation. I've had enough to do with Kim over the past several weeks to think he wouldn't stop at that. And if he had second thoughts on murder—which he would—Zhao would have convinced him it could be done without danger. It was merely a question of activating certain connections, bringing to bear certain resources. Zhao knew people who were very good at what they did, and took pleasure in their work. They were on call. Yes, it was a challenge to carry this off on such short notice, but the greater the challenge, the more intense the pleasure. Have you ever seen Zhao's eyes glow in the dark? Phone calls were made, probably to Russia. An order was placed. Money transferred. On the evening of October thirteenth, the goods showed up at Hong Kong Airport—a Korean-Russian who was unusually good with a knife."

"Full stop, Inspector. You're telling me Zhao put out this order? Not Kim?"

"Does it matter?"

"It might."

"Then you'll have to pursue it on your own. I have no way of knowing for sure. Kim is basically weak. If there hadn't been someone to push him along, he wouldn't have gone ahead with any of the murders on his own, not this one or the ones that followed. You want me to keep going?"

Kang nodded. "Do you have a name for this Korean-Russian killer?"

"Tanya."

"You're sure?"

"You asked for a name, Kang. That's the name I came up with."

"How? How would you know that? Did you meet this person?"

"No. But I got close."

"How?"

"Pork buns. There was an MSS officer who kept an eye on the Russian prostitutes. He had lists of the girls, what they wore, how they worked, whether they had any clients that were on the watch alerts. Mostly, things were routine, so he ate pork buns and snoozed. Past midnight on October fourteenth, he noticed a new girl, a blonde. She didn't dress like the others, didn't walk like them, and only worked for a few hours before she disappeared. He never saw her again. He has an agreement with the Russian pimp who runs that group to be kept up to date on new faces. Who was the blond girl? The pimp was real nervous, said he'd only taken her on as a favor for a friend, but she was strange and he didn't want her to scare away clients. He said her name was Tanya."

"Tanya. I should have known."

Kang knew Tanya? I felt like I had stepped off the continental shelf.

"After she killed him," Kang was feeling his way here, "they killed her?"

"Yes, only it wasn't a her. She was a he."

"Tanya was a him?" Kang looked stunned. "You know this?"

"No, but I'm willing to bet. Someone with our boy's appearance was on the ferry from the airport the thirteenth. He wouldn't have gone to the airport, but the killer might have come from there. He came in as a male, maybe actually as a Korean from Russia, though the passport was probably fake. That's getting to be depressing, all of the phony passports. Why do we bother with them?"

"Forget passports. What about the killer?"

"After he landed in Macau, he went somewhere to change. I don't know where, but I think I know who helped him. He was on the streets for a couple of hours. After that, he showed up at the Hotel Nam Lo, trooping up and down the stairs a few times to make sure the front desk clerk didn't miss him. Her."

"How do you know this?"

"Someone told me, someone who had no reason to lie. They didn't say it in so many words, because they didn't know what they were telling me. And I didn't know what they were telling me at the time."

"This whole theory has a lot of supposition."

"Life is uncertain, Kang, and theories have holes. That's the way it is. Maybe it doesn't seem to hang together because the plan wasn't thought out ahead of time. As I said, the whole thing was probably put together in the hurry. They had a skill set that had to be matched with physical attribution, but basically they would take what they could get—essentially, any assassin who answered the phone and didn't mind wearing a wig. They must have danced around the room when they came up with Tanya. They made clear that for full payment, it had to be a quick and dirty job—very dirty. They wanted a lot of blood. That had to be part of the story. Depravity piled on depravity. Yes, and when it was done, they killed him. Her."

"Why?"

"Panic maybe, though in this case, I wouldn't rule out blood-lust. Someone should check to see if the Macau police located the lungs."

"Both sets?"

"Good point. There should be enough body parts for two—I wouldn't bet on all the right parts, though. This case is so weird, I wouldn't be surprised if the autopsy reports mention an extra set of arms."

The waiter had moved into hearing distance. He had turned very pale. Kang waved him away, again.

"The thing that still puzzles me," I said, "is how they got both bodies out. The tapes from the hallway security cameras showed someone leaving with two suitcases. How could he walk out pulling luggage that contained his own torso? Another thing, our boy only had one suitcase when he checked in. Where do you suppose the extra came from? I think someone supplied it afterwards. I think I know who."

"You saw the tapes?"

"No, but I think I will—soon. What happens now?"

"A lot of uncertainty. A whole lot." Kang drummed his fingers on the table. "A whole fucking lot."

"I've been wondering, who benefits? And I'm not talking about motive exactly. Think about it. No one benefits, but everyone benefits. When you lay everything on this fancy tablecloth, it's just the least bad of all the possible outcomes for a lot of people. I'd say that if you trim the fat, you end up with three basic possibilities."

"Maybe."

"First, there could be a smooth transition to new leadership. That's what Kim keeps harping on. He's obsessed with it. So, let's say Kim's people do take over, that they don't screw up more than normal, and that no one around here cares. That's bad for the Chinese; Pang's ghost is unhappy and restless, but unless they want to use force, there's nothing Beijing can do about it."

Kang thought about it. "Unlikely."

"Sure it's unlikely. I didn't say it was likely, did I? I said it was possible. The reason it won't happen is because there are too many people who—dissatisfied or not with what they have right now—aren't ready to bend over and take what the South Koreans are going to give them. The second possibility is more likely. It's what we might call *transition interruptus*. That's Latin. The Pope uses it."

Kang put his hands together.

"From what I can tell and a few things I read, Pang's people have plans to move in so quickly that no one knows what hit them. That will be very bad for Kim, bad enough for him to lose his pension. Seoul would be furious but hapless, completely paralyzed."

"I'd say this second scenario is also unlikely."

"So would I, because it wouldn't take more than a week for people up here to decide that even if they're hungry, they don't want Chinese food every night. They'll become sullen and from there they'll go active. It will be messy and the Chinese don't like mess, so they will bail out as quickly as they can."

"Give me something likely, will you?"

"Third choice, someone pops up out of nowhere. That's actually very common and I'd say likely. A skunk colonel decides his star has risen, and that he is tired of listening to old men. Everyone connected with Kim or Pang is eliminated, either in bed or over dessert. That is also very common. Then the whole thing starts over again. In the end, it's not the worst outcome for Pang's people; they can live with more of the same. Zhao is terribly unhappy; too bad for him. Kim is unhappy; too bad for him. The Russian in the northeast is found dead of food poisoning—Chinese fish."

"You figured this out on your own?"

"I had a little help."

"There's only one problem, Inspector. You still don't know what you don't know. And what you don't know makes none of it plausible."

"Irrational, implausible. Who cares? You're missing the point. What am I going to do about it?"

"What are *you* going to do about it?" Kang moved around some silverware. "Excuse me, I thought this was about history and the future of tens of millions of people. But no, obviously, it is not. It is about *you*."

"I didn't mean it that way. You know what I meant."

"No, actually, I don't know what you meant. I'm beginning to think I made a mistake by getting you involved." He picked up the spoon and the knife and moved them off to one side together. "When we first met years ago, Inspector, I said I'd been watching you for a long time."

"We were on the phone. I remember because the operator

was playing games with me. You suggested we meet at the Koryo Hotel."

Kang applauded softly. "Very good, Inspector. What else do you remember?"

"Everyone was watching me in those days, it seemed. People in my sector used to say they always knew when I was around. Streets became busy; sidewalks filled with surveillance teams jostling each other. Sometimes I would turn around and the whole line would trip over itself trying to duck into doorways."

"Only I wasn't in that line. Keeping track of where you went or who you saw didn't interest me. I needed to find out who you became, to watch for signs that the seeds your grandfather planted took root. It was partially his idea."

There was no sound; it happened silently, in an instant. The past shattered and was gone.

"I didn't know your grandfather very well. We only met a few times. He told me you had potential, but that it would be slow to show up. Like one of the old gingko trees on the temple grounds, he said."

I heard Kang, I knew he was telling the truth, but I wasn't at the table with him. I was above it, hovering, watching autumn's cruelest trick—the emptiness at the end of time. This was the betrayal. This was the lie, the only lie that could have torn my self from my being, and I never imagined it. I never saw it coming.

"No," I heard my voice. "I'll bet what he said was, 'You've got to look at a tree, listen to it, see how it grew, before you know how to use the wood.' I know how his mind worked. And now?" I was back in the chair. I made sure to sound calm. The core of my existence was suddenly gone, but I could be calm. At least I could preserve that much dignity. "Do you think the time has come to harvest the lumber? What should I become? A writing desk, on which you can sign orders for executions?"

Kang kept his eyes on me. They were lazy, his body slack, still the bear watching the rabbit.

"Or no, not a desk. That's too obvious. I know! Let's make me into a table on which to spread the victory meal. Oak is fine for that, better than gingko. Did my grandfather tell you I was to be an oak plank?" I laughed, and that was my mistake. The laughter split the calm in two, and out of the breach slipped a murderous anger I thought I had given up a long time ago. My entire existence nothing but the whim of an old man who had lost his son? Raised for what? No better than my brother mindlessly following sacred political texts, worse than him for believing I was different. Trained, shaped, pruned—why? To be an instrument of what hand, to hold what weapon, to slay what hope in the name of what myth? "Elm! That's it! I should have known. Elm might split if used too soon. It has to be seasoned." I held up a hand, my right hand, the one I used to sand the wooden cars and boats smooth to the touch. The hand was old, veined, bent; surely it was not mine. "Tell me, was that part of the plan as well, to wait until I was seasoned?" I picked up a knife from the table and sliced my flesh. "A miter cut is what he always suggested. Makes a strong joint, he would say." The knife was very dull. I sliced my arm again.

"O!" Kang leaped from the chair and grabbed for the knife.

I jerked it away from him. A little blood came down my arm, not much. "Trees are passive. But I am not. Trees are forgiving. But I am not, not anymore. Do you think I don't realize what this means?" I laughed again. Another mistake. More anger poured through, it widened the breach. "Let me tell you a story."

"Not right now." Kang looked at my arm. "We have other things to worry about."

"Wrong again. Again and again and again." I began shaking, shouting, bellowing like an ox, blood boiling, heat burning away shields built during nights of terrible fear. "This is a story of betrayal. It is vast, Kang, and so very complicated." I knew what I had to say. I didn't know all the words, but I knew where they would lead.

Kang spoke calmly, as if nothing had happened. "Always complicated, these stories. It wouldn't be betrayal otherwise."

"You!" I was practically screaming in his face. I couldn't think of anything else to say to that. "You!" The other customers looked away. The waiter folded and unfolded napkins. The cook came out of the kitchen and stared.

"On second thought, perhaps it would be better if you proceed, Inspector." Kang sat down, though he stayed poised to jump up again if I reached for the knife. "Why don't you make yourself comfortable? A long story is best told . . ." He paused. "Never mind; however you wish. Tell it however you wish. Sit, don't sit, trot around the room like a wounded unicorn if it will do any good."

I began. The other customers put down their silverware to listen. The words flowed out.

"There was once a king who cried when he was happy and who smiled when he was mad. He had his subjects whipped when he was pleased with them. He soothed them and treated them with huge banquets when he was angry. At first, there was confusion in the kingdom. People were not sure of themselves. They stumbled through the months, never clear on how to approach the throne, or whether to approach it at all. At the end of a year, they understood. As more time passed, it became inconvenient to deal one way with the king and another way among themselves. They adapted. Children learned to cry when they were happy, to jump with joy when their parents screamed at them with rage, because rage was approval and all children seek that. When lovers sat cooing at each other in the park, passersby knew they were furious and hurried on. If the king nodded in agreement at your petition, the next day you were led to the execution grounds, where the condemned laughed and their relatives told jokes. The other countries did not know how to deal with such an upside-down place. Wise men were consulted. Diplomats went through special training before being assigned to the court, lest they smile when they should frown and cause a war.

"The king finally died. People stood on the street corners and cheered when his coffin went by, pulled by a long line of white horses decked with ribbons and bright bouquets. The prince did handsprings at the funeral and ordered the royal musicians to play only quick marches for the whole period of mourning, which according to tradition was to last for three years, and thus went on for six.

"Foreigners who observed this did not know what to make of it. You see, they said knowingly to each other, it was inevitable. All the time the people were pretending to be happy when they were actually sad."

Kang said nothing for a moment. The other diners resumed their meals. The cook returned to the kitchen. "You should write it down," Kang said finally. All at once, he looked alarmed. "Are you all right?"

4

Kang stood over me, a question mark spinning above his head.

"What the hell?" I said. I was on the floor. From there, I could see the legs on all the tables. Rarely do you see so many table legs from that perspective. They were all imperfect. No wonder the tables wobbled.

"You passed out, Inspector. I don't think this is good. I think you need to see someone."

"Help me up." I was too weak to lift my hand, or maybe it was no longer connected. It was someone else's hand. Had we been introduced, this old hand and me? "What wills me to come back, do you think?" I said after Kang pulled me to my feet and put me in the chair with the loose armrest. "What is this awful fascination I have with light and air? I could have stayed where I was, but for some reason I'm back. Weeds do that."

"A curse, I know, Inspector. An affliction." He was taking my pulse, nodding his head to keep count.

"For a moment, you know, I really wasn't here. Maybe longer. I could have closed the door behind me. I should have."

"No, you weren't gone. You were hovering. That's what we all do in autumn, isn't it?" He let my arm drop. "Whatever it was, you're back among us, and your color is getting better. It couldn't get any worse than it was. Did you finish the story?"

"What story?"

"It was about betrayal, but rather complex."

"Ah, betrayal. Oak, perhaps." My head was still clearing.

"You are the one who knows his way around a forest, Inspector, not me."

"And you are the one who knows his way around betrayals. Can I have a glass of water? Tell me, these days what makes you think you aren't in the betrayed column? After what happened in Macau, you could be next."

He produced a glass half-filled. "Ask me again tomorrow. I woke up this morning; that told me I'd make it through today. If I wake up tomorrow as well, I'll figure the same. It doesn't worry me, though, which way it swings. You have your door. I have mine. I always have."

"This armrest is driving me crazy. These chairs were made in China; I can tell. They think they can run this country? Don't make me laugh."

"Relax, Inspector; don't get excited. You might disappear again otherwise."

"You disappeared, Kang, and not for a couple of minutes. Why did you come back? Why do you care what goes on here? Don't tell me you're suddenly a patriot. You're not a believer. And you're not here on your own; that's what I think. Who is paying you?"

"I didn't leave because I wanted to, you may recall. It wasn't my choice to stay away so long."

"It never struck me that you were someone who was too particular about borders, or about your paymaster. Major Kim told me—"

Kang looked away. "Nothing Kim says matters." He said this softly, like he had turned out the lights in a room he never wanted to see again.

"You know him pretty well, I take it."

I waited, but nothing came back. The question simply dissolved in the space between us. "Let me guess. You had a joint operation, but it didn't go well. And now you're working against him."

"I'll say this only once. Never believe anything he tells you. Nothing. Ever."

"My grandfather was suspicious of oak trees. He said that they were too complex to be trusted." I thought about it. "And me? You believe anything I say? I'm not all that complex, really. You've been watching me; you should know that much."

"For the moment, I believe whatever it is that keeps me alive. That should be your credo, too."

"I don't need it. I'll find something else. Maybe something halfway in between."

"A piece of advice, Inspector—stay out of the middle. In times like this, it is the middle that gets crushed. When this is finally over, the countryside will be littered with the corpses of people who chose too late."

"You're about to give me a choice, is that it? Don't bother. I don't join and I don't jump. I don't know if that's my fate or my upbringing. If you have doubts about me, don't. I'm not with Kim, and I'm not scared of him."

"Here." Kang handed me a napkin to put against the cut. "Take this in case you finally decide it's worth getting out of the middle." He stood up to go. "No sense bleeding to death right now."

5

"Let's suppose the Chinese moved in. Would that be so bad? It wouldn't be the end of the world. You don't want the Chinese here in large numbers, of course, or with their ponderous influence."

"I don't want them in any numbers, and neither do you." Kang had helped me back to my hotel room. He was leaning against pressed wood.

"You also don't want the South to take over."

"Why should we? We'll be treated like dirt for a generation. Look how long it took them to stop sneering at Cholla people."

"Then what's left?"

"We've been on our own for a long time. We can do better. We're not completely stupid after all these years." Kang had started down one road of thought, but I could see he changed his mind at the last minute. "You realize, Inspector, that this can't have a happy ending. There is no clean solution. It's over the edge of the cliff already."

"Pity." He must know about Li.

"I mean, especially for you. It can only end badly."

"Compared to what?" I said. "If you're trying to scare me into jumping in line behind you, forget it. I told you: I don't jump; I don't join. That's probably why I survived on the mountain. The more I think about it, the more I realize I was lucky to be there."

"The problem is, you might not be lucky forever. Life is a series of remembered tasks. What if you forget to inhale one day?"

"Don't worry; I plan it out every morning when I wake up. So many breaths. So many heartbeats. So many trips to the bathroom. It's too hard to dole out laughter daily, so I put it on a monthly ration. By the end of the month, people find me dour."

Kang had a pistol in his belt. He put it on the desk. "What about surprise? What's the quota for fear this month? Pain?"

"Overfulfilled. I've already borrowed against next month. I told you, if you're trying to scare me, forget it."

Kang moved to the window and looked outside. "This hotel. You like it?"

"It's all right. You said so yourself."

"I'd say you might want to consider moving to a new room. Even better, move out altogether; find a quieter place, something with a better character, maybe. It's up to you, but that's what I say." He looked at the pistol, then at me. "You have something to protect yourself with in these troubled times?"

"My aura of invincibility."

"Useful, but carry this when you go out from now on." He took an extra clip out of his pocket. "If you use these up and need more, it means you're out of luck, so don't bother looking around for the exit door. Keep one for yourself. I'll be in touch." He stepped into the hall and, from the sound of another door slamming shut, took the stairs.

I didn't have a suitcase, but I also didn't have much in the way of clothes, so I put everything in the laundry bag. There was no sense checking out, since Kim, or at least his accounting department, was paying the bill. Downstairs, the bird clerk looked up as I walked by.

"It's no problem for us to do the laundry," she said. "Just dial six."

"I thought six was room service."

She held up one finger.

"Never mind. I prefer to do the laundry myself. Go down to the river and beat it on the rocks, that's how we washed our things in the old days."

"There are no rocks."

"No? That's progress. Every damn river in the country is filled with rocks except this one." I smiled at her. She wasn't bad looking when you saw her in the afternoon light. "Say, don't I know you from up in Rajin? Didn't you used to sing at the casino?"

"Me? I've never been up there." She seemed pleased.

I hoisted the bag over my shoulder. "I've always done my own laundry."

"You kidding me?"

"Sure, it's how we did things. My grandfather, who you probably never heard of, said he hadn't spent all that time in the forest fighting Japs just to make sure someone else would wash his shorts."

"He said that? What about your mother?"

"She died in the war."

"Oh." The clerk looked serious. "You shouldn't call them Japs."

"Pardon me?"

"Japs. You shouldn't say that. We get Japanese tourists these days, older ones, not many, but more and more. They like to come and look around at places they used to live, where they went to school, that sort of thing. We're not supposed to offend them."

A car, two cars roared into the parking lot. A lot of doors slammed all at once.

"You'd better get back here." The clerk opened a door behind the counter. I moved quickly to see what she meant. There was a small space and what looked like a passageway, though it was too dark to see where it led. "Do it!" she hissed. "Now!"

I disappeared inside, and the door shut behind me.

"You can't go up there," I heard the clerk say.

"The hell we can't." A clatter of footsteps up the stairs. A few minutes later, footsteps coming down, not nearly as fast. "Where is he?" It was Major Kim's voice. He was out of breath.

"I don't know. He left a few minutes ago."

"Where'd he go?"

"Out."

"What out? Where did he go?"

"How should I know? You don't pay us to put tracking devices in their undershirts."

There was a slap and a yelp. "You were supposed to keep him here."

"Yeah." This time it was the thin man. "You were supposed to keep him here."

"He didn't take well to stalling tactics, all right? He left. He said he was going to do his laundry down by the riverside. That's what I know. You hit me again and I'll report you."

Another slap, another yelp. From the sound of his voice, Kim had moved around the counter and was standing right outside the little door. "You people had better get it straight who's in charge from now on. What happened to these TV monitors? You're supposed to be taping everyone who comes in here."

"They're not on."

"I can see that. When did they go off?"

"Yesterday, day before, who knows? I'm not a technician. We put in a request for maintenance, but they're sealed, so someone special has to open them. He hasn't shown up. Hey! Let go of me."

"You screw with me once more, you'll end up in a camp, you understand? And they aren't nice, those guards. Get these monitors fixed. Everything else better be working, too. I'll be back to check. And you," I was guessing he had pointed a finger at the thin man, "you go down to the river and pick him up. If he gets out of your sight again, you're going to be trading recipes with the crabs at the bottom of the West Sea."

The car engines started up, and tires screamed out of the parking lot. A minute later, the clerk opened the little door and looked in. "You heard that?"

I came out and straightened up. "I heard."

"One of these days, I'm going to put a bullet in his skull."

"Good for you. Since when are we friends?"

"Beats me. I only do what I'm told."

"By whom?"

"Someone better than him." She rubbed her cheek.

"If you don't mind my asking, what's the handy little closet under there?"

"It leads into the main monitoring panels for the audio and video surveillance in all the room—phones, lamps, phony sprinkler heads."

"TVs in the bathroom," I said.

She shrugged. "Most of the time, whole floors in a hotel are devoted to monitors and transcribers and so forth, but these owners didn't want to sacrifice profits. They must have had a lot of clout, because Security ended up with everything crammed into a room at the end of that tunnel."

"Thanks."

"You need another place to stay. Don't leave me a forwarding address; I don't want to know. If I were you, I wouldn't leave by the front door."

"Where?"

"There's a back exit." She fiddled with a dial on one of the monitors and a picture appeared. "Nobody around. They'd be in plain sight if they were back there."

"I thought the monitors weren't working."

She twirled the dial again and the picture disappeared. "They're not."

6

The back door of the hotel opened onto a narrow street that snaked past a school and a collection of buildings that were under major repair. I wanted to get to the SSD offices, not the headquarters but a nondescript compound behind a sagging brick wall where the technical offices were located. Security was not as tight there as it was at the main building. I knew that because when I was still working at the Ministry I occasionally had gone to the compound on business. Assuming the compound was still there. Assuming the procedures hadn't changed in five years. One thing, I knew, was working in my favor—bureaucratic time. Mountains might crumble, but regulations were for the ages. Five years was nothing for a bureaucracy. It wasn't even worth opening a file.

As I emerged onto a main street, I heard a car slam on its brakes and watched in amazement as a blue Nissan with right-hand drive shot across six lanes up onto the sidewalk in front of me.

"Get in." It was the thin man, and he was breathing heavily. "We thought you were at the river doing laundry."

"I was, but I had to go back for some bleach. You don't mind giving me a lift? Where'd you get this car?"

"We had a deal. You broke it. I'm going to bust your legs so you can't do that again."

"No, you're not. You're going to take me to SSD Compound Three. They just phoned about some photographs. Step on it."

7

The guard at the front gate held up his hand and frowned.

"I told you we'd never get in. My plates are the wrong ones for this compound. Now I'll have to argue with this moron." The thin man started to open his door.

"Wait; don't get out. Stay in the car. He's not used to looking in a right-hand window at a driver. If you get out, you give the guard the advantage."

"I do?"

"Make him come over here. Growl at him." I gave it some thought. "Give him one of your stares."

The guard frowned again and looked more closely at the license plate.

"Don't worry," I muttered between clenched teeth. "He's getting nervous. He'll come over to your side any minute and ask for ID. Tell him to get lost."

"What? He'll call in his commander, and they'll take me away in chains."

"They don't have chains. All they have is those nose rings. Just say we need to see H4. See if that does any good."

The thin man put his hand to his nose as the guard walked over.

"ID." Every guard since time began sounded angry when he said that. It wasn't anything personal.

I wasn't too worried, but the thin man looked rattled. "I'm here with a headquarters visitor. He has official business with H4."

The guard took a step back and saluted. "Next time, get a fucking blue pass for the windshield."

I smiled as we drove in. "See, that wasn't so difficult. Park over on the side. That's where I used to put my car. Someone will come out of the building to complain, but if you lock the doors, there isn't anything they can do. Move as if you've been here a hundred times before."

"Say, you know your way around. I'm impressed."

"Do whatever I tell you. Once we get into the photography section, you sit in the waiting room. They have collections of real good pictures, if you know what I mean."

The offices of H4—"Silver Mountain Tractor Parts" as it was known to outsiders—were on the second floor. That was where SSD doctored photographs for use in operations. It was also where photographs were checked to make sure someone else hadn't monkeyed with them. The people in H4 were very good at what they did. If they said they needed a new, state-of-the-art machine to keep up with the opposition, they got a new machine.

The door to the second floor from the stairway was locked. "This one is compliments of me," the thin man said. He took out a leather pouch with several small tools in it, selected one, and opened the door. "We're even."

"Even," I said. "There's the waiting room. Go in there and look important. I'll be out in a few minutes."

The third door down the hall was open. The desks hadn't changed; nothing had changed, not even the rounded shoulders of the man sitting with his back to the door, peering through a microscope.

I knocked softly. "Can anyone come in?"

The man swiveled around in his chair. "Long time, Inspector." He stood up. "Who let you through the front gate?"

"Nice way to greet an old friend. Have a minute?"

"Sure. That's probably how long we'll have before the guards come up and drag you away."

"Not to worry. I'm here with someone from SSD headquarters."

"That so? I suppose they're in the toilet powdering their nose."

"Actually, they're in the waiting room."

"You don't mind if I look? The last time you and I did business, they lifted my file for investigation and my rations were suspended for two months because you weren't properly escorted." He walked down the hall. In a minute, he was back. "OK, your escort is swooning over the photographs. We can talk. What can I do for you?"

"A little background."

"As in information? That I can't do. Pictures we can discuss. Information is something else. You know that."

"All right, pictures. If I wanted to modify pictures from a hotel security camera, what would I have to do?"

"Depends on the camera. If it's an old one that takes photos every few seconds, it doesn't much matter. The photos are crap and the time between the frames makes it nearly impossible to get a believable continuity. We don't touch them anymore. There are only a few hotels in the city that haven't changed over to the new technology yet."

"What about hotels overseas?"

"We don't have access."

"Nowhere?"

He scratched his head. "Mostly nowhere."

"How about Macau?"

"MSS doesn't like us fooling with their stuff."

"But you do."

"I don't pay attention to what's on the film or where it's from. The job description comes in on the orders, I push a few buttons on the machine, zip, zap, a new reality is born."

"If I was in a new five-star hotel in Macau and I wanted to evade the hallway security cameras, could I do it?"

"Sure. All you'd have to do is call the control room and tell them to turn off such and such a station."

"But that would leave a gap, a blank spot. Everyone would know."

"An empty inside corridor is an empty inside corridor. It looks the same all the time. No problem with changes in shadows. Once in a while a maid walks by. If you don't really care, you just put in a stock scene. No one can tell with the new digital stuff. They say they can, but they can't. If you are going up against some-one who is more careful, double-checks the schedule of the help and that sort of thing, then you have to be more careful, too. That takes some coordination with the locals. But it can be done."

"Zip. Zap. Coordination?"

"You know, a local service. Friends in the right places."

"Gangsters?"

"You're asking for information, O. No information about gangsters asking for film to be altered from Macau. I can't share that sort of thing with someone like you, no matter how many times you ask. Nothing about suitcases, either. Now, get out of

here, and take your friend with you. You'd better wipe his chin;
I think he's drooling all over his shirt."

A small word of appreciation was on my lips when a huge
explosion rattled the building and knocked us both off our feet.

"What the fuck?" My friend picked himself from the floor.
"It will take weeks to recalibrate everything after that. This is
delicate equipment." An alarm began to sound in the hall. "That's
it; you'd better get out of here before they start shooting first
and then forget what the questions were."

8

By the time the thin man and I got downstairs to the car, there
was full-blown panic in the compound. The guard who had admitted us was lying on the ground, his face bleeding from flying
glass. Another guard had his pistol out and was pointing it at
pedestrians who were running past, shouting and crying.

No one looked twice when the thin man's car made a tight
turn and flew out the front gate.

"Some photographs!" The thin man shook his head in admi-
ration. "I'm going to get myself transferred."

"Did you hear the explosion, or were you too busy turning
pages?"

"I heard it." He pointed at a cloud of smoke billowing over
the city. "Must have been an awful jolt over there."

"Isn't that where my hotel is?"

There wasn't much left. One side of the building had been
sheared away, and the roof was in danger of caving in at any moment. I spotted Kang in a crowd of people pushing against a
police cordon that had been thrown up in front of the parking
lot. No one had any training for this sort of thing, and all the
cops looked nervous. The officer in charge was running up and
down the line bellowing at his men to keep everyone back.

"I'll get out here," I said to the thin man.

"Oh, no. I'm not letting you out of my sight again."

"I'll be right there." I pointed to the crowd. "There's no way I'm going back up to my room, and I can't go anywhere else until I have another place to stay, can I?"

"I'll park. If when I get back you're gone, I'm putting you on a shoot-on-sight list."

"Since when is there such a thing?"

"Since right now. If you think I don't have the authority to do it, try me."

"You spit, I'll raise my hand."

I jumped out of the car and hurried over to Kang. "This is your doing. That's why you told me to get another room."

Kang seemed unperturbed. "No. We were going to cause some damage, scare the fish in that ugly rug, but not blow the whole damned place up. Half the staff was killed. Someone else did this. I wouldn't put it past Kim to have set the bomb so he could blame us."

"Kim might do something like that. I'll tell you for sure who would—Zhao."

9

Kang had given me directions to Zhao's apartment house. "We want him as much as you do," Kang said, "but you've got a funny look in your eyes. I'll give you a ten-minute head start. If he's in the open—which I doubt—do whatever you want. If he's in his hole, don't try anything heroic. Or stupid. And don't forget, we're right behind you."

The explosion had pulled all of the official security off almost every building in town, including Zhao's. The viper was asleep, curled up on a sunny chair in the lobby. That's good, I thought. Bombs don't impress snakes.

The woman at the front desk started to say something, but I pointed to the viper and put a finger to my lips. "Shhhh. He spits poison if he wakes up all at once," I whispered. "I'm supposed to tell Mr. Zhao what that big noise was all about."

She pointed upstairs.

The apartment wasn't on the top floor; it was the top floor. There was no hallway. The elevator doors opened silently and directly into a library filled with books from floor to ceiling.

I meant to say, "Get up, you bastard," but when I saw the library all that came out was, "You read?"

Zhao was in a chair—red leather. "Sometimes, when there's nothing else." He didn't seem surprised to see me. "I don't like books, though. You know why?"

It didn't seem to me that this was the exchange I should have with Zhao just before shooting him between the eyes.

"I'll tell you why." Zhao turned off the small reading lamp beside him. That plunged the room into darkness. "A book is what? Lots of words, but only one word at a time. You read a word; then you read the next word."

"You've got that part down pretty well." I pulled the pistol out of my belt and eased myself back a few steps.

"Same with people talking—one word at a time. Only there you can watch their faces." He looked at me closely. I don't know how I knew he was looking at me, but it felt obvious. "You can see what their hands are doing, or their eyes. Eyes are a give-away. Whenever one of my guys has screwed up bad and is trying to convince me not to drop him off a boat, there are a lot of words of regret, but it's his eyes that tell me if he really means it. It's so much better than any written confession. I always tell people, 'Listen to their lips, but watch their eyes.'"

"One of those snappy four-character sayings, right?"'

"You think I'm joking? Try listening to a symphony sometime. You can't do anything like that with a book, not even close. The same goes for a painting. Sure, it gets done one brushstroke at a time, that's how it's painted, but I'm talking about the effect. You stand back, what do you see? Brushstrokes? No, you see a painting. You follow?"

"I got your point."

"No, you didn't. You think I'm spouting theory." Zhao's eyes followed me as I edged along the wall. "But this is reality we're talking about. Books aren't real; that's what I'm telling you. Words are never real. If I say, 'I shot you,' what the fuck do you care? But if I put a bullet in your heart, that's real. Am I right?"

"I suppose." Standing still might help. Maybe he couldn't really see me but tracked movement like a bat or a shark.

"You better suppose. A bullet in your heart—that's an image. Words aren't even that. Words are words. And books are what? Words. I'll say it again. You can't get faster, or slower, or louder, or softer. Here's a word. Here's another word. It's like throwing fish to a seal."

10

The elevator door must have opened. I couldn't hear it, but there was something new—a change in air pressure, or maybe the faint whip of a viper's tongue. I pressed myself so far against the wall that the paint squeaked.

"Breathe normally," Zhao laughed. It wasn't the sound of anything this side of hell. "Just relax and close your eyes."

No, I wasn't going to do that. Kim said I couldn't stop the flow of history. Maybe not, but I could make sure Zhao wouldn't be part of it.

"Inspector? It won't be long now. Give Pang my regards when you see him."

A light went on, a bright orange light that made the whole room look like the middle of a burning city. I turned my head and there, standing a meter away, was Zhao's number three, the pupils of his orange eyes as big as saucers. He was holding a saw, not for wood but for cutting through bone. His mouth opened. I fired twice. Then there was a third shot, a fourth. The viper wasn't moving, I had my finger off the trigger, but there was still one more shot, very loud considering it was a room full of books. If Zhao was trying to shoot me in the back, he was taking his sweet time about it.

The room became supremely still for a moment. I turned around, and there was Zhao. He was sitting back in his leather chair, only I wouldn't say it was a fighting posture or even one to show how relaxed he was. His eyes were open, but he wasn't seeing any words. He wasn't seeing anything. Greta stood off to his right, a pistol at her side.

"That's done," she said. "You all right?"

"Me? I'm fine. Did Zhao even know you were there?"

"I doubt it. Did you?" She walked over to the elevator. "Let's get out of here." She tossed me a book of matches. "You want to burn down the building?"

The thought never crossed my mind. "No, I think we'll call things even at this point. Are we leaving the bodies here like this?"

"Let Major Kim deal with it."

When we got down to the lobby, the lady at the desk was skimming a magazine. She flipped the pages as we walked by. Out on the street, Greta looked up at the top floor. "That orange light is still on. I hope it fries his eyes out." She turned to me. "You hungry? We can get some *mandu* now. I'll call Kang from the restaurant."

11

"One thing I don't understand." A plate of dumplings sat in front of me, barely touched. I had discovered that near-death experiences did not whet my appetite. Greta didn't seem to have that problem. "I know why the young man wanted that room—so he could see the fort. And I know someone standing along the front of the fort could see his room. But for what?"

She took a small light from her pocket. "It's got a powerful beam, very concentrated." She clicked it on once, twice, three times. "That's it. Three times. That was all he needed to be sure that we were waiting for him. All he had to do was click his light once to show me he was there. I waited in the fort every night, but there was nothing."

"Why was the message so crucial? Why didn't you arrange for him to go to the window and send his signal when he arrived?"

"We didn't know for sure we'd make it on the first day. And we had to make sure that someone else didn't see the light and report it to the police. The message was from a song we used to sing when he was a child. He and I were cousins."

Something creaked in my memory, a rusty hinge too old to repair. What had Luís told me? Maybe the young man had been standing at the window to signal a long-lost relative. Luís actually had said that. And I had dismissed it as Macanese sarcasm. What did I know about Macanese sarcasm?

Greta looked at the *mandu* on my plate. "Are you going to eat that?"

"I liked it better when we were having pastry. Go on." I pushed the dish to her side of the table. "You were telling me about the family ties."

"I was with him a lot when he was growing up. Later, I went away to school in Europe and decided not to come home."

"That's where you met Kang."

"He said I was about the same age his daughter was when they took her away. You were there that night, Inspector. You saw what happened."

"I only saw the aftermath, the furniture wrecked, the flowers she put on the tables scattered across the floor." I didn't mention the book in French, facedown as if she'd placed it carefully on the counter when they crashed through the door. "One thing I still can't figure out. Why did he invite Tanya to his room?"

"Maybe he didn't. Maybe Tanya just knocked on his door. I think the whole story about him inviting a prostitute to his room, having dinner, the whole thing is a lie, part of the effort to destroy his image."

"There are receipts in his handwriting for the room service charge."

"There are a hundred ways to forge a receipt. Zhao probably owned a string of print shops that turned out phony receipts. No one pays attention when signing those things anyway. The signatures all look like four-year-olds did them. They're easy to forge."

"You don't think we know what happened that night. Neither do I."

She helped herself to one of my *mandu*.

"I don't think we'll ever know."

12

"Everything is coming apart at the same time, Kang, all at once. It's exactly like the hotel. Boom! And anything left standing is only there by inertia."

"That's how it might look to some people."

"You don't think so?"

"Things appear; then they disappear. That's how the universe does its business, Inspector. Evolutionary change is a nice idea, but it isn't the way the world works itself into a new order. I wouldn't let it upset me. That's why people age; they worry about things they have no control over."

"I take it you think you have a place in the new order."

"No, I don't know. Unless what we're talking about is chaos. For that, we both have a reserved seat."

"You expect Kim to stay and fight?"

"He and his friends will fry all of us if we let them. So, we don't let them."

"You really think you're going to defeat the whole South Korean army? They'll pour across the border. We'll be up to our necks in troops and bureaucrats and religious zealots and helping hands."

"We have ways."

"When you left, did you think you'd be back?"

"I left behind what existed then. But this is now, and we're going to shape what comes next."

"That's what people always think. That's what they thought the last time. That's what they'll think the next time."

"It's a wheel; it goes around."

"You're going to ask me to join?"

"No. It was considered but rejected."

Chapter Five

Because it was so late in the year and I had nowhere to go, Kang arranged for me to stay in an apartment near his until the spring. By late April, I had returned to the mountain, in a truck with a load of lumber and a small box of tools. The new house took more than three months to build. It was smaller than the old one, darker on cloudy days, though the window faced south this time, not east, which meant there would be more sunlight in the winter. The army brought up another phone line; the new phone arrived a couple of weeks later. Kang called me a several times a week at first—to get my views, he said—but then there was less and less to say.

Soon after it was decided that I would move back to the mountain, I learned that my brother had died the year before, while I had been in Prague. Kang had known but had held off telling me. I made the trip to the cemetery in October, on the first anniversary of my brother's death, and was surprised to meet a man, middle-aged, who was standing silently, his head bowed, in front of the marker.

The weather was perfect, the sky boundlessly high and blue. "A pleasant day," I said when the man looked up and acknowledged my presence. "Did you know this person?"

"He was my father. And you?" The man studied my face closely.

"You are his brother; I can see it from the eyes. We have a picture of my great-grandfather at home. You both had his eyes."

We shook hands, though I was too stunned to say much more than, "It is a pleasure to meet you." When he asked if I lived nearby, I said merely that my home was outside of Pyongyang, several hours' drive away. We left it at that.

As we walked together out of the cemetery, he put his hand on my arm. "I'm afraid I was not completely truthful with you. I am not his son, that is, not his real son."

"How do you mean?"

"He never married my mother." '

"I see." I pointed to a bench. "Why don't we sit and enjoy the air for a few minutes. I'm sure no one here will mind." Once we were seated, I spread my arms on the wooden rail and lifted my face to the sun. "If you don't mind my asking, how old are you?"

"I am forty-nine. My father—your brother—was assigned to the border region in 1969, soon after the clashes. He did something that helped defuse the situation and he arranged for food to be brought to Koreans living on the Chinese side."

"Your father told you this, I suppose."

"No, he never mentioned these things. I heard them from other people. While he was there, he fell in love with a woman. Afterward, he came twice a year to see me and to give my mother support. We saw him every year until I was twenty. Then I went away to school, and it became more difficult."

"Why would it be difficult? You were in Pyongyang, I imagine."

"In Pyongyang? No, I was in Beijing."

A breeze came down the hill and scattered the leaves that the groundskeepers had raked into a tidy pile. "Your mother, she is well?"

"She is."

"And she lives where?"

"In Yanji."

"Aha, I see. She is Korean?"

"Half-Korean, half-Chinese."

I smiled, and then I laughed. It was a happy laugh, the sound of an old tree budding in the spring. "Some Chinese blood is a good thing," I said. "Your great-grandmother had Chinese blood, did you know that?"

It was only days later, when I was back in my house, looking at the moon as it rose through the gap between the tall pine trees, that I realized the man at the grave was not just my brother's son. He was my nephew and I his uncle.

That night, I dreamed of my grandfather and wondered even as I slept if he had dreamed of his grandfather, and he of his, and so on back in time. It was interesting, I thought to myself, that at the end we dream of the beginning.

Macau

2009

"A latter-day John le Carré."
—The Tampa Tribune

"Each Inspector O novel is a strange new trip through the looking glass." —*Booklist* (starred review)

MINOTAUR BOOKS
A THOMAS DUNNE BOOK

CPSIA information can be obtained
at www.ICGtesting.com
Printed in the USA
LVOW12s1548270117
522415LV00001B/117/P